Memoirs of a Crimefighter

Seth Andrew Jacob

memoirsofacrimefighter.com
sethandrewjacob.com
@sethandrewjacob

Cover Design by Dylan Todd
Cover Illustrations by Ramon Villalobos
Edited by Adam P. Knave, and Lillian Cohen-Moore
Formatting by Polgarus Studio

DISCLAIMER:

No secret identities are revealed in these memoirs. Any first names given are false ones created for this text. The content of these memoirs is not intended to libel any superhero, supervillain, or superhuman, living or dead.

Chapter 1:
Spandex Wasteland

The night that I found out my father died started out like any other night. I had just finished a routine patrol with my superhero team, The Millenials. Well, we called it a "patrol", that's not really the right word for it. It's more like the alcohol and drug fueled antics of people in their twenties on a Saturday night, except with a liberal dose of superpowers thrown into the mix. There's no law against flying under the influence, but there probably should be.

As we walked into The Domino Mask, the DJ was playing a weird remix of the theme from the Superb 6 cartoon show, and the dance floor was packed. I pushed through throngs of inebriated superheroes to get to the bar. Ex-sidekicks let off the built up steam of a repressed youth by drinking a lot more than they probably should. Some obvious spandex tourists who had no powers or superhero careers danced in clusters of expensive, impractical costumes. Elastic, gyrating limbs stretched to the pounding beat and entwined their way through the dance floor. Red heat vision eyes pulsated rhythmically and gave off waves of warmth, and capes fluttered as dancers ascended above the crowd.

I made my way to the bar and struggled to get the busy bartender's attention. Joe Metal sat down on the bar stool next to me with a resounding clang. One of my teammates, Joe Metal was known for his state of the art exoskeleton armor. He didn't actually have any superpowers, but he designed and built his suit of sleek, highly advanced armor from scratch.

"Hey, Spectacle. The video of the Master Boson fight's already got like a couple thousand views," Joe gave me a look that all but screamed *Told you so* as he leaned over the bar and grabbed a couple of glasses for us.

"Not this again, Joe." Joe Metal's armor recorded all of our fights with supervillains, and he uploaded the footage to YouTube religiously. We made a lot of money from the ad revenue on these videos. If there's one thing I've learned as a superhero, it's that the internet loves a good super-brawl.

However, the vast majority of the money that The Millenials makes comes from collecting rewards for taking out buffoons like this Master Boson guy, a ninja wannabe with low level nuclear powers that we caught trying to rob a liquor store earlier that night. The superhero-industrial complex works like this: it's cheaper for the government to just pay us to handle these maniacs than it is to try to police, register, and regulate the hordes of costumed narcissists calling themselves superheroes. Why spend billions of dollars per year trying to arrest superpowered vigilantes when you can pay us to take care of superpowered criminals at a fraction of the cost?

Joe flicked his wrist, and a spigot jutted out of his armor. He aimed it at each of the glasses and copious amounts of vodka streamed out.

"Just hear me out, bro. We've had a decent amount of success by taking advantage of social media. Isn't it time we took it to the next level?" Joe downed his glass in one quick motion.

"I've heard it all before, Joe…I'm all for the social media stuff, you know that. I just don't want to go as far with it as you do." I smelled the glass of vodka Joe poured for me and then took a sip. I couldn't help but be skeptical of liquor contained in the same exoskeleton that had multiple uranium reactors.

Joe shot some vodka into our teammate Insight's glass while she took a selfie with our other teammate, Mr. Mercurial. Her forehead pulsed with purple telekinetic energy as she levitated her phone in the air in front of her with her mind, and you could tell that she was going out of her way to radiate a little more light than necessary for the benefit of the camera. She had just redesigned her costume, and she was showing off her new modern hippy meets superhero style.

She had her arm around Mr. Mercurial, whose entire body was made up of silvery flowing fluid. Mr. Mercurial stretched his chrome smile wider than humanly possible, and his metallic, mirror-like eyes bugged out of his head like he was a living cartoon. It was blatantly obvious as they kept taking pictures that Insight and Mr. Mercurial were deliberately staying out of this conversation. They had heard it all before.

"Spectacle, it's inevitable. Sooner or later, everyone is going to be doing what I do. Everyone will be live streaming every waking moment of their lives," Joe pointed the spigot in his wrist at his glass and filled it up again. His eyes flitted back and forth as he poured. He was reading text that his armor fed into his optic nerves, probably tweets or texts or tumblr posts. Joe was constantly immersed in the stream. Sometimes it was hard to draw a line where Joe ended and the internet began.

"Alright, fine, Joe. Let's say everyone starts live streaming everything all the time. What about privacy? What about these little things called secret identities? Maybe you've heard of them?"

"Come on, Spectacle. Don't be such a rube. The world is growing more and more connected every day, and it's the people who cultivate a familiar, relatable online persona who rise above the noise," Joe held his glass up as if he was making a toast.

"Secret identities are going extinct. Privacy is dead. Long live the social media superhero!" Joe laughed as he drank from his glass. A drop of vodka rolled down his chin and landed on the titanium collar of his armor.

"Sounds to me like you're getting ambitious, Joe. Remember when we started The Millennials? Remember what we agreed on?"

"Of course I remember, it's not about that, it's just—"

"I'm not trying to be a dick or anything, but I'd really like to hear you say it," I said. To be honest, I was definitely being a dick. Joe looked down at his glass and sloshed the liquid around in it. The excitement had drained from him.

"No archenemies," Joe answered sullenly.

"That's right. No archenemies. We never wanted The Millenials to be the next Superb 6. We never wanted to have to deal with insanely powerful assholes obsessed with killing us because daddy never gave them enough hugs." I drained my glass and held it out for Joe to refill while I made my point.

"Ambitious moves like the one you're talking about put more eyes on us. It gets us more attention, and that's the opposite of what we want. We want to be under the radar, Joe." My phone started buzzing in my pocket while I was talking, but I let it ring a few more times so that I could finish my argument.

"We don't want to be a major league superhero team because being in the major leagues gets you killed. I don't know about you, but I'm happy fighting low level hacks and making decent money. I don't need a bunch of psychotic, absurdly powerful bastards getting all infatuated with the idea of being my 'archenemy'." I pulled out my vibrating phone, and Joe's eyes went back to scanning the invisible text in front of him while I took the call.

He was retreating to the stream for the moment, but I knew that this discussion wasn't over. Joe was always getting excited about these ideas he had about the future of superheroes. He would become almost manic about his latest internet marketing scheme to break into the upper ranks of the crimefighting community, but he usually got distracted and moved onto the next idea before he could follow through with the first one.

I answered the call from the number I didn't recognize, and I don't know what I was expecting, but it wasn't that. The man on the phone told me something that I wasn't prepared to hear, and the thumping music in the bar faded to a drone like I was listening to it under water.

"Yes. I understand. I'll be there…thank you, of course." I hung up, and my phone slipped out of my hand and landed on the bar with a slap.

"Hey…whoa, are you okay man?" Mr. Mercurial sat down next to me at the bar while I was on the phone and I hadn't even noticed. His silvery brow wrinkled with concern.

"Yeah, I'm fine. That was nothing." Of course, I was lying to Mr. Mercurial, and probably to myself too. I was anything but fine. The man on the phone was my father's lawyer, and he just informed me that my father had died of a drug overdose.

The rest of that night is a blur. Immediately after the call from my father's lawyer, I began to drink with the reckless abandon characteristic of a person trying to obliterate any discernible memory of themselves or their problems. It's easy to say in hindsight that I was making the worst decision in that situation, but at the time it felt like a pretty good idea.

I have smears of memory from that night. I remember Mr. Mercurial trying out bits from his stand up comedy routine on us, and I remember laughing at his jokes much harder than they deserved to be laughed at. I remember being outside of the Domino Mask and smoking a cigarette with Insight. Insight looked at me with that purple telepathic gleam in her eye that she gets when she's receiving strong mental vibes from someone, and she asked me if everything was alright. I remember lying to her and taking another drink while forcing my jumbled, drunken thoughts on something else, anything else. I remember Joe Metal taking a lot of pictures of us, pictures that later showed up online, and I remember faking an unconvincing look of happiness. I remember bits and pieces of a conversation I had with Insight about the philosophy of superheroes and what she called "superhuman consciousness" while she took drops of SUHP. I remember a spiraling feeling as I stumbled home to my apartment, like my world had spun out of orbit and the sun was drifting farther and farther away from me.

I woke up feeling like a nuclear bomb had gone off inside my skull. I could barely think, and my phone was blaring an alarm. For a few seconds, I wondered which one of my asshole teammates set the alarm on my phone to mess with me, and then it came back to me. I set the alarm because I had agreed to meet with my father's lawyer.

About thirty minutes, one thoroughly unpleasant vomiting session, and approximately a gallon of water later, I was sitting in front of my father's lawyer. His office was a cramped and musty room filled with stacks of paper. He was a nice, middle aged man who had a touch of a hoarding problem.

"I'm so sorry for your loss," he said, and his eyes were filled with a deep well of genuine sympathy.

"What happened exactly?"

"Well…I'm sure you've heard of soup? Your father had a bit of a soup habit, and I'm afraid an older man's heart can only take so much soup…again, I'm so sorry."

Soup, or SUHP, is Synthetic Ultra Human Potentiator. It's a drug used by many superheroes and supervillains that temporarily induces a euphoric high, mild hallucinations, and increased superhuman abilities in the user. I had no idea that my father, who I thought was a stock broker, had ever used it in his life.

"My father…was a souphead? Since when?"

He was taken aback. He looked at me as if the circumstances of the discussion had just radically changed. He just realized that we weren't on the same page. We weren't even in the same book.

"Look…son…I don't know exactly how to tell you this. Have you spoken to your mother recently?"

"She died in a car crash when I was very young. So no, no I haven't spoken to her recently."

"I'm sorry…I wasn't aware of that. I always had the sense that your father wasn't the, ah, sharing type but…anyway. I had an idea that your father wasn't close with you when I was listed as his emergency contact and the hospital called me, I thought, well, you know…but…this is…I mean…"

"Just tell me."

The lawyer got up from behind the desk, and he walked over to me. He took a deep breath, resting a hand on my shoulder.

"Your father was a costumed crimefighter. Have you ever heard of Jack Titan?"

I chuckled. My head felt like it was going to explode with the pressure of the headache I had, I thought I might throw up again, and I was little bit offended by the lawyer's joke, but still, I couldn't help but laugh a little.

"Son…I know this isn't easy to wrap your head around…" He cleared his throat.

"Wait, hold on a second. You're seriously telling me that my father was a superhero?"

"…masked vigilantes need legal counsel more than you would think. You'd be surprised how many frivolous super-criminal law suits superheroes have on their plate. Supervillains are constantly suing for assault, hospital bills, even emotional damage. Supervillains are notoriously litigious."

My father was a stock broker, or rather, he always told me that he was a stock broker. I didn't know what to say.

"I was one of the few people that he trusted with his secret...God, I'm so sorry, he should have been the one to tell you this..."

The cluttered office whirled around me. I almost passed out. This was all too much to handle.

"I know this must be an incredibly difficult time for you, and you, ah, honestly, I understand you had a late night. We have a lot of things to discuss...your father left everything to you, his apartment, his money, and his, uh, crimefighting paraphernalia. Get some rest, okay?"

I stood up and walked out of the lawyer's office. I was flying on autopilot as I got out of there. My body made its way past his secretary, to the elevator, and out of the building, but I wasn't there. The overpowering shock had shut me down. I never had a close relationship with my father, but I thought I had some vague idea of who he was. Now he was dead, and he lived a secret life as a superhero that I never knew about, that I would never know. And on top of that, I was living the same secret life, and he would never know either. I collapsed to the street outside of the building and vomited for a second time.

There's only so much a superhuman constitution can take.

Chapter 2:
A Portrait of the Superhero as a Young Man

The night that my superpowers manifested was one of the best nights of my life. I was seventeen years old, stuck in an all-boys boarding school in the dead of winter, and bored out of my mind. A friend of mine on the track team had smuggled a stash of SUHP into school. He was using it to improve his 100 meter dash times and get an edge over other teams at track meets, but I had a different use in mind.

I managed to sneak out of the dorm after lights out without being noticed. Hundreds of acres of forest surrounded the school, and I took a vial of soup with me into the white, snowy woods so I could experiment with a little privacy. I can still remember crunching my way through the snow in the immersive silence of the night. I could barely see where I was going in the darkness, and the small flashlight I had didn't help much. When you're in a boarding school, alone time is a precious commodity, and the isolation of the forest made me feel like I had just found an endless supply of that resource. It was refreshing.

I strayed off of the path and trod through the snow for a while, deeper and deeper into the trees, until I felt comfortable that there was no chance of being spotted. If a student was found out of the dorm after lights out and wandering out into the woods by himself to do illegal drugs, it was guaranteed that you would be expelled, and probably sent to some sort of reform school. Still, I have to admit that the threat of getting caught only added to the excitement.

I brushed the snow off of a fallen tree and sat down on the log. Just for a moment, I appreciated the scenery. Being alone in the middle of a snow covered forest is almost like being on another planet. You're all bundled up in winter gear like an astronaut in a space suit, all you can hear is the sound of your own breath, each footprint leaves a mark in the territory that might be discovered by some other explorer. It's a landscape that is simultaneously harsh and stunningly beautiful, and I felt like I was millions of miles from civilization.

I took the small vial of soup out of my jacket pocket. I shook the little plastic bottle and watched the clear liquid slosh around. It struck me as so strange that this stuff was responsible for so much radical change in society. SUHP was first created in 1938 by scientists who were trying to come up with medically useful compounds, and instead, they accidentally created a drug that temporarily unlocks superhuman potential in the DNA of ordinary people. I read somewhere that the first scientist who took soup accidentally spilled a huge dose on himself, and he thought he was having a stroke when he started smelling ultrasonic frequencies and seeing gamma rays.

It wasn't until the Harvard SUHP Project in the 60's that they discovered that SUHP activates dormant sequences of genes within the vast stretches of junk DNA in the human genome. In most people, SUHP temporarily switches on genes that will give them a random set of mild superpowers for a few hours as well as a euphoric high and hallucinations...but a small percentage of the population has a genetic predisposition to having those genes stay on permanently. The superhero boom of the 60's was partially because of the growing legions of soupheads as the drug gained popularity, but it was also because a tiny fraction of those millions of SUHP users unlocked extraordinary genetic potential that transformed them forever.

I had no reason to think that I had any superhuman potential lurking in my gene pool as I opened the vial and drank the soup. I had no idea that my father was one of the participants of the Harvard SUHP project decades before I was born, and that the drug released superhuman potential within him that sparked his superhero career as "Jack Titan, Man of Myth." I sat there somewhat skeptically as I waited for the stuff to start working, completely unaware that I was about to experience the genetic equivalent of being struck by lightning.

I was starting to think that my friend ripped me off and I was about to walk back to the dorm when it hit me. It was like the snow painted forest was suddenly on fire, burning with cool white flames that danced on every naked branch and pale green fir. Everything looked like I had been seeing it on a low resolution, black and white TV for my entire life and I didn't even know it. Now, that old bulky box had been replaced by a crystal clear HD TV with radiant colors. More than that, I felt strong, impossibly strong, like my muscles were tightly coiled titanium springs just waiting to explode into action.

I stood up from the log, I took a deep breath, and then purely on instinct, I jumped. I jumped so high that I was looking down on acres of forest like a giant striding across the countryside, and then the tops of the trees came racing at me as I fell back down to Earth. I landed on an ice covered branch, the force of my fall snapped it like a pencil. I tumbled down through the bare arms of the tree until I snagged the trunk with an unreasonably strong grip that cracked half century old wood. I hung there on the side of the tree, at least 40 feet off of the ground, just in uncontrollable awe at both the drug enhanced vision of the wintery forest and the amazing things I was doing.

Then I pushed off of the bark with both feet like a swimmer pushing off of the starting block. Trees glided by me as I flew through the air, and newly enhanced superhuman reflexes made them all seem like they were moving past me in slow motion. It was all like a strange dream except that it felt more real than anything I had experienced in my entire life, like I had been playing a video game since the moment I was born but I had just put down the controller and stepped into reality. I felt hypercharged with energy like I had been injected with a thousand cups of coffee but there was no jitteriness, there was only an incredible clarity and focus unlike anything I had ever known.

I reached out for a nearby branch and latched onto it. I spun around it like a trained gymnast once, twice, three times before letting go and catapulting high above the trees. For a split second, I hovered above the forest and I could see the school on the horizon. It was so small and far away. Then, I plummeted back down into the woods and I scraped the side of a fir to slow my descent like it was the most natural thing.

I crouched in the snow and caught my breath. I should have been freezing cold, but I could barely feel the sting of the winter air on my cheeks. I felt intoxicated, not just with the high of the soup, but with power, power like a galaxy of fiery burning suns spinning around inside of my chest. I stood up and walked over to a nearby tree stump. It was a huge, ancient thing anchored deep into the ground. I clenched a fist, and steam ebbed off of my hand because of the unnatural amount of heat generated by muscles experiencing superhuman strength for the first time.

I pulled back my fist, and I jabbed at the frigid tree trunk. The stump exploded into a cloud of icy splinters, and I'm lucky that I squinted enough to block the hail of shards rocketing in every direction. Still, a few splinters had lodged into my face and my knuckles. Stunned, I looked at my fist like it was the first time I had seen it. I opened my fist and flexed fingers strong enough to crunch steel like a beer can, and I looked at where the stump used to be. It was just a jagged mess of shattered wood, and I couldn't believe that I had just done that.

For a few more hours, I experimented with what I thought was temporary superhuman agility and strength. I ran and leapt through the forest, and all conscious thought dissipated. I was like a wild animal on the loose in its natural habitat, just letting the shapes and colors of the winter forest wash over me. There were no doubts or anxieties or concerns with my everyday life. There was only the exhilarating rush of incredible movement, of strength beyond description, of a physical potential unchained by a lifetime of an inarticulate restraint, of liberation.

I lost track of time, and when the intoxicating effects of the drug wore off, I found myself sitting in the top of a tree. The sun was beginning to rise, and I realized that I had to get back to my dorm room before someone discovered that I was missing, if they hadn't already. I jumped off of the branch and as I was falling I was hit with a sudden panic. Too late it occurred to me that the powers must have worn off by now, and as the ground rushed at me, I thought I would be seriously injured by the fall. I slammed into the snowy floor of the forest…and to my surprise, I felt fine. I just thought that I got lucky and there was still a bit of the soup working its way through my system. I started to walk back to campus, unaware that superhuman sections of my DNA had just been startled awake from a deep sleep.

Chapter 3:
Trophy Room

"For every action, there is an equal and opposite reaction…!"

I was watching Master Boson launch into his stale supervillain spiel on the video Joe Metal had uploaded onto The Millennials' website, and if there's one thing that's not good for a downward spiral, it's obsessing over what the internet thinks about you. My father died two weeks ago, and I proceeded to aggressively preoccupy myself with work. Every day, I would go after low level losers like Master Boson, sometimes with The Millennials, sometimes by myself, and I barely stopped to sleep or eat. There were often periods when no supercrime was going down in the city, and these were the times that I would torment myself with these videos. Meanwhile, the voice mails piled up.

I sat up from my couch and paused the video, stopping Master Boson's horrendously bad rant. Then, I made the worst mistake I could possibly make…I scrolled down to the comments section to see what people were saying about me. I cannot stress this enough to any up and coming superheroes reading this: do not read the comments. I'd bet good money that reading comments on the internet is what drives a lot of supervillains to do more than half the crazy shit that they do.

I stood up from the couch and stretched my legs. My one bedroom apartment had deteriorated from a relatively nice place into a shithole of epic proportions. Although I never kept it in perfectly clean condition, there was at least an effort to keep it presentable. When I first got the place, I decorated it in a minimalist style with post modern art that ironically referenced superhero culture. What was an apartment that you could bring people to after a night out had become an inexcusable mess of clothes all over the floor, empty pizza boxes, discarded beer bottles, plates of half eaten food, and a stink of body odor spreading like fungus.

I stepped over one of my dirty costumes that had laid on the floor next to my coffee table where I dropped it a week ago and walked into the kitchen, which reeked of unwashed dishes. I opened the fridge and took out a beer (one of the only known cures for the common internet comment). I popped the cap off of the bottle with a super strength flick of my thumb, and didn't even bother to pay attention to where it landed. A third of the beer was gone by the time I sat back down on the couch to pore over the internet's infinite wisdom.

I pored over them, and predictably, they were varying shades of "I hate this" to "I love this" with very little middle ground in between the two extremes. The beer bottle was empty when I had reached my tolerance for internet comments, and I pushed the power button on my laptop to put it into sleep mode. The screen turned to a reflective black, and my unshaven face looked back at me from the dark surface. My black hair was matted and greasy, heavy bags were visible under my eyes even through the black mask stuck on my face. There was a mustard stain on the collar of my dark navy costume jacket, and the skin tight blue spandex underneath the jacket was covered in dried sweat marks. I slapped my laptop shut.

I was about to microwave some ravioli before heading back out to take out my frustrations on the first unlucky supervillain that I could get my hands on when I heard someone knocking at my door. I paused for a moment. I wasn't expecting anyone, and my place certainly wasn't in any condition for visitors. I walked over to the door and looked through the eye hole to see Ultra Lady, a superheroine I had never even met. The eye hole warped my view of her like a fish eye lens, but still, she was strikingly beautiful in her iconic red and white costume despite the distortion.

"Are you going to open the door? I know you're standing there. Even if I couldn't hear your heartbeat with my ultra-hearing, I can smell you through the door. Jesus Christ, when was the last time you showered, kid?"

She must have heard my heart rate suddenly double. There was a lump in my throat, and I tried and failed to gain my composure before opening the door slightly with the chainlock still on.

"Uhm…can I help you?"

"Are you serious? Come on, let me in. I want to talk to you about something."

I hesitated. I wasn't exactly in the right state of mind to have company, and I couldn't understand for the life of me why Ultra Lady, *THE* Ultra Lady would want to talk to me. Ultra Lady was about five years older than me, and if I was a C-list superhero, then she was A-list. Realistically, she wasn't even on the same grading scale as me. Ultra Lady was on a meteoric rise to the upper echelon of the superhero community. She recently joined the Superb 6, replacing Doc Hyper, who had just retired, and she was gifted in every way. She was invulnerable, she could lift over a hundred tons and was easily one of the strongest crimefighters in the game, plus she could fly and move at super speeds rivaling the now retired Doc Hyper. She could hear electrons bounce off of each other and see lightyears away, and as if all of that wasn't enough, she was also stunningly gorgeous. She was the Indestructible Woman, the Lady of the Future. What could she want from me?

"Listen, I know we don't know each other, and I don't want to…I don't want to offend you or anything, but I knew your father. And I just want to talk to you for five minutes. If you don't like what you hear, I'll leave."

I closed the door and slid the chain lock off, then I opened it for Ultra Lady. Her disgust with the state of my apartment was instantly apparent as she walked with me to the couch. The sight of her walking through my messy, garbage ridden apartment in a pristine white cape and her radiant red costume was a stark contrast, like seeing Athena stroll around a landfill.

"So you knew my dad?"

"Yeah. Yeah I did, briefly. He was a reserve member of the Superb 6 and we had a few…team ups."

"Oh, 'team ups'? Is that what the kids are calling it these days?"

"…it wasn't like that. Your dad, he was kind of like a mentor to me."

"That's nice for you," I got up from the couch and got another beer from the fridge. I held one up, offering it to her, but she just looked at me with disapproval so strong that it could have been another superpower. "Ultra-disdain".

"Look. I get it. I know you must be going through some shit right now…your dad just died, and it's pretty obvious that no one in the superhero community is even aware that you are his son. At least, no one at his funeral seemed to know that The Spectacle is Jack Titan's son. The funeral I just came from, by the way."

I drank my beer, and said nothing.

"Your father's lawyer was there. I spoke to him, and he mentioned that Jack had a son. I didn't even know he had kids…he was never the sharing type."

"Yeah, tell me about it," I said. Ultra Lady looked at me with eyes that could watch bullets crawl like snails, and all my body language must have been making my emotions a flashing neon sign for her to read in slow motion.

"Oh my god. You didn't know, did you? You didn't know that your dad was Jack Titan."

I briefly considered lying to her, but that ultra-hearing would have heard the lie in my heart beats. I nodded, and took a long drink of my beer.

"God…no wonder you didn't go to the funeral." Ultra Lady shifted uncomfortably on the couch. There was an awkward silence, and I got the impression that she was wavering between leaving and giving in to the urge to say something that I might take the wrong way.

"Okay. I came here to give my condolences, and okay, maybe I was also curious to see what Jack's son was like and why he wouldn't even show up to his father's funeral…but I think you should have this." Ultra Lady reached into a pocket in her cape and pulled out a piece of golden rope, about two feet long, joined in the center with a little oval scrap of leather.

"He called this his 'golden sling'. You should have seen him use it." She handed it to me, and I turned the sling over in my hands. The leather patch in the center of the two gold painted ropes had the initials "J.T." embroidered onto it in yellow thread.

"Jack would put a little piece of debris in this thing and I swear, he could hit a comma on a page two hundred yards away. It was unreal how he would whip that sling with super strength and just rocket projectiles."

"How did you get it...?"

"On one of our team ups, things went a little sour. We were fighting...The Punster and his henchmen, I'm sure you've heard of him. Jack lost his golden sling during the fighting, and when it was all over, I managed to get it back. He told me to keep it and put it 'in my trophy room'...he said he had a million of them."

I rubbed my thumb over the yellow "J.T." stitching. There was still a big part of me that refused to believe that my dad was a superhero, but holding his "golden sling" in my hands hammered home the reality of it. He was always stitching his name into his things. When I was young, I used to watch him stitch his initials into his shirts and his socks.

"Thank you. I actually...I really appreciate this."

"Of course...I probably shouldn't say this, but...you know, if you need someone to talk to, you can call me. I didn't know him that well, but I could tell you a couple of stories about your dad." Ultra Lady's intense waves of ultra-disdain had faded and were replaced by a look of pity. She got up from the couch and floated a few inches off of the floor to avoid stepping on dirty clothes and garbage as she left.

"And it's not my place to say this, but get your shit together man. You can't just *not* go to your father's funeral."

"I'm a superhero, I can do anything. I can leap tall buildings in a single bound, I can bend steel with my—"

"Don't be a smart ass, Spectacle." Ultra Lady opened the door and softly landed on the ground. Her white boots squeaked as she touched down on the tile floor, and she lingered with a white gloved hand on the doorknob.

"If you want to know more about your dad, the information is out there. There were people at the funeral who knew him way better than I did. But you've got to stop wallowing in self pity." She walked through the door and closed it behind her without looking back.

I sat there holding the golden sling in my trash cluttered apartment. I was angry, angry that Ultra Lady would talk to me like that. Who was she to come down from the space station headquarters of the Superb 6, like a pompous goddess descending from Olympus, to self righteously lecture me about my life? I was angry that my father never told me that he was a superhero. I was angry that the superheroes at my father's funeral probably knew him better than I did. I couldn't see it at the time, but most of all, I was angry at myself. I was furious for letting myself fall to pieces like this. I was raging at the idea that Ultra Lady was right.

I put the golden sling in my costume jacket pocket, and I took out my phone. For the past two weeks, I had been avoiding calls from my dad's lawyer and letting his texts and voice mails build up. The voice mails he was leaving painted an interesting picture. They began passive aggressively with the lawyer politely requesting that I meet with him again to deal with funeral issues and go over my father's will. Then, as time passed, his messages gradually mutated from respectfully tolerant to flat out yelling at me for neglecting the logistics of my father's death. I couldn't help but giggle at his frustration, but I also felt a flood of guilt as it dawned on me that I couldn't just be willfully oblivious to these things.

After an extremely tense phone call with the lawyer, who was less than happy to hear from me after weeks of me ignoring his calls, I took a walk across town to my father's apartment. He had warned me that unless I went there and collected his belongings, which my father had left to me, his possessions would mostly likely be thrown out by the owners of the building.

"And you don't want that. Trust me. Check in his sock drawer, go look in his little walk in closet, and you'll see what I mean," he explained with more than a hint of bitter amusement in his tone of voice.

Although it wasn't the home I grew up in, my father's apartment was a place I had been many times. I lived there for a few months during the summer before I went to college. I even had a key, but I had never been there with the knowledge that my father was a superhero. I turned the key in the lock, and the lawyer's cryptic comments made me anticipate a scene of utility belts and Titan-computers and spare costumes in glass cases. When I opened the door, what I saw was the ordinary apartment that I had seen many times before.

The place just looked like the upper middle class home of a sixty year old stock broker. I walked into the apartment, and just like the many times I had been here before, there were no signs whatsoever of a superhero career. There were barely any signs of a person living there. The place was immaculately clean; the cupboards were empty, the fridge was vacant except for a jar of pickles with an expiration date that had passed almost a year ago, the wood floors were so well kept that they gleamed like a mirror. The TV remote was perfectly perched on the arm of his white leather couch, magazines were flawlessly fanned out on his glass coffee table, even his flat screen was free of smudges and looked like it had just been brought home from the store. Nothing was out of place.

I sat down on his pristine white couch. It didn't seem like there was anything here that I would miss if it was thrown away. Sure, he had nice furniture and expensive things, but none of those things were worth it to me to keep if I had to constantly be reminded of my father's death. The leather creaked as I got up from the couch and walked into my father's bedroom, to investigate the walk in closet that the lawyer had mentioned.

My father's bedroom seemed just as unlived in as the rest of his place. I looked around for the walk in closet that the lawyer had mentioned, but I was surprised to find that he didn't even have a closet. That seemed extremely strange to me. What kind of bedroom doesn't have a closet? He did have an uncommonly large dresser that was almost as tall as me, and I opened the top drawer which was filled with socks. The black socks each had my father's initials stitched into them on the ankle in blue thread, and I rifled around in the drawer but found nothing.

I almost gave up looking for anything of any importance when I found a single black sock with my father's initials in gold thread instead of blue. It seemed a little weird, so I started to pick up the sock to see if maybe there was something inside of it, when I realized that it was caught on something. I didn't want to pull too hard and rip it, so I cleared away the other socks and saw that there was a metallic wire attached to the heel of the sock. The wire led into the back of the drawer where it disappeared through a small, almost pinhole sized opening in the wood.

I gently tugged on the wire, and there was a loud clank like a giant door was unlocking. The entire dresser shifted a few inches away from the wall. I pulled on the back of the dresser, and it pivoted away from the wall on hinges. The unusually tall dresser was blocking the opening to the huge walk in closet, and I was confronted by what looked like a miniature superhero headquarters.

A wall of the room was plastered with clippings from the career of Jack Titan. One article was from early in my father's career and it had a photograph of him as a young man. The headline read "Jack Titan Apprehends The Punster" and the photograph showed him in his Jack Titan costume. It was so bizarre to see him, maybe only a few years older than I was then, decked out in this Greek warrior themed superhero costume. It consisted of a tight fitting toga with gold embroidering, leather greaves on his shins and bronze braces on his forearms, a golden mask and a golden wreath atop a head of long, curly brown hair that was gray my entire life, and a silver chest plate. The silver chest plate had bold, stylized "JT" symbols etched onto both shoulders. The photographer had caught him right as he was flinging his golden sling.

The wall of this small room was teeming with clippings from newspapers, magazines, and even a bunch of print outs from online news sources spanning Jack Titan's entire career. When the lawyer told me that my father was Jack Titan, I recognized the name, but I thought that he was a relatively obscure superhero. This wall of clippings told a different story. They spelled out the narrative of my father's career from a low level costumed crimefighter to a respected mainstay of the superhero community. I was dumbfounded by the amount of material here. I could have spent months reading over the myriad articles. It was too much to take in all at once, but it was easy to see that a thread ran through the narrative in front of me. Over and over again, Jack Titan faced The Punster.

I wasn't familiar with The Punster, but there were dozens of headlines detailing their various encounters. There were a few pictures of the supervillain. He was a skinny, bald man in a purple turtleneck with a big, gaudy green "P!" emblazoned on the chest, and he had a creepy look of crazed enthusiasm. The crimes he committed were all pun themed, and the headline writers clearly had their fun with that. There were article titles like, "Jack Titan

Squishes Punster's 'Play Dough' Counterfeiting Scheme", "The Punster's Giant 'Antdroid' Bugs Downtown,", and, "Jack Titan Testifies Against Punster, Gives Him a Pun for his Money."

It was obvious that this hidden room was where my father had been spending the majority of his time. There was a mattress on the floor with a crumpled blanket on it, empty water bottles were strewn everywhere, a pile of protein bar wrappers had built up in the corner, and there were more than a few used up vials of soup. There was none of the sterile, impossibly clean order that characterized the rest of the apartment. I stepped over the mattress and the insane amount of empty soup vials littered around it. There were enough of them to put a small whale into a coma, and I tried to ignore them as I made my way to the back wall of the room where I saw his Jack Titan apparel.

His silver chest plate hung on a hook on the wall, and on closer inspection, I could see that it was a slab of kevlar coated in shiny paint. His golden mask and wreath dangled on a hook next to the chest plate. The rest of his armor, the greaves, the bronze braces, and a pair of Grecian sandals sat on a narrow shelf built into the wall. There was a heap of his golden slings, at least twenty of them, at the far end of the shelf. Underneath the shelf, there was a big cardboard box.

The box was labeled "Trophy Room" in black marker. If I could have spent months reading through all the articles pinned to the wall, then I could have spent a lifetime poring over the stuff packed into that box. It looked like my father saved everything. The first thing that I noticed was a brittle, ancient plastic ID badge from his participation in the Harvard SUHP project in the early 60's. His eighteen year old, beardless baby face awkwardly smiled at me on the yellowing ID badge. He looked impossibly young, almost a decade younger than I was at that moment, and it was unreal for me to see the undeniable proof that my dad was once the opposite of the stoic, aloof adult that I always knew.

There were countless photographs of my father scattered throughout that box. A lot of them were from so early on in his superhero career that they were still in black and white. His Jack Titan costume in those first years was so bad that it looked like it was held together by tape and paper clips. His beard hadn't really filled in yet, and he was holding his Golden Sling clumsily, like he couldn't even pretend that he knew how to use it correctly...but in each of those photos, he looked so happy. Even in black and white, it was easy to see that excitement, that electrifying thrill of putting on a silly costume and transforming into more than a normal person, that charge of confidence you get when your absurd outfit screams at the world, "*I am a superhero, I dare you to tell me I'm not!*" It was easy to recognize it on his boyish face, even through his cheap, spray painted gold mask, because I'd had the same look on my own face.

There were piles and piles of photos of him with other superheroes, some of whom I recognized, and others that I had never even heard of who must have faded away into obscurity over the decades. My dad, having the time of his life at hole in the wall bars and house parties with superheroes who are living legends today. Drunk and smiling with his arm around Beyond Man. Sitting at a dirty bar with Queen Quantum, years before she could afford to bedazzle her Cosmic Crown with real four karat diamonds. I saw him with global icons like Doc Hyper and Sleight of Hand and even Anhur, who hated to be photographed unless he was with a beautiful woman, beating a supervillain to a pulp, or both.

I saw him in candid snapshots with the people who went on to become the founding members of the Superb 6 and some of the most iconic superheroes in the history of costumed crimefighting. Today, you never see photographic evidence of these people cutting loose like this, and believe me, armies of paparazzi have tried. Today, you'll see them on the cover of magazines and on billboards and if you're lucky, flying up in the sky above you, but you won't see them gawkily dancing in dive bars with people like my dad. It was so weird to see these people like that, these celebrities who we look at like gods watching over us in their Superb 6 satellite, but back then, they were all just a bunch of goofy kids.

I flipped through the stacks of photographs, and it was like looking through a slide show of my dad's entire life. I saw him grow up from a teenage superhero, just an amateur in a bed sheet toga and a card board chest plate, to a full fledged professional in his mid twenties with a tailor made costume that was so good that he really did look like a Titan plucked right out of Greek Mythology. I saw him grow older and older and I saw that look, that pure, vibrant joy of being a superhero, melt from his face. And finally, I saw pictures of my dad approaching the age he was when I was born, and that somber, poker faced man that I knew showed his face.

And then there were the mementos, the endless mementos. The limited edition Jack Titan action figure, complete with 8 points of articulation, real removable metal armor, and sling throwing action. A ticket stub from the premiere of the Beyond Man movie. An invitation to the opening of the Kirby Museum of Superhero History. There was a compound camera eye from The Punster's giant rampaging insect robot, his "Antroid." A shiny green scale from one of Dragon General's wings, and one of The Abnormalite's razor sharp fangs, which made me a little proud, because my dad probably punched it right out of that monster's mouth. There was a note from Mistress Gorgon that was half love letter, and half death threat. And there was a pair of brass knuckles with an engraving from Anhur that read, "To Jack Titan: May your fist be blessed by Ra, and hit as hard as the Titans of old." There were so many more wonderful things in there, so many weird trinkets and trophies. Everything that my dad kept from an entire lifetime of costumed crimefighting was crammed into that box.

Then, beneath all of the photos, beneath the mountains of relics saved over the course of my dad's whole life, I found the mother lode. I found dozens of spiral notebooks buried at the bottom of that box, and each of them was filled with his writing about his life as a superhero. Everything he ever did in costume, he wrote about. There couldn't have been less than half a million words in those notebooks. I skimmed through one of them, and I read about things as mundane as stopping Dragon General and his Reptilian Guard from robbing an armored car, and as downright psychedelic as the time Doctor Delusion dosed him and the Superb 6 with his hallucinogenic, SUHP tipped daydream darts. I flipped through the hundreds of pages of my father's hand written notes, and it hit me. He was really gone. These notebooks, they were all that was left.

I lost track of time while I looked through that box. I realized that it contained everything of my father's that I wanted to keep. If anything remained of him, it wasn't in the antiseptic apartment outside of that room. It was pinned up to those walls, and it was stuffed into that box marked Trophy Room. Everything outside of that hidden room could be sold for whatever cash I could get for it, but the things on those walls and in that box were priceless and irreplaceable. I gathered up all of the articles on the walls, I took his Golden Slings, his wreath and mask, his pieces of armor, and I threw it all in that box marked Trophy Room. The last chance to know my father that I had consisted of everything in that cardboard box, and the worst part is that I didn't even know how important it was to me until it was taken away.

Chapter 4:
On the House

"Sorry kid, we're at capacity." The bouncer outside of "The Flasked Crusader" took one look at me, and the scowl on his face made it obvious that he wasn't even going to consider letting me into the bar.

The bar was in a part of town that even a superhero doesn't want to be in after dark, and I was there because of a matchbox I had found in the box of my father's stuff. The matchbox was at the top of the mountains of things jammed into the box, and it had a recent date and time written on it in his handwriting. I thought that he must have met someone there recently, and if I wanted find out more about my father, going to one of his regular hangouts was probably a good place to start. I was intimidated by how much material was in that box, but I thought if I could talk to someone he actually knew, if I could sit down and just have a conversation with someone he might have even considered a friend, that would be better than studying his volumes of scribbles. I thought wrong.

"Uh, there's no way you can let me in?" I asked him, and I looked around at the deserted street outside of the Flasked Crusader. No one was trying to get into this dive.

"I said get out of my face," the bouncer said, and he turned his attention back to his phone. He was a big guy…six and a half feet tall and two hundred and fifty pounds if he weighed an ounce. Normally, that wouldn't faze me (size isn't a factor when you've got super strength), but his skin was also a thick hide of blueish green scales. He was a superhuman, and I couldn't be sure what his abilities were. Maybe he could just breath under water. Or maybe he could breath fire.

"I guess this is a waste of time, but can you tell me why you—"

"Yo, I'm not gonna say this again. This place isn't for you. Look at you, you're a hipster vigilante, you're a little snot nosed do gooder and I don't need you startin' any shit with some of the less than heroic types in this establishment. So walk. *Now.*" The bouncer glared at me, and the snake-like, slit pupils of his eyes made his stare even more intense. After a good ten seconds of this, he looked back at his phone and it was as if I wasn't even standing there.

I considered slipping the guy some money to get in, but after a pocket search, I realized that I hadn't brought any cash. I just had my Millennials team credit card which was issued to me by the Crimefighter Credit Union. The

Crimefighter Credit Union, or the CCU, handles the banking for the entire superhero community. It was established to protect everyone's secret identities from corporately owned banks, and to process the checks we collect from the government for catching supervillains with warrants on their heads. The whole superhero-industrial complex would collapse without the CCU, but the credit card they issued me wasn't going to convince this charming gentlemen to do me any favors.

"Hey man, I'm really not going to cause any trouble, I just want to get a drink inside..."

The bouncer looked up at me, and then he spit on the sidewalk. His spit was hot pink, and the asphalt sizzled where it landed. A few seconds later, his acidic loogie had burned a hole right through the sidewalk.

"Next one's in your eye," the bouncer cleared his throat, and then he was right back to his phone.

I was about to give up and walk away when I happened to catch a glimpse of his phone screen. He was looking at Professor Dinosaur's website, a supervillain that The Millennials had put behind bars twice in the past year. I recognized it from Professor Dinosaur's distinctive symbol, a stylized T-Rex brand that the scaly villain wore on his tweed jacket like the crest of some nonexistent dinosaur university.

"It's none of my business, but if you're thinking about applying to be Professor Dinosaur's henchman, I'd reconsider. You're better off being a bouncer," I remarked, and then I marched away, pissed off that this guy was forcing me to give up on this lead.

"Wait wait, hold up kid, why d'you say that?" The bouncer called after me, and I stopped walking.

"Nothing, don't worry about it man," I bent my knees and hunched down as I prepared to leap away from this god forsaken hell hole of a bar. Just as I was about to jump, a huge scale covered hand fell on my shoulder and held me to the ground.

"Seriously bro, what's wrong with being this Dino guy's henchman?" The bouncer's eyes were filled with a childlike curiosity that clashed with his predatory reptilian pupils.

I brushed his hand off my shoulder and tried to hide the chills that ran through me when I scraped his gross snake skin.

"Here's the thing about Professor Dinosaur: he's sloppy as fuck. The superhero group I'm with, we've caught this guy a few times and it's embarrassingly easy. Almost doesn't seem fair," I answered.

"So what? All these villain douchebags get caught. I just want some quick, easy money," the bouncer leaned against the wall and resumed ignoring me, but with a dash of disappointment that I couldn't give him any useful information on his potential employer.

Doubt paralyzed me. I could give this guy advice, and he might let me into the Flasked Crusader, but then he would end up being a more effective henchman for a more dangerous supervillain. If he worked for Professor

Dinosaur, that pretentious faux-intellectual would all but guarantee that this bouncer would end up in jail, probably in some half baked attempt to steal a stegosaurus skeleton. I should have walked away, but I just had to know why my dad would come to this place.

"Professor Dinosaur doesn't really pay that well…that's why he's constantly getting caught. His henchman are always these inexperienced, young guys."

I had the bouncer's attention again.

"You're trying to get work with a, ahm, you know, a reptile themed guy right? If I were you, I'd take a look at Dragon General."

"Why? Why Dragon General instead of this dinosaur guy?"

"Dragon General's slippery. Dude's hard to catch, not like Professor Dinosaur. Dinosaur's always taking hostages and trying to hurt civilians…that shit's fucked up. And it gets the attention of a lot of heroes. Dragon General's different. He's efficient, he just gets his money then he splits, he's not interested in taking out his frustrations on regular people."

The bouncer was intrigued, and I was already regretting this, but I'd gone too far to stop now.

"Plus, all Dragon General's henchmen have good teeth."

"Uh…" The bouncer was confused.

"*Good dental.* He calls his henchmen his Reptilian Guard, and I'm pretty sure he keeps the same dudes on staff. That means the pay's good enough to keep them around. You're superhuman too, so I bet you'd be like a henchman officer or some shit. Better pay, maybe?"

The bouncer squinted at me. I think he was trying to figure out if I was making fun of him, and for what felt like forever, he didn't say anything. I thought he was going to hit me.

"You're alright, kid," he slapped me on the shoulder with one of his meaty, snake skinned hands.

I talked with the bouncer for a few more minutes, just shooting the shit with the guy, and it occurred to me that I'd probably be fighting him sometime in the near future. Turns out his name was Joel, and although he seemed like a nice enough dude once you got past his whole tough guy schtick, I wouldn't want him coughing up that hot pink acid on me. He finally let me into the Flasked Crusader, and as soon as I stepped foot in the place, I knew that I was so far out of my element that I might as well be in another dimension. It was dimly lit, grimy, and it smelled like hard liquor, blood, and energy blasts. The youngest person in the bar had to be double my age, and although nearly everyone there was in costume, I didn't recognize most of them. I walked towards the bar and from the dirty looks I was getting, it was abundantly clear that I was not welcome there.

I sat down on a wooden bar stool, and it dawned on me that there were a lot of supervillains in the room. I saw The Abnormalite, a pink skinned monstrosity of a man with fangs, four arms, and eight eyes, playing pool with The Immaterial Man, who was a fog cloud in the vague shape of a person. The Abnormalite gave me the stink eye with half of his eyes while the other half carefully lined up a shot on the pool table. The Immaterial Man watched as The Abnormalite sank the eight ball in the side pocket (or at least I think he was watching, it's hard to tell with a humanoid puff of smoke). I spotted superheroes mingled in with other villains I was less familiar with, and these superheroes barely even qualified for the name...they were really more of the "anti-hero" type. These were the kinds of heroes that you don't see on the cover of magazines, that you'll never catch tweeting or making an appearance on a talk show or signing autographs for kids. In the crimefighter circles I usually run in, anti-hero is a dirty word.

Their costumes had skulls and sharp metal spikes and chains and knives strapped to their hips as well as absurdly large guns and if I'm not mistaken, one guy had a live grenade dangling from his utility belt. I recognized Sergeant Silence, an anti-hero pushing 70 whose hardcore, merciless treatment of villains practically caused the term "anti-hero" to be coined just to describe his particular class of crazy. I'm not ashamed to say that the hair on the back of my neck stood up at the sight of him drinking by himself in a booth in his combat camo and with his flamethrower harnessed to his crooked, age bent back. All these anti-hero guys were so grizzled and brimming with so much rage that it would be funny if I wasn't afraid that one of them might try to cut me just for showing my face there. What could my father possibly be doing in a place like this?

"What'll you have?" The bartender was a middle aged, stocky woman. She seemed a little bored by me, like she had seen young superheroes get chewed up and spit out by this place so many times that it was getting old.

"I'll just have a beer. Whatever you have on tap," I responded. She brought me the beer, and plopped the glass on the bar.

"Hey, can I ask you a question?"

"You're a little young for me, sweetheart…besides, I don't date superheroes anyway," She snickered while she started mixing a drink.

"No…no, I was just curious…have you ever seen Jack Titan in here?"

The glass she was holding slipped out of her hand, and she spilled a half made drink all over the bar. She leered at me with suspicion, and then she started over on the drink.

"Maybe. I'm not sure. Why do you want to know?"

"Well. He passed away recently, and I know he came here, so…you know, he was my dad, so I'm sort of trying to find out more about him…" I drank my beer and I suddenly felt like my stomach was a cement mixer, churning with nervousness and panic. This whole plan felt like a massive mistake.

"I don't know what to tell you. He's never been in here," she responded, and she wouldn't make eye contact with me as she remade the drink.

"Oh…is it possible that he was in here on a night you weren't working?"

"I'm the only bartender here, I work every night, sorry." She finished the drink and carried it over to The Abnormalite. I saw her discreetly whisper something to The Immaterial Man as he was racking up the balls for another game, and he pivoted his hazy fog head in my direction. Then, I heard a phone ring in the back room of the bar, and the bartender walked so fast to answer it that she was almost running.

I sat there drinking my beer, and I wasn't exactly sure what to do next. I wasn't ready to give up yet, but I also wasn't prepared to strike up a conversation with any of these upstanding, friendly citizens. I tried distracting myself by looking at my phone, but The Immaterial Man and The Abnormalite were staring at me, and it was making me extremely uneasy. The bartender casually strolled out from the back room of the bar right when I was about to bolt.

"Can I get you another?" Her attitude had radically changed. Everything about her was now screaming friendliness.

"Uh, sure," I was leaning heavily towards leaving. No one here had any information on my father, and even if they did, they weren't going to share it with me. The bartender refilled my glass, she gently placed it in front of me, and then she leaned in conspiratorially, like she was about to tell me a secret.

"You know, I did know Jack Titan. Don't take this the wrong way, but I actually fought him a bunch of times. I was a henchman, well henchwoman, with The Punster. My name's Jane, by the way."

"Yeah? Nice to meet you, I'm…ah, The Spectacle."

"Sure you are. Yeah, I was one of The Punster's Goons. Back in the day, Punster had a gang of henchmen, he called us Goons, he dressed us up in these hazmat suit uniforms with these tanks of goo that you could spray at the capes to slow em' down. You know, 'goo', 'Goons.' It was part of his pun thing."

"Right," Something about the way Jane had just turned the switch from "extremely standoffish" to "aggressively outgoing" was unsettling.

"Whatever happened to The Punster?" I asked her. The Punster was in so many of my dad's clippings, and I was curious what happened to the wordplay obsessed supervillain.

"He, you know, he passed a few years ago. He was, you know, ah…old."

"Okay…yeah, that makes sense."

"Yeah."

"Think you could tell me anything about my dad, like why he was here?"

"Oh sure, sure, I could tell you loads of stories!"

For the next few hours, Jane spun tales about my father that were endlessly amusing. She told me about the time The Punster built a giant, ant-shaped android called the "Antdroid" that almost killed my father. She told me about the time Punster had Jack Titan in a huge vise, and how he kept screaming "Jack *Tighten!* Jack *Tighten!*" over and over as it squeezed the life out of him until he was able to break the metal contraption through sheer physical strength. She told me about the first time Jack Titan faced the Goons and how they almost drowned him in a sea of immobilizing, chemical goo which The Punster synthesized himself. She told me story after story about my father and The Punster's demented, pun-themed schemes, and she poured me beer after beer to go along with them.

I thought that I was learning the things that I had set out to learn. I thought that I was getting to know the man that my father was as Jane weaved an epic narrative of Jack Titan versus The Punster. The way she told it, they were archenemies on an almost mythical scale. Time and again, Jack Titan fought the mad Punster. He escaped his pun death traps and he foiled his boundless supply of pun schemes that would have been admirably creative if they weren't fueled by a deranged, pun obsessed criminal mind. The way she told it, my father was a flawless hero who bravely fought a cackling caricature of a villain. Jane served me a pretty lie, and I ate it up without realizing that it was all a distraction.

Eventually, Jane ran out of legends of my father, and by the time that she did, I was inexcusably drunk. When I tried to pay my tab, she said that it was "on the house," and even in my drunken stupor, that seemed odd to me. I didn't question it. I should have known then what had happened, but I just staggered out of the Flasked

Crusader, oblivious to the sideways glances of grimacing supervillains and anti-heroes. Joel the bouncer gave me a friendly nod and thanked me for the Dragon General recommendation, and I leapt away from the Flasked Crusader. I wasn't just drunk on the free beer I had been guzzling for the past few hours. I was drunk on the false assumption that I had achieved my goal. I thought I had just found out a wealth of information about my late father. I vaulted from rooftop to rooftop, loaded to the gills and lucky that I didn't slip and fall, and I was filled with a sense of satisfaction and achievement that was about to be shattered.

When I made it back to my apartment, I couldn't even get my key into the lock. I was tempted to tear the door off the hinges, but I finally managed to unlock it, and stumble into my bedroom. I fell onto my bed and the room spun around me. My booze drowned brain was seconds away from sinking into a deep, dreamless sleep when I noticed something that jolted me completely awake. My father's box marked Trophy Room was missing. I got out of bed and walked over to my desk where I had left the box. A single vial of soup was sitting where the box had been.

Super strength is a funny thing. Sometimes, it's like the entire world is made out of mist. Up to a certain point, everything feels like it weighs nothing. You punch a wall, and your fist goes through it as if it was a curtain of vapor. You lift up a few tons of steel and concrete like a kid carrying a big ball of cotton candy. Sometimes, super strength is thrilling…but when you're angry, it's the height of frustration.

I threw the vial of soup against the wall so hard that the glass exploded into a fine dust and the liquid inside vaporized instantly. I slammed my fist on the middle of the desk and it split in half and collapsed in on itself. My bookshelf was next, and I just sliced at it with a stiff hand like cutting ice cream with a red hot knife. The shelves fell apart and the books burst into confetti and rained around me. I snatched the metal doorknob of my bedroom door and I squeezed it like a stress ball. The fist sized doorknob crunched in my hand to a little sphere the size of a grape. There was no conscious thought, nothing left of what I think of as "me", there was just indescribable rage and an endless frustration at the fact that no matter how much I broke, I just felt like I was swinging at shadows.

Chapter 5:
Delusions and Illusions

I woke up feeling very silly. I had yet another hangover, I was surrounded by smashed furniture, and I felt like an idiot. I thought I could just waltz into that bar and find out what I wanted to know. All I accomplished was getting the attention of someone in that bar who called Jane and had her distract me with hours of bullshit while someone was in my place stealing the box of my father's superhero stuff. A wealth of information about my father's superhero career was lost because I was cocky and naïve.

I got out of bed, still dressed in my Spectacle costume that I had passed out in, and looked around at the wreckage that was the undeniable evidence of my little temper tantrum. It all seemed so senseless. My father was dead, and learning all about his secret superhero life wasn't going to change that. I stepped over the ruins of my book shelves and into the main room of my apartment, and it occurred to me that any one of the people in the Flasked Crusader could have been responsible for stealing the box.

The bar was filled with supervillains and anti-heroes. Who knows how many grudges my father had built up over the years? How could I know why someone would want to steal the box of his stuff when I had barely even begun to look through the volumes of journals, endless mementos, and decades of photos? How did they even know that I had the box and where I live? Who can predict the whims of bat shit crazy people who dress up in brightly colored spandex, people who are so incredibly narcissistic that they seriously think that they can rule the world?

Maybe it was as simple as a collector of superhero memorabilia seeing an opportunity to add to their collection. At that point, I really didn't care anymore. I was over it, I was done living in the past and trying to find out about my father's superhero career that he hid from me my entire life. I sat down on my couch, took a deep breath, and just tried to put it all out of my mind. I reached into my costume jacket pocket and took out my phone…the match book that led me to the Flasked Crusader caught on my phone and fell into my lap. I held it in my hand, and as I looked at the little flap of stiff paper, I knew that it was one of the last remnants of my father that I would ever possess.

I carefully turned the match book over in my hands, like it was some sort of sacred relic, and I looked at the crude drawing of a superhero drinking from a flask on its cover. My father had written a recent date on the flask, and I rubbed my fingers over pen indentations that his hand had made only a month ago. For a few minutes, I sat there examining the matchbook and reflecting on it. Then, I ripped it in half. I was ready to let go of this stupid crusade to understand my father's superhero life, but right as I was about to tear the halves into even smaller pieces, I noticed something that made me hesitate.

Someone had written something on the inside of the matchbook. There was an address and an apartment number, and below it a note that read:

"Stop by any time."

I still gripped the piece of stiff paper in my fingers, and a tiny rip was starting where I was pulling at it. I wanted to finish what I started and destroy both the address and the note, I really did, but I just couldn't do it. I couldn't let go of my stupid crusade, not when there was still the smallest of leads available to me. I just had to know.

I put in a few hours of crime fighting with The Millennials, who had become understandably annoyed by my erratic behavior, but I skipped the obligatory post-patrol bar hopping. Instead, I went to the address in the matchbook. It was a surprisingly nice building, nicer than the building that I lived in and even the one that my father lived in. It was in a neighborhood that was one of the wealthiest areas of the city. As I jumped onto the roof of the thirty story building overlooking the park, I wondered what a person this filthy rich would be doing in a place as low class as the Flasked Crusader.

I thought it would be best to just bypass talking to the doorman. I didn't even know who I was here to see, and I couldn't imagine that any explanation I could offer would get the doorman to let me up ("Uh, I found this address in a box of my dead dad's stuff?"). So, I popped the doorknob off of the door on the roof and I took the stairs to the apartment. Even the stairwell seemed opulent, with its tasteful wallpaper and polished railings.

When I arrived at the apartment, I knocked on the front door, and excitement surged through me. I didn't know who was going to answer that door, but my imagination had already cooked up a few scenarios. Maybe it was a member of the Superb 6 who was interested in making Jack Titan a full time member of the team. Maybe it was a famous reporter looking to tell the story of Jack Titan, or maybe to offer him a job as some sort of gonzo superhero journalist covering crimefighter culture from the inside. Maybe it was a woman?

The peephole turned dark as the mystery person behind the door evaluated me. Half a minute passed as I felt eyes judging me through the peephole. Then the door swung open, and a kid, maybe nineteen years old, was standing in front of me. He was wearing big, mirrored aviator sunglasses, a neon green, tennis ball colored hoodie with the hood practically swallowing his head, and khaki golf shorts with the letter "D" printed on them hundreds of times in a repeating pattern. He was probably a full foot shorter than me, and he had a wispy mustache.

"Well?"

"Uh…are your parents home?"

The kid's head tilted and his forehead furrowed in surprise. Then he started giggling.

"No, my parents aren't home. Are you selling girl scout cookies?"

"No, I um—"

"Because if you are, I'll take a dozen boxes of thin mints. I'll eat the shit out of some thin mints, you know what'm saying?"

"Uh…my dad, Jack Titan, I found this address in a matchbook with his stuff? He died recently, and I'm just sort of—"

"Oh fuck. He died? Oh fuck. For real? Let me take a look at that." The kid grabbed the half of the matchbook with his address on it right out of my hands. Even through the mirrored aviators, I could see a look of recognition on his face as he read the square of stiff paper.

"…come in here," he commanded, and I walked into his apartment.

When he answered the door, my first thought was that this kid had rich parents who indulged his terrible fashion sense. His apartment made it clear that this was not the case. It was decorated by a young person who had an unlimited budget, but severely limited taste. The main room was a massive space with a big glass window overlooking the park, but he spared no expense to ugly up this gorgeous apartment. He had several bean bag chairs, each the same tennis ball green as his hoodie, lying around on his nice wood floors. There was a long, gold colored couch in the center of the room facing a white wall. There was a metal statue of a naked woman, except for a bright red cape and a yellow utility belt slung around her bronzed hips, by the door. He had a replica of the refrigerator sized crime computer from the Superb 6 cartoon show, complete with useless flashing lights and glowing vacuum tubes, but it'd been converted into a keg. On the far wall, an enormous Warhol-style grid of his face in all different color palettes leered over his apartment.

"Take a seat man. Can I get you something to drink?" The kid guided me to his gold couch which faced a big, blank wall. There were video game controllers on the glass coffee table in front of the couch, a couple issues of the superhero gossip rag Spandex, and a bong designed to look like some sort of cosmic, reality altering weapon.

"No, I'm fine. I actually just wanted to ask you about—"

"Water, coffee?"

"No, really, I'm cool, I just—"

"Beer? Club soda? Sparkling water?"

This kid was deliberately trying to get under my skin. It was working. He took a seat on a nearby bean bag chair and grinned at me.

"I'm sorry man...you're a superhero, and I kind of just fell back into my natural instincts to fuck with you, you feel me? You know, because I'm a supervillain and all."

"...Right."

The kid got up and extended a fist for me to bump. I saw that the knuckles of his right hand had the letters, "D-E-L-U" tattooed on them. I reluctantly bumped his fist, and he sat back down on his yellow bean bag chair, almost disappearing into it like a chameleon because his hoodie was the same ugly color.

"I'm Dr. Delusion...you've probably heard of me."

"I'm The Spectacle, and I've heard of *a* Dr. Delusion, but I'm pretty sure he was a lot older than you. Also, I'm pretty sure you're not a doctor."

"Yeah, that's my dad. So we've actually got a little bit in common. Except *my* dad wants me to continue on the Dr. Delusion name, *yours* apparently didn't want you running around as little Jacky Titan Junior. Am I right?"

I didn't say anything because I was restraining an almost uncontrollable urge to throttle this annoying, snot nosed incarnation of Dr. Delusion.

"Fuck, I did it again, my bad. You gotta understand, every time I deal with you cape types it's a negative experience." Dr. Delusion's smile twisted at the corners of his lips and teetered on the edge of a snarl.

"So yeah, I did actually know your dad a little. Can I ask, just out of curiosity, what you thought a guy like me was doing talking to an old timer like him?"

"You know, I don't even know what I'm doing talking to a *guy like you*."

"Fair enough, I deserve that I guess. All this villain, hero bullshit aside though, I get it man, I want to help you find out whatever you want to know. Can we just play nice in the spirit of that, know what'm sayin'?"

"Alright. So why were you meeting him at the Flasked Crusader?"

"Drugs," Dr. Delusion answered, and he pulled a plastic baggie out of his hoodie front pocket. It was filled with SUHP crystals. Crystal SUHP, called "bouillon cubes" on the streets, is the solid form of the substance that only the most hardcore of soupheads prefer. Because you smoke crystal SUHP, it's absorbed into the bloodstream almost instantly, and it gets you ten times higher. It also has ten times the overdose rate.

"Oh," I replied, and suddenly this kid's opulent apartment made a little more sense.

"Yeah, your dad had a hell of a soup habit. He must have been running through a gallon a week, and I guess his old supplier went out of business. Actually, that's a lie, I know his old supplier went out of business. *I put him out of business.*" Dr. Delusion laughed and jiggled the bag of crystalline SUHP. He watched the clear crystals bounce around in the bag, and he had a giddy look of greed like he was playing with a bag of diamonds.

"Well, that's great for you, Dr. Delusion," I was ready to leave. I was convinced that I had rushed into another dead end, and I was wishing that I had finished tearing up that matchbook.

"Yeah, I'm always looking to expand my clientele. I was put in touch with your dad and I was gonna sell him some bouillon cubes, but he never showed. How did he die, if you don't mind me asking?"

"Soup overdose." I stared right at Dr. Delusion's aviators to try to psyche him out with eye contact even through the mirrored lenses. Usually, I try to avoid getting personal with supervillains, but this kid was making it hard to not hate him.

"Oh man, that sucks." Dr. Delusion dropped the bag of crystal soup, the "bouillon cubes", into his lap like he was so depressed to hear this news that he couldn't hold it in his hands anymore. It was a good performance, but I wasn't buying it.

"Yeah. It does. You don't happen to know anything else that would be helpful, like anyone else he was seeing or places he was hanging out, do you?"

"…Nah, nah man. I wish I could help, I really do."

"Well, I appreciate your help, Doctor. I'm sure you have a lot of patients to see today, so I'll get out of your hair." I got up from the gold couch, but Dr. Delusion jumped up from the bean bag chair to stop me from leaving.

"Hey, don't be like that. Hang out for a while," Dr. Delusion grabbed a remote off of the glass coffee table, and pointed it at the ceiling. I looked up and saw that he had a projector attached to his high ceiling, and the blank wall in front of his couch lit up. The screen of a computer was projected onto the wall.

"You seem like a cool guy, despite the hero thing. No reason we can't be bros, right? Come on man, let's watch some Netflix on this new projector I got." I turned my back to him and starting walking towards the front door of Dr. Delusion's apartment, completely ignoring this plea for friendship from this loathsome kid.

"Sorry man, I don't really hang out with drug dealers. It's kind of an unwritten rule for me," I reached for the doorknob, but when my hand touched it, I recoiled in horror at what I saw. My father's head was attached to the door where the doorknob should have been. His eyes were bulging out of his head.

"Spectacle, I've gotta insist you stick around," Dr. Delusion sneered, and I whirled around to see that he had strapped a small gas mask over his nose and mouth. I suddenly felt weak in my legs, like my knee joints had transformed into sponges, and I hugged the Superb 6 crime computer to keep from falling to the floor. Dr. Delusion walked towards me as I struggled to stay upright.

"Did you know that if you change around a few molecules in the SUHP formula, the new compound will cause debilitating vertigo, erratic fluctuations in superhuman ability, and severe visual hallucinations?" Dr. Delusion nudged me on the shoulder, and I dropped hard onto the wood floors.

"Right now, my proprietary blend of SUHP is pumping through the air conditioning of this room, suspended in water vapor. It's not quite a design classic like my pop's daydream darts, but still...pretty cool, right? You would not believe what it costs to get a contractor to set this up. It's goddamn highway robbery." Dr. Delusion crouched in front of me as I clawed at the floor and tried to push myself up off of the ground.

"Why?" I stammered. Dr. Delusion's reflective aviators now looked like bright spotlights shining into my face and blinding me.

"Why does anyone do anything ever? Money, Spectacle. You think I'm just gonna let you walk out of here? You really think I buy this whole soul searching, finding your father crap? Especially with the way he died, and all the shit you've been talking about my business? I'm not going to let you ruin my insanely profitable business because your daddy can't handle his soup and you need a little revenge on an innocent drug dealer." Dr. Delusion grabbed me by the collar of my costume jacket, hoisted me to my feet, and then shoved me across the room. I tripped on one of his bean bag chairs and fell on the foam filled blob. I tried to get up off of the bean bag chair, but the squishy thing seemed to be pouring through my fingers like it was made out of thick, tennis ball colored gravy. Dr. Delusion plopped down onto a nearby bean bag chair, and he started fiddling with his phone.

"Check this out. You're gonna love this, Spectacle. I've got this place set up so I can control everything with my phone." Dr. Delusion was talking to me like a proud child showing off his toys to a friend on a sleepover. It was like the most normal thing in the world to him, yet I was doing everything I could to power through the effects of a crippling drug surging through my central nervous system.

I succeeded in getting off of the bean bag chair which felt like a blob of viscous yellow liquid sucking me in and dripping off of my body, but I could just barely stand. The huge apartment was rotating around me and tilting and it was taking everything I had to keep myself on my feet. I made the mistake of looking towards the window, I thought maybe I could try to break through the glass and escape, but the park looked like an alien jungle with mutant purple pterodactyls soaring over the trees which were vibrating and pulsating. The buildings of the city skyline, which I routinely jumped across like playing hopscotch, now seemed to be piercing the stratosphere and thousands of times taller than I knew they were. Looking at the spires with their morphing textures and rearranging architecture made me nauseous, and I vomited all over Dr. Delusion's copies of Spandex Magazine. A cover story about Queen Quantum's possible baby bump was covered in my vomit which glowed and steamed like radioactive waste.

"Oh come on! Keep it together Spectacle. For fuck's sake, we're just getting started," Dr. Delusion fumed as he did something on his phone, as if my reaction to his drug was the height of rudeness. I had fallen to the ground again, and I was bracing myself on his glass coffee table which rippled underneath my gloved fingers like the surface of a pond.

"Alright, what do you make of this, Spectacle?" Dr. Delusion gestured at the projected screen, and I looked up from the quivering glass of the coffee table.

An old photo of my father was plastered on the wall in light and looming over me. I recognized the photo from my father's wall of clippings. Dr. Delusion probably found it in a simple Google search. The photo, however, was substantially different under the influence of Dr. Delusion's SUHP compound. The features of my father's face were decaying, the flesh was rotting off of his cheek bones, maggots pushed through his putrid skin and fell off of the wall and onto the floor. He was beckoning me with a pale, dead hand. His eyes were brimming with fire and rage and disappointment, and I was filled with a terror so indescribably powerful that the word "terror" doesn't even feel adequate. I couldn't look away from the horrible vision.

"Oh man, you should see your face right now," Dr. Delusion giggled.

"If you're gonna kill me, just kill me you sick fuck," I spit this out, but I still couldn't face Dr. Delusion. My eyes were locked in place by my father's haunting gaze.

"Naw, that's not the way this works. I'm a supervillain, and I've got you right where I want you. It's kind of a villain tradition for me to fuck with you as much as possible before I kill you." Dr. Delusion stood up and backhanded me in the face. I spun around and slammed my head on the wood floors…but still, as soon as my skull pounded against the floor, my eyes locked right back onto my father's searing glare.

"And I'm all…about…tradition!" Dr. Delusion screamed this and his voice cracked as he swiftly kicked me in the stomach.

Blackness was sneaking in around the edges, but I fought to stay conscious and to suck some of the air he had kicked out of me back into my lungs. Dr. Delusion strutted around me and I tried to crawl away. He paused, fiddled with his phone again, and the projected image of my father in his youth was replaced with a tight shot on his face as an older man. Jack Titan's golden wreath didn't look regal here, the SUHP distorted it into a crown of razor sharp, gilded leaves cutting into his forehead and temples and iridescent blood trickled down his face. Again, his eyes were blazing with flames and they oozed so much anguish that it physically hurt me, but even still, I couldn't look away. His mouth was twisted in pain and agony. I pawed at the floor and tried to drag myself away, away from this phantom, away from this wispy mustached, second generation Dr. Delusion, but all my super strength had left me. Some small, drug choked part of my rational mind whispered that this nightmare wraith of my father wasn't real, but it was a very quiet voice overpowered by a chorus of horror.

"Man, this was a real let down. Usually, I have to put in at least a little effort to figure out what's gonna freak you capes out. This was really too easy." Dr. Delusion knelt down next to me. I took a swing at his face, but my depth perception was all fucked up and my fist didn't even graze his gas masked face. He put his fists together and thrust them in front of my face…I flinched and he laughed, and I saw that "D-E-L-U-S-I-O-N" was tattooed across the eight knuckles of his fists.

"See this? This is the last thing you're ever gonna see…the last thing that dozens of lower tier, spandex clowns just like you saw when they tried to fuck around with my multimillion dollar drug business." The letters spelling out delusion on his knuckles radiated a sickly, red light that burned into my retinas like a brand.

Then, Dr. Delusion walked out of the room, and even still, my father's heartbreaking eyes locked me in place like a tractor beam. They were bursting with so much despair, like he was trying to communicate some profound truth to me but I couldn't hear it. I just couldn't understand what it was he was trying to tell me. Molten tears of lava flowed out of his eyes and down his decomposing face, and he started clamping his eyes shut and opening them again. It was so strange. He wasn't blinking, he was closing his eyes tight for a few seconds and then opening them again.

"Here we go. Did you ever think it would end this way, Spectacle? Not with an epic super brawl to the death with some kinda mutated monster, not surrounded on all sides by your worst enemies, not bravely sacrificing your life to save the world. Just a plastic baggie and little ol' me," Dr. Delusion came back into the room holding a large, plastic zip lock bag. Dr. Delusion sat down behind me, and he slipped the plastic bag over my head. He gripped the plastic around my throat and through the clear plastic, I saw the fifteen foot tall projection of my father closed and opened his eyes even faster than before.

My lungs scorched as I gasped for oxygen. I thrashed around on the floor as Dr. Delusion choked the life out of me, but I couldn't focus, I couldn't summon the super strength that I needed to save myself. My mind was possessed by the projection of my father on the wall that had been amplified by the SUHP compound into a hallucination so ghastly, so frightening that I couldn't look away, I couldn't concentrate on anything but that look of desperation he was giving me from beyond the grave. I closed my eyes, partly out of an involuntary response to being starved of oxygen, and partly because I was accepting what seemed inevitable…and that's when it hit me.

The fog cleared from my mind as soon as I closed my eyes. The hallucinatory spirit of my father no longer paralyzed me. I don't believe in ghosts, I don't believe in gods and devils, I don't believe anything is truly "supernatural." I believe that everything, even some of the crazier shit I've seen in my line of work, can ultimately be explained by science…but I won't lie to you. In that moment when my eyes were closed and a calm washed over me, my drug addled brain was convinced that my father had been trying to send me a message from the afterlife.

I kept my eyes closed and I grabbed Dr. Delusion's skinny wrists and squeezed as hard as I could. I felt his wrist bones crack and crunch like brittle twigs. He let out a high pitched whine and let go of my throat. In the darkness, I peeled off the plastic bag and gulped sweet, precious air. Dr. Delusion was howling somewhere behind me, and I spun around and fired a fist towards the sound of his shrill squealing. My fist bashed against his forehead and silenced his shrieks. I felt around, with my eyes still closed, and picked him up off of the ground by the folds of his hoodie.

"Turn off the drugs. *Now.*"

"I can't, you idiot! You broke my fucking wrists! How am I supposed to use my phone to turn off the vapor flow?"

"Figure out a way. Work through the pain, or I swear to god…" My voice must have been conveying just how insanely angry I was because I didn't get a chance to finish the threat before I heard Dr. Delusion tapping on his phone.

"There. It's off. What now? Are you gonna kill me, hero?"

I snagged his gas mask without opening my eyes. I started pulling it off of his face.

"Okay, okay I'll turn it off for real! If you want to get any information about your daddy out of me, you don't want to expose me to this shit," Dr. Delusion fumbled around with his phone again while I held onto his gas mask, ready to pull it off at the slightest sign of trouble.

"Alright, it's seriously off this time. Can you blame me for trying?" I began to slip off Dr. Delusion's gas mask.

"Woah woah woah, give it a few minutes, let the vapor dissipate a— "

"Why should I?! Why shouldn't I let you take a good whiff?"

"Pay attention, dummy, I just told you: I know a little bit about dear old daddy, and I might not be as talkative if you dope me to the gills."

His voice sounded like he was telling the truth, but I would have liked to see his face to be sure. The last thing I wanted to do was trust the scrawny, drug peddling bastard who had just tried to murder me, but if he knew anything, I had to pry it out of him.

"Okay. Talk."

"Hold your horses, Spectacle. First let's discuss my terms…information for amnesty? What do you say, Specta—"

I gave his rib cage a super strength flick with my index finger and I heard a pop.

"Fuck! I think you just broke one of my ribs! Goddamn it, are you fucking kidding me?!"

"Just tell me what you know, Delusion, and try not to pass out from the pain."

"Alright, alright…all I know is…I heard from some people that your dad, he was a regular at this superhuman underground fighting ring, okay?"

"Where?"

"It's under…under 100 Ton Gym," Dr. Delusion passed out while I held him up by the folds of his hoodie.

I tossed him onto his gaudy golden couch with my eyes still tightly closed. I tied him up with some zip ties that I keep in one of my costume jacket's inside pockets, just to be totally safe, which was not an easy thing to do blind. I sat down on the couch, took a deep breath of relief, and rested for a few minutes to shake off the effects of the airborne SUHP. I kept my eyes closed as a precaution, but there were still some minor visuals assailing me in the darkness. There were floating geometric shapes piecing together and rearranging and exploding apart like a little psychedelic laser light show just for me. I saw the half destroyed matchbook tumble by the colorful shapes as if it were in the weightless vacuum of outer space. I saw the vague outline of my father drifting at me in the darkness, but this time, he wasn't a morbid terror. This time there was warmth in his eyes and a smile on his face, and maybe even a hint of pride. Then, he was gone.

Chapter 6:
Amateur Hour

I put on a costume for the first time almost a year after my powers manifested. Comics and movies make it seem like it's totally feasible to be a high school superhero, but the truth is that it's a time management impossibility. I was a senior in high school, and I had to deal with schoolwork, applying to college, standardized tests, constant extracurricular responsibilities, not to mention girls. On top of all of that, I was attending a boarding school that regimented every hour of every day and kept tabs on students' whereabouts at all times. There was no room in that packed schedule for gallivanting around in brightly colored tights. And even if there was, that wasn't even something that registered as a possible lifestyle choice for me.

It was more than just a matter of having no free time. I had spent a year in semi-denial about my superpowers, instead I remained convinced for a long, long time that it was all a lingering aftereffect of that first SUHP trip. I kept telling myself that I was having SUHP flashbacks, that a minuscule amount must still be in my system somehow, even though I knew that was absurd and scientifically impossible. I kept telling myself that there was no way that I really was going to live the rest of my life as a superhuman.

I felt like I had no one to talk about it with, and although I tried not to, I thought about it constantly. I would try to mention SUHP whenever the topic of drugs came up, which tends to happen with teenage boys a lot, and not so subtly wonder out loud if anyone we knew had permanent superpowers from taking it. It was always an idea that everybody laughed off. No one ever copped to having superpowers, and statistically speaking, it's likely that I really was one of only a few people in the entire school who had a genetic predisposition to superhuman ability.

The summer after I graduated high school was a strange time for me. I was living with my dad at his apartment in the city until college started in the fall, and with all that free time on my hands, I was coming to terms with the fact that these things I could do were not going to wear off. This is who I am now, I kept thinking over and over again, and I knew that the rough ideas I had about my future meant nothing. I used to think that I would go to school to be a lawyer…but how could I now?

How could I sit in classrooms and offices and courtrooms for the rest of my life when I could do the things that I could do? Who could go into work from 9 to 5 when you could be leaping hundreds of feet through the air over rooftops with the city lights glittering below you? What would happen when my mind drifted during those long, lawyer hours and I'd see myself stopping dangerous mad men in colorful costumes with my bare hands while crowds cheered for me like I was a glorious spandex demigod? I could try to keep my head down and live a normal life, but how do you live a normal life when you know with every fiber of your being that you're not a normal man?

Pop culture has given us this idea that the young superhero stitches together a superhero persona over the course of a long weekend. He just sits down at his desk and draws on a sketch pad and just like that, his superhero identity is born fully formed on the page. He whips out a thread and a needle and some fabric and before you know it, the montage is over and he can start beating up bad guys. If you're a young, superpowered kid and you're thinking about becoming a superhero, I can't stress enough that this was the complete opposite of how it was for me.

It took over a month of agonizing to create what eventually became "The Spectacle." I went through dozens of superhero names before I found one that wasn't taken and wasn't also embarrassingly stupid. I have no artistic talent whatsoever and designing a superhero costume was a maddening process. I destroyed a notebook full of crudely drawn Spectacle prototypes to spare myself the excruciating torment that the internet would deliver if those sketches ever got out. Slowly but surely, The

Spectacle emerged from mountains of crumpled notebook paper.

Once I finally settled on a costume design that didn't make me look like a complete idiot, I spent another week clumsily piecing it together. Although the design I was working from is the same one that I use today, that first attempt was a shameful excuse for a costume. I couldn't sew spandex for shit, I butchered the cursive "The Spectacle" writing on the breast of the blue jacket, the yellow piping on the red spandex pants was just shamefully bad, the black domino mask was too big and it kept slipping down my face…but it was good enough to get me started.

Writing about the first time that you put on a costume and went out looking for criminals to punch in the head is like writing about sex. You're never going to capture the thrill of the act, not in a million years of writing and rewriting, and anyone who hasn't done it isn't going to understand unless they do it themselves. With that in mind, let's talk about one of the best nights of my life, the night that I stopped wanting to be a superhero and became one, and how everything that could go wrong, did.

I slipped into the costume on the roof of my dad's building so he wouldn't notice me leaving the apartment in it. My entire body was shaking and my heart was racing faster than a hummingbird with a coke habit as I put on the ill fitting thing. I had watched hours of footage of superheroes leaping from building to building, but nothing prepares you for that moment when you're standing on a rooftop and you're looking at the ledge and you're trying to force yourself to start running towards it. Intellectually, I knew that I could make the jump from the rooftop I was standing on to the one across the street. I had made jumps five times that distance in the woods at school while testing the limits of my newfound powers after lights out. Intellectually, I knew that I could do it, but try telling that to the screeching voice in your head telling you that you're about to plummet to your death.

After a good twenty minutes of psyching myself up, I ran towards the edge of the roof as fast as I could. My brain was a beehive that had been hit like a piñata before I started sprinting, but once I finally forced myself to move, I stopped thinking. My thoughts evaporated, and there was only the pounding of my feet on the cement roof, my rapid, sharp breaths going in and out, in and out, the rushing of wind on my masked face, the honks and engines and squealing brakes and traffic sounds hundreds of feet below, and the edge of the rooftop racing towards me. Then—I jumped.

I felt like I was weightless as I shot across the air above the city street. For a split second, I felt incredibly calm as I saw the city spread out below me, and then gravity began clawing at me once again. I was falling towards the building across the street, and as I flew at it, I realized something that erased any sense of calm I had and replaced it with sheer panic. I had jumped too far, and I was about to overshoot the rooftop.

I kicked my feet and flailed my arms as I missed the far edge of the rooftop by a few inches, and suddenly I was sailing past it. Here's where I'd like to say that my life flashed before my eyes, or that I had some sort of profound epiphany that I needed to survive so I could dedicate my life to the fight for truth and justice, but honestly, all I was thinking was "FUCK." I fell past the rooftop I was aiming for and across a dark alley and before I even knew what was happening, I crashed onto the roof of a building below the one I had intended to land on.

I tumbled on the gravelly roof and skidded across it before clanking my head into an air conditioning unit. I sat there for a few seconds, legitimately surprised to still be alive, and then I burst into uncontrollable laughter. My whole body ached from the rough landing, my head hurt from denting the aluminum casing of the air conditioning unit, adrenaline gushed through my veins like river rapids, and death had almost taken me in a supremely humiliating way...but I felt amazing, I felt vibrant, I felt so *alive.*

I sprung to my feet immediately and started running for the next jump. I launched off of the rooftop and towards the wall of a much taller building. I hit the reflective windows of the wall and pushed off of them, propelling myself even farther and higher. I landed again on a window ledge, but this time, I hit the ground running at a full clip. It got easier and easier every time I hurled myself from one building to another.

Everything became so fluid, my mind didn't have space for anything but spotting the next roof to land on, the next flagpole to swing from, the next billboard to bounce off, and I lost myself in the organic process. Even the mistakes, the smallest of slips on damp concrete or the misjudging of angles, they seamlessly folded into it all and became starting points for the next move. It's like when a musician plays a wrong note in a solo, and he toys with it and it evolves into this amazing riff that repeats throughout the song. I started to flow as I rocketed from building to building, across traffic filled city streets, deliberately falling dozens of stories before touching down on a balcony and starting it all over again. Even as I type this, I know it sounds pretentious, but the lines started to blur between me and the city.

Hours had passed and I had traveled halfway across the city when I saw him. I was catching my breath while sitting on the ledge of a rooftop when I happened to notice an armored car on the street swerve and then screech to a stop. The back doors of the armored car swung open, and The Whimsy stepped out of the vehicle with a duffel bag stuffed with stacks of cash. Even from so many stories up, I recognized The Whimsy from the research I had done on costumed crimefighting, research that mostly consisted of reading back issues of Spandex.

I was instantly convinced that I could take him. The Whimsy was always portrayed in Spandex as a joke of a costumed criminal. One issue described him as "the self proclaimed 'ironic supervillain'" in an article titled, "Five Worst Villain Costumes of the Year." He clocked in at number three, which was a generous place to put him on that list considering that his costume consisted of a neon blue polo shirt, a plaid fanny pack, skinny jeans, one of those bulky, 90's watches that say the time out loud in a bad robot voice, and neon pink framed sunglasses. The Whimsy was just a 16 year old, wannabe supervillain who had been in and out of super-juvie since he was 13. His fanny pack full of ironic, high tech gadgets was an amusing novelty, but I was confident that my powers would make this kid an easy first win for The Spectacle.

The street clogged with traffic as the armored car sat in the middle of the road. The Whimsy took a brief glance in his neon pink sunglasses at the two armed guards scrambling out of the vehicle. The truck was overflowing with purple knock out gas. The coughing armed guards tried to take aim at him, but they passed out on the street before they could fire a single shot, and then The Whimsy ran. I bounded off of the ledge, into the branches of a tree, and then onto the top of a cab. The top of the cab rang out with a hollow bang with the impact of my weight, and I saw The Whimsy look over his shoulder at me as he weaved in and out of bumper to bumper traffic. We made eye contact for a fraction of a second, and then I was after him, ricocheting off of one car to another like a skipping stone across a lake.

The Whimsy managed to turn the corner of the street and make it out of my line of sight before I could reach him. I touched down on the roof of the armored car, and then flung myself off of it and towards the corner where The Whimsy made a sharp left to lose me. I bashed into a newspaper vending machine with my hip as I made a running landing on the sidewalk, it fell over on its side, and the glass of the box shattered. Papers with the front page headline, "Superb 6 Stop Mistress Gorgon's Subway Rampage" spilled out into the busy intersection. I pivoted around the corner and spotted The Whimsy kneeling down and tying the laces of his retro, neon teal and yellow high top sneakers. I took a few steps towards him when I saw that he wasn't tying his shoes...he was squeezing the rubber bulbs on the tongues of his shoes. I had just enough time to wonder why he would be bothering with those archaic shoe pumps that pretty much did nothing when the bottoms of his sneakers emitted a pulse of bright white light.

Suddenly, The Whimsy exploded away from me in a flash of white energy from the treads of his high tops. In less than a second, he was a tiny dot arcing through the city skyscrapers.

"Son of a bitch," I muttered, and then I ran after him as fast as I could on the sidewalk. I was trying to build up momentum for one big jump so I could tackle The Whimsy out of the sky. He was so far ahead of me now that he looked like a bouncing strobe light the size of a flea. I was really starting to pick up some speed as I put everything I had into this sprint, I sidestepped pedestrians who strolled by me at a glacial pace, I hopped right over a little old lady who dropped her purse like she was a hurdle, I was moving faster than I ever had in my life, and then, when I felt like I couldn't possibly run any faster, I sprang into the air in the direction of the tiny blip of light that was The Whimsy.

I tore through the sky at him like a bullet, and I saw him look over his shoulder at me and reach for his fanny pack when I slammed into him in mid air. My weight overwhelmed the energy propulsion in his shoes and we plummeted towards the street. Fortunately for us both, I had grabbed onto him pretty tightly, and I controlled our descent despite his struggling. The landing on an empty stretch of sidewalk was rough on my knees, but I kept The Whimsy from hurting himself in the fall.

"Alright, tough guy, you fought the good fight but now it's time to—" The Whimsy stopped fighting against my superhuman grip on his blue polo shirt, and he pushed a button on his bulky, old school watch. The watch blasted sound in my face so loud that it cut me off in the middle of my hackneyed attempt at superhero banter.

"The…time…is…two…oh…seven…A…M," the robot voice blared in my ears in a mind-numbingly loud ultrasonic frequency. I threw up my hands to block my ears and The Whimsy pulled away from me, keeping his wrist aimed at my head.

The ear-piercing sound vibrated my eyes and made the street around me foggy and unfocused. My ear drums felt like they were being stabbed with red hot needles. My whole skull reverberated with the ultrasonic waves of the 90's robot voice reading out the time again and again, and I felt warm blood trickle out of my nose.

"*The...time...is...two...oh...seven...A...M...*" The Whimsy was a hazy blur, and he backed away slowly as the booming voice jack hammered into my head.

"Stop," I couldn't even hear myself say this through the deafening ultrasonic sound.

"***The...time...is...two...oh...eight...A...M...***"

Right when I thought my brain was going to burst, the robot voice trailed off to a high pitched whine, and then it faded out completely. My eyes stopped vibrating and The Whimsy shook his wrist, tapped the screen of his bulky watch, and then he shrugged at me. The bottoms of his high top sneakers started glowing with white energy again.

Before he could pop up into the air again, I lunged for his fanny pack and looped my fingers around its plaid belt. The white energy pulsed on the bottom of his shoes and his feet flew out from under him while I held him down by his fanny pack. While I fought against the force of whatever crazy hover technology was in his sneakers, The Whimsy whipped his phone out of his pocket. The bright light pulsating from the bottom of his shoes fizzled out, and I lowered him to the ground while he typed on his phone in the most casual way.

"Kid, what the hell are you doing? Jesus Christ, stop texting and tweeting or whatever, I'm in the middle of citizen arresting you here." The Whimsy held up one finger, as if I was rudely interrupting some important text conversation and he'd be with me in one second, and I honestly was taken aback. This was just a little sixteen year old kid, and he was beaten. What was I supposed to do?

Punch him in the face? In the moment, that seemed a little harsh.

The Whimsy's phone flashed as if he was snapping a picture of me while I tried to figure out what to do with him. Then, the flash on his phone started flickering rapidly and the light got brighter and brighter until it was so blindingly bright that it was leaving huge blotches of purple in my vision. Again, The Whimsy started backing away from me as I tried to block my eyes from the extremely bright flashing. He was disappearing from me in the blinding after images, and out of just pure frustration at this point, I barreled forward and punched at the source of the light.

I landed a lucky blind shot and shattered the glass on the back of the phone which seemed to break that infuriating LED flash. The Whimsy unzipped his plaid fanny pack and started to snake a hand into it to pull out his next absurdly annoying and painful trinket, but I grabbed at it and just tore that tacky thing off his waist.

"Alright. Okay. That's enough of that bullshit. Uh. Drop the duffel bag, and put your hands on your head." I tossed the fanny pack aside, and The Whimsy reluctantly took the duffel bag off of his shoulder. He let it drop to the asphalt, and then he raised his clenched fists in front of him.

"I'm sorry…what are you doing? You want to fight me? You're all out of your party tricks, you don't want to fight a dude with superpowers, Whimsy." I walked towards him, not even remotely threatened by his fighting stance, and I threw a sloppy punch at his jaw.

The Whimsy bobbed his head out of the way, and he jabbed me right in my bleeding nose. I was stunned by the blow, but also shocked that he was able to land it. Everything I read about The Whimsy made me think that he relied on corny super-gadgets, but this kid was clearly reacting with superhuman reflexes. His jab was like a lightning bolt. The Whimsy had superpowers, and I had no idea what they were.

I swung wildly at him, just trying to end this fight before it spun out of control, and The Whimsy skipped out of the way of my punch. I threw a left cross which hit the air next to him as he danced around me, and then I just started punching at a rapid fire pace. I didn't even scrape him with a punch. He was so much faster than me. Fighting The Whimsy was like trying to hit a fly that just buzzes away before you can raise your hand to slap it.

I was getting frustrated. I was winded from throwing all these super strength punches that didn't connect, The Whimsy's total silence was driving me crazy, and that's when he started hitting back. He hit me in the jaw with a right hook that I didn't even see coming, he battered me with jab after jab, and even with my own superhuman reaction time, I was helpless against his undeniably greater super speed. Thankfully, The Whimsy didn't seem to have any super strength, otherwise his flurry of punches probably would have killed me, but I'm not invulnerable.

His barrage of blows to the head were messing me up in a big way, and I knew that I couldn't take much more.

I'm not proud to say it, but I panicked. A fight or flight urge came over me as he peppered me with punches, and flight was looking pretty appealing. The Whimsy pulled back his fist for what might have been a knockout blow, and I just leapt up and over him. I didn't look back as I landed on a rooftop behind The Whimsy, and I proceeded to run straight home. I changed into my regular clothes on the rooftop, and when I walked back into my dad's apartment, he didn't even notice my swollen face and profusely bleeding nose. He barely looked up from the spiral notebook he was writing in to ask where I had been, and I barely put in the effort to make up an excuse about being at a friend's house. My first night as a superhero ended with me icing my puffy, aching face and mulling over all the mistakes I had made, but despite the pain and the embarrassment, I went to sleep excited to go out and try again as soon as possible.

Chapter 7:
The Titanson

If you think going to the gym is intimidating, try going to a superhero gym. 100 Ton Gym was the kind of place where the average bench press weight was roughly equal to that of a midsize SUV. If you were running on one of the treadmills, it's likely that the person next to you would be clocking in at just under the speed of sound. I worked out at 100 Ton Gym for a month without seeing a single sign of the superhuman cage fighting that Dr. Delusion claimed was underneath the place. The only thing that I discovered was that superheroes take their work out routines a little too seriously.

After a month, my life had pretty much returned to normal, or as normal as it could be when a couple times a week I'd be fist fighting with crazies like Master Boson. I had stopped going to 100 Ton Gym in the hopes of discovering this underground super fighting ring that Dr. Delusion told me about, and I was actually there on this particular night because I genuinely liked working out there. It wasn't the nicest place. Beyond Man's franchise of gyms for superhumans, "Extradimensional Fitness," was much cleaner, had more staff, more advanced equipment, and a delightful juice bar, but it was a little too sterile for me. 100 Ton gym had character. It had this weird vibe that hit you when you walked through the doors, this feeling that superhumans had been coming there since the superhero boom of the 60's, and you could sense the history in the air. Or maybe it was just the mild stink of half a century of super-sweat.

I walked into the gym that night with no real intention of finding out information on a hypothetical cage fighting ring or my father's trophy room box. It had been a slow couple of days for crimefighting, and I just wanted to get in a little exercise rather than sit around reading internet comments about myself. I pushed through the doors of 100 Ton Gym and walked through the entrance hall that had ancient carpeting, and wallpaper that had been peeling off the walls since before I was born.

The hallway walls were lined with old framed pictures of superheroes who used to be regulars at the gym. There was a funny photo from the 70's of Doc Hyper standing next to a treadmill that he accidentally tore to pieces with his super speed. There was a photo of Queen Quantum in the 60's before she was a founding member of the Superb 6 and she was still an up and coming superheroine. She was smiling for the camera and lifting a three ton weight on her pinky with her strong force manipulation power. There was even a picture of Jack Titan with his arm slung around the owner of 100 Ton Gym. The place could use an interior decorator and a serious remodeling, but it had a history that was appealing to me.

I noticed that there were a lot of superheroes in the gym that night as I made my way over to the rack of dumbbells. Crystallor was doing pull ups with multiple tons of metagravity weights strapped to his jagged legs, and the sound of his crystalline fingers crunching around the metal bar was like fingernails on a chalkboard. The Sci-Fighter was boxing a force field infused punching bag that lit up with energy each time his nanomachine powered fists struck it. I was surprised to see Anhur, a founding member of the Superb 6 and supposedly the Egyptian god of war, was doing clean and jerks in the corner. He was lifting a barbell that had an absurd amount of metagravity weights on it, simulating the force of at least 500 tons, and I had to wonder what a superhero of his caliber would be doing there. I hadn't seen him there before, and it was unreal to actually see Anhur in person with his Egyptian, four feathered headdress, his fine, gold and blue linens wrapped around his waist like a skirt, and his "mystical" spear laying at his feet as he raised an insane amount of weight above his head.

I took off my costume jacket, and I stretched a little while trying very hard not to give away how star struck I was by Anhur. Then, I picked a metagravity dumbbell up off of the rack that simulated about a ton, and I started doing curls with it. I was focused on keeping the proper form while curling roughly 2000 pounds of artificial weight, just watching my arm in one of the mirrors to make sure I was executing the super strength curl correctly, and I almost dropped the dumbbell when I saw something strange behind me. Forcing myself to act calm, I stopped curling the metagravity dumbbell, and I gently put it back on the rack while I watched in the mirror. I pretended to admire my bicep in the mirror, but I was actually using the mirror to observe something behind me that I hadn't seen in the month I had been working out there.

I saw five superheroes walk out of the office of the gym...but it was a tiny, cramped office, and there was no way that all five of these spandex meatheads could have all fit into that little room. They were laughing as they filed out of the office. One of them had a bleeding split lip, and another had used his cape as a sling for a broken arm. The five of them looked like they had just gotten into a fight with The Abnormalite, but they weren't acting like it. They were acting like little kids who just had a great time on the playground, and they were still brimming with energy and excitement from a particularly rousing game of dodgeball.

Anhur lowered the 500 ton metagravity barbell to the floor like it was made out of styrofoam. One of the five superheroes, the one with the split lip dripping blood down his chin, discretely whispered something to Anhur. Anhur let out a thunderous laugh, he picked up his spear, and he enthusiastically walked into the small office with a spring in his step. The five superheroes left, loudly giving each other shit and punching each other in the shoulders and generally annoying the superhuman patrons of the gym, and Anhur slammed the office door behind him.

I sat on a bench for a few minutes and stared at the door. I looked around at the other superheroes going through their meticulously planned workout routines. No one seemed to notice or care about the five superheroes who climbed out of that office like it was a clown car. No one showed any sign of concern that Anhur had disappeared into the same office. I made eye contact with Crystallor, and then I sort of nodded at the office door. Crystallor was taking a break in between sets and keeping track of his reps in a notebook, and he shrugged his quartz-like shoulders at me. He was the only person in the room who even came close to acknowledging that something weird just went down. The Millennials had teamed up with Crystallor a few times, so I felt comfortable getting up from the bench and going over to see if he knew what was up.

"Don't even ask, Spectacle," Crystallor dropped his notebook and got up from the titanium reinforced bench that was supporting his eight foot tall, massive mineralized body.

"I didn't say anything yet, Crystallor," I tried to keep my voice down as Crystallor slid 50 tons of metagravity weights onto a barbell.

"C'mon bro…leave me alone…I don't want to…start any…shit!" Crystallor talked to me while squatting with 50 tons on his glittering, crystal shoulders.

"Crystallor, bro, level with me..." Crystallor finished his set of squats and glared at me as he lowered the barbell off of his shoulders.

"...is this that underground fighting thing I heard—"

"Heh, no I haven't heard if anyone good is playing tonight at the Domino Mask." Crystallor loudly interrupted me, and he nervously glanced around us to make sure that no one heard me. Then, he motioned for me to sit down with him on the bulky titanium bench. He opened up his workout notebook and pretended to show me the details of his routine.

"Look...we got a good thing going on here, and I can get you in, but you gotta be cool. This deal isn't exactly legal, Spectacle," Crystallor murmured to me while pointing randomly at his chicken scratch records of reps and sets.

"You get me?" Crystallor slapped his notebook shut and stood up from the bench. He looked at me with concern, and his crystalline brow wrinkled like tectonic plates mashing together.

"I got you, I can be cool," I stood up with him, and Crystallor led me over to the office door.

It seemed like most of the weightlifting crimefighters in the gym weren't paying attention, and it occurred to me as I walked into the office with Crystallor that only a few of them must be aware of this secret arrangement. He shut the door behind us, and Anhur wasn't inside. Crystallor guided me through the small, seemingly normal but cluttered office to a closet door at the back of the room.

He opened the closet door, and behind it was a dimly lit flight of stairs that led down beneath the gym. Crystallor went down first, I followed him and gently closed the closet door. His crystal body sparkled in the darkness of the staircase that only had a little bit of light seeping in through the crack of the closet door. We must have descended at least three floors into the ground before we reached a door at the bottom of the stairs. The door had a sign on it with a yellow and black nuclear radiation symbol on it. The sign had "Fallout Shelter" printed on it in thick capital letters.

"Alright. Just act like you're supposed to be here." Crystallor knocked on the door four times with his jagged, clear knuckles. He waited a moment, and knocked a fifth time.

Then, he opened the door, and we walked into a room packed with superheroes. It was a surprisingly big space with gray concrete walls, and there was a circular cage in the center of the room. Superheroes surrounded the ring in a multicolored sea of bright spandex, watching and cheering and screaming as Anhur and Photoneer fought inside the cage. Crystallor and I pushed through the crowds of superheroes to get a closer look, and I felt waves of force ripple outward from the ring with each super strength punch.

Photoneer floated a foot above the ground in front of Anhur. Photoneer, the "Master of Light," was not in great shape. He looked like he had just gone twelve rounds with Anhur, but the so called god of war had gone down there only a few minutes ago. Photoneer was wobbling in the air as he hovered around Anhur. His gold and silver costume torn to shreds in what must have been an intensely one sided brawl, his golden gloves sheered away at the knuckles from punching invulnerable skin with enough force to shatter the face of a mountain, and it looked like a stiff breeze would be all Anhur would need to knock the punch drunk Master of Light out of the air. Photoneer pulled his radiant, light saturated fist back for a haymaker, and Anhur just swatted him to the ground with a flick of his spear. The light drained from Photoneer like a light bulb going out as he lost consciousness. The crowd of superheroes went absolutely ape shit.

Anhur threw his huge, brown arms into the air and screamed triumphantly. He stomped around the ring in a little victory lap, shaking his spear at the crowd vigorously, and his every pore was oozing swagger and confidence. A couple of superheroes dragged Photoneer out of the ring, and Anhur, who didn't even look like his opponent had touched him with a single photon, strode out of the ring and into the mob of masked crimefighters. He was surrounded by the grumbles of losers who had bet on Photoneer and lost, and the frenzied excitement of those who had bet big on Anhur and won. Their faith in the alleged Egyptian god of war had been rewarded.

"Alright man. Try to mingle a bit, I'm gonna place a few bets. Daddy needs a new pair of shoes, and you would not believe how expensive crystal resistant size 25's are." Crystallor moved his way through the crowd, shook

Anhur's hand and congratulated him on his win, and then the two of them made their way to Silver Scribe.

Apparently, he was doing the bookkeeping for this highly illegal superhuman fighting ring. I saw him furiously writing in his glowing Hyper-Tome, and then he handed a fat wad of cash to Anhur. Anhur stuffed the money into the blue and gold fabric wrapped around his waist, and he spoke to Crystallor for a second. Crystallor raised an angular eyebrow while Anhur talked to him, and then he looked at me while he responded to him. Anhur chuckled, he turned away from Crystallor while he talked to Silver Scribe about arranging his next fight, and then Anhur started walking directly towards me.

"You! Boy! My condolences!" Anhur put a hand on my shoulder, and I was almost in shock that he was actually talking to me.

"Your…uh, I'm sorry, for what?"

"For your father's death…you are the Spectacle, yes? The Titanson?" Anhur frowned in confusion, and his Pharaoh-like, black beard shifted with his facial expression. I couldn't help but laugh at the word "Titanson."

"Heh, yeah, yeah I guess I am the Titanson. Yeah, my dad was Jack Titan."

"Ultra Lady mentioned your name to me at the most recent gathering of the Superb 6. He was a great man, your father. I have no doubt that Anubis will weigh his heart in the Underworld, and he shall find it balanced with Ma'at, the feather of truth."

"Uh, right. Whatever you say. I mean, thank you, I appreciate the kind words."

"You doubt me, boy?" Anhur's eyes blazed at me. He did not look happy with my less than enthusiastic answer.

"No....well, kind of. I don't really believe in, you know, the underworld, or gods."

"Excuse me? You don't believe in gods? You are speaking to the god of war, boy! You are addressing Anhur, the Slayer of Enemies! Anhur, the Sky Bearer! Your very father was descended from the Titans themselves!" Anhur was fuming now. His body language became extremely aggressive, and honestly, he was scaring the shit out of me.

"...I don't want to be disrespectful or anything, we don't have to talk about this...if you knew my dad, actually I'd love to ask you about him—"

"Titanson, do not change the subject. You cannot insult me to my face and then switch to the paltry small talk of tiny minds. Tell me true...what is this no gods nonsense of yours?"

"I mean...what can I say, I don't believe in gods, I don't believe in heaven or hell. No disrespect intended, but personally, I don't think you're really the Egyptian god of war."

"Oh? Then what am I? No, really, boy, tell me. Do not coat it in sweet sugars."

"I think you're just some Egyptian guy who took SUHP and unlocked an enormous genetic potential for superhuman ability. I mean I get it, I've read the articles about you, I know that you do this whole ancient god of war character, and it's a great marketing strategy. I dunno, maybe I'm wrong. Maybe you really are thousands of years old, but I'm pretty sure you're just a dude from Cairo who happens to be genetically gifted with an insane amount of superhuman power. Again, I'm not trying to be disrespectful, this is just what I believe."

Anhur was taken aback. He didn't know what to say to me, and he looked like he wanted to jab that spear of his straight through my heart. Some superheroes around us looked uneasy and tried to pretend like they weren't listening to our conversation. A space around us cleared as a lot of nearby superheroes decided that it was an excellent time to get in line to talk to Silver Scribe about placing their next bets. I was sweating bullets, but what can I say? He asked. I even tried to change the subject.

"You dishonor your father greatly, boy. Jack Titan was descended from the mighty Titans! He carried on a legacy established by his forebearer Prometheus! He was a man of honor! We fought many battles together! He was like a brother to me...and you not only besmirch me, Anhur, the god of war, but you spit on the memory of your own father?"

"It's not like that, I'm pretty sure that my dad didn't think he was related to actual Titans, I think it was just like a cool theme that he ran with...don't take it personally Anhur, really, I'm a huge fan of yours—" Anhur raised a hand in my face and cut me off mid-sentence.

"Boy, you are no Titanson. No son of Jack Titan, the Man of Myth, would be so insolent, so…dishonorable. And look at you…Jack Titan was a man, a man who would make his Titan ancestors proud. He was the spitting image of Atlas. You? You're just a weaselly little child."

Anhur took a final look at me and scowled like I was a bag of flaming shit that he had just found on the front porch of his pyramid. He turned away from me, and I still can't believe I was stupid enough to do this, but I grabbed him by the arm.

"Release me, or I swear by the burning light of Ra that I will pound that hand into a fine paste," Anhur whirled around and his eyes were filled with such an intense rage that there was no doubt in my mind that he would follow through on his threat, and I let go of his arm…but I just couldn't let go of my stupid search for information on my dad.

"Sorry, I just…you said you knew my dad really well? I've been sort of trying to find out about his superhero career, like the places he hung out and the people he knew, and a box of his stuff was stolen, and well, anything you could tell me might help…"

Anhur smiled at me, and somehow his smile was even scarier than his wrath-filled glare.

"You want me to tell you about your father? I don't even believe that you are Jack Titan's son! Why should I waste one minute of my immortal life speaking with some illegitimate bastard boy who insults my divinity and the titanic blood of my fallen friend?"

"...Anhur, please. I don't know what to say...I'm just asking for a little information, he was my dad and, you know, you keep talking about honor...I'm trying to honor him. I want to take back a box that was filled with his life's work. I want to find the son of a bitch who stole it and beat the shit out of him. You can understand that, right?"

Anhur stroked his black, conic beard. He looked away from me and at the empty ring in the middle of the room, and then he looked back at me with that terrifying, broad smile.

"Let us strike a bargain, boy. You prove to me that you are truly the Titanson, and I shall tell you everything that you could want to know, and more."

"Come on, what do you want from me? You want to go do a blood test? How can I prove that I'm really Jack Titan's son?"

Anhur looked at the ring, and he nodded his four feathered headdress in its direction.

"Fight me. The only way that you can truly know a man, or in your case a disrespectful boy, is to face them in combat. If you are the Titanson, I will know."

"You've got to be kidding me. Fight you? This is fucking ridiculous."

My entire superhero career has been built on the foundation of a very simple rule: never fight villains that are more powerful than you. I learned my lesson when I put on a mask for the first time and got my ass handed to me by The Whimsy. If you want to survive as a superhero, you have to choose your battles carefully. You want to pick fights with villains that you know you can beat. These crimefighters that think they can go up against absurdly powerful villains by themselves because they have this childish, romantic idea of the "honorable" superhero? 99 times out of 100, they die. They die in horribly gruesome ways like having the valves of their heart turned intangible by The Immaterial Man. They end up torn limb from limb and burned to death by people like Dragon General. Always fight villains that are weaker than you. Trust me, if you want to have a lengthy superhero career, you don't want to be a hero.

"Okay, Anhur. Let's do this," I said to Anhur, and every rational part of my mind was wailing in protest. Agreeing to fight Anhur, a man who could juggle airplanes like ping pong balls, was an insane violation of my one simple rule, but I just couldn't help myself. If he knew anything about my father and whoever had taken the box that held his life's work, then I just had to know what it was.

"Ha! Don't worry, boy, I shall go easy on you. By the end of the night, you'll only be in a hospital and not a grave." Anhur was filled with glee, and he practically skipped over to the Silver Scribe to set up the fight. I started sweating bullets as I watched him demand that the Silver Scribe arrange a match immediately. The surrounding superheroes erupted into a frenzy of placing bets on Anhur. Crystallor had a look of horror on his rocky face. My heart was pounding in my chest like a jackhammer and I could barely register what was going on around me.

Before I could get a chance to come to my senses and back out of the fight, I was ushered through the crowd of clamoring superheroes and towards the ring in the center of the room. I saw Crystallor angrily arguing with Silver Scribe as I was pushed through the open gate of the ring, but Silver Scribe had already taken his bets and he wasn't calling off the fight. I stepped onto the blood-spattered rubber padding of the ring, and Anhur followed me in. He closed the gate behind him, and the light of a force field flowed through the fence like a wave as the door slammed shut. Some minuscule part of my mind realized that the fence surrounding the ring was reinforced with a force field that kept the destructive, superpowered cage fights from demolishing the building.

Anhur stood in front of me relishing the borderline hysteria of the cheering crimefighters around us. Anhur looked like he lived for this. He started twirling his spear around and shouting back at them and pumping up the crowd even more. I suddenly felt a stifling heat in the room and I couldn't catch my breath. There was an unbridled joy in Anhur's eyes as he soaked up the fervor of the audience, and then he abruptly stopped his terrifying, guttural screaming that was riling up the spectators. The room quieted down slightly, and Anhur pointed the blunt end of his spear at me. He just looked me right in the eye, and that moment seemed to stretch out for an eternity.

Then Anhur charged at me and swung the blunt end of his spear at me. I instinctively leaned back and out of the way of the wooden rod, and Anhur backhanded me in the face with his free hand. I was thrown from my feet and against the force field infused fence which lit up with pulses of energy as I slammed into it. I fell back down onto the rubber padding of the ring and I felt like I had just been hit by a bus. Anhur laughed that booming laugh of his, and then he swung at me again with the spear like he was trying to hit a home run and I was the baseball.

I quickly sidestepped out of the way, and that first hit to the face had jostled all the shock out of me. My mind was racing, I was desperately trying to come up with a way out of this situation I had foolishly stepped into as Anhur viciously swung his spear at me again. I jumped over the spear and pivoted in mid-air to dodge as Anhur threw a punch at me. I landed on the rubber mat and I jabbed at Anhur's midsection while he was over extended from his punch, and it was like bashing my fist against a brick wall. Anhur laughed again, and this time the crowd of superheroes outside the ring laughed too as I pulled back my fist in pain.

Anhur continued cackling as he started to rapidly swing his spear at me again and again like he was a blindfolded kid at a birthday party trying to beat the candy out of a pinata. I jumped and ducked and dodged out of the way of his wild swings, Anhur was starting to get frustrated by my superior speed and agility as I danced around him, he angrily raised the wooden rod high above his head and brought it down so fast and so hard that I was barely able to bounce out of the way. It slammed into the floor, the blue rubber padding where it struck disintegrated, and the concrete below the padding cracked in a spider web pattern. One blow as powerful as that would definitely knock me out cold, and probably pulverize a few bones in the process. I realized that my only option was to fight Anhur like The Whimsy fought me all those years ago. I was much weaker than him, but taking advantage of my speed was my only chance to end this fight without an obscene hospital bill.

Anhur tossed his spear aside, and I could tell that he wasn't treating this like a joke anymore. He started throwing punches at me with such ferocity that I was having trouble bobbing out of the path of his massive brown fists. My superhuman reflexes were much sharper than Anhur's, but every one of his incredibly powerful punches was proving to me that he was easily the strongest person I had ever fought in my life. He missed me with a left hook that connected with the cage, the force field burst into blinding light from the sheer power of the punch, and the shockwave knocked me to the ground. The crowd roared, the wind was knocked out of me, and Anhur raised one of his sandaled feet like he was going to stomp the life out of me.

I rolled out of the way right as Anhur's foot crashed onto the rubber mat with a bang like cannon fire. I sprung to my feet, maneuvered to the side of Anhur before he could react, and just started pummeling him in the rib cage with rapid fire punches. I put everything I had into that flurry of punches. I hit Anhur's nearly invulnerable midsection as many times as I could in the minuscule window of time I had before he could react, and after I had landed at least a dozen strikes, each of which could have punched a hole in a sheet of steel, my knuckles were on fire like hot, ground up glass had been injected into my fists. I poured all my strength and speed into that series of body shots…but when it was over, Anhur slapped me away from him and I fell back up against the fence. It was clear that he was barely fazed by my shower of punches. At best, he looked slightly annoyed.

"I am supremely disappointed in you, Spectacle Titanson. I was looking forward to a challenge, not a coward leaping away from me." Anhur knelt down and picked up his spear. I was backed up against the force field infused cage wall, and the last thing I needed was for Anhur to pick up his little beating stick. I knew I couldn't keep dodging him in these close quarters for much longer, and that spear dramatically increased his reach. I had to try to stall.

"Oh, so now you believe I'm the Titanson?" I asked. Anhur chuckled at this, and he rhythmically slapped his spear in his hand as he walked towards me.

"Perhaps."

"Oh, okay. Well, then I've proved my point with this fight, haven't I? I accept your forfeit graciously, oh Anhur, Mighty Slayer of Enemies." Fury washed over Anhur's face like the flooding water of the river Nile, and I immediately regretted being such a smart ass.

Anhur feinted left, and I started to move out of his way when he slammed the side of his spear into my shoulder from the right. The pain was so incredible that my whole world almost went black, the fabric of my costume jacket was shredded where the wooden rod struck me, and I fell to the rubber mat.

"I must say, Spectacle Titanson, you put in a good fight...but the time has come for me to end that fight." I crawled away from Anhur as he ambled towards me, and the crowd around the cage lost their minds.

Even I was pretty sure that Anhur was about to give me a considerably bad concussion and finish this joke of a fight. I clawed at the rubber mat to pull myself away from him, and something fell out of my jacket pocket through the huge tear in its fabric. I was exhausted and wracked with pain on the right side of my upper body, so it took me a second to recognize the thing as it slipped through the hole in my jacket and fell onto the rubber mat.

It was my father's Golden Sling. When Ultra Lady gave it to me months ago, I put it in my costume jacket pocket and forgot it was even there. I grabbed the sling and a piece of concrete debris from the small crater that Anhur had made when he brought his spear down on the floor earlier. It was a longshot, but as I got to my knees and looked up at Anhur preparing to crack me in the face with the blunt end of his spear, I knew it was the only option I had left. I slipped the shard of concrete into the leather patch, Anhur thrust his spear towards my head, and I swung that Golden Sling around like my life depended on it. I let go and fired that rock at Anhur's face with all the superhuman strength that I had left in my beaten body.

The shard hit Anhur's forehead and exploded into a fine mist of gray sand. He missed me with the spear by centimeters, I felt the wooden rod graze my hair, Anhur looked dumbfounded as little flecks of concrete fell off of his dust covered forehead, and the audience gasped. Anhur pulled back his spear, presumably to try to pound me in my beautiful face again, and then he went a bit cross-eyed. He raised a hand to his forehead, and a little bit of blood oozed out of the spot where I had nailed him with the rock. Anhur looked at his blood covered fingers in absolute disbelief, and then he looked down at me. I looked up at him with a sheepish grin.

"This is…no one…no one has spilled god-blood since the last great Horus War. I…I forfeit! All hail Spectacle Titanson!"

Anhur grabbed me and hoisted me to my feet. He thrust my arm up into the air, which hurt like a bitch given the fact that he had just bashed the shit out of my other shoulder, but I didn't think that was exactly the right time to complain.

"All hail Spectacle Titanson, son of Jack Titan! All hail Spectacle Titanson, the second coming of the Man of Myth! All hail the Mighty Spectacle, he who draws blood from gods!" The entire crowd of superheroes groaned in collective disappointment. A lot of them were downright furious with this result and boos filled the small room. Clearly, not many of them had bet on me.

"Whatever you say, man," I spit out through a bleeding smile, and Anhur helped me hobble my way out of the cage.

"I haven't seen a mortal wield a sling like that since, well, since your father and I met, all those years ago," Anhur said as he helped me out of the cage and down the steps. I was struck by the sincere nostalgia in his voice.

"Are you out of your goddamn mind? What the hell is wrong with you? Are you trying to get yourself killed?" Crystallor said as he clomped up to me with his giant, quartz feet through thick clusters of superheroes who were complaining to Silver Scribe about the outcome of the fight.

"Your friend fought honorably, Crystal Golem! You should be proud to call yourself a comrade of the Titanson," Anhur ruffled my hair with one of his giant brown hands that he had just been trying to break my skull with only minutes earlier.

"So…you were close with my dad, or…?"

"Ah yes, our bargain. I did know your father quite well, Titanson. Our battle has shown me that you are truly his rightful heir, and I would be honored to tell you the stories of Jack Titan's greatness. The Man of Myth was like a brother to me, and his son deserves to know the truth."

Anhur launched into a series of stories while we watched several more superhuman brawls. In the Flasked

Crusader, Jane sold me pretty lies about my father like he was a saint in a golden mask. Anhur didn't bullshit me at all. In fact, despite lying about being the Egyptian god of war, the man didn't seem to be capable of saying anything other than exactly what was on his mind.

He told me about their first team up in the early 60's against Mistress Gorgon, and how Jack Titan's sexual relationship with the serpent haired woman almost got the both of them imprisoned in a block of her supra-stone. He told me about how he had actually invited Jack Titan to be a founding member of the Superb 6, but he flat out refused because he thought "this superhero team thing is never gonna take off". He told me about their battles with The Shill and his gang of corporately sponsored hench-CEOs, and how Jack Titan's incessant goading of The Shill caused him to launch a targeted advertising campaign that made the general public believe that the Man of Myth was a cross-dressing communist. He told me about the countless times that Jack Titan dealt with The Punster's psychotic schemes, and he told me how much my father hated that pun obsessed supervillain. Anhur told me that he thought Jack Titan's boundless hatred of The Punster impaired his judgment, and maybe even fueled the fire of their rivalry when it could have just fizzled out, if only he would have let it.

Anhur told me hours of stories about my father, and the man he described wasn't a flawless hero like the sugar coated legend that Jane used to distract me. Anhur painted a picture of a man whose personal neuroses kept him from being the A-list superhero that he could have been, a man who was as manic, as obsessed with fighting crime, as the supervillains were with committing crimes. Yet there was clearly admiration in Anhur's tone, there was an appreciation for "a cleverness on par with Odysseus," "more courage than Achilles could muster in a lifetime," and something else, an inherent goodness that Anhur tried to convey to me but ultimately failed to put into words. In spite of all his faults, Anhur really did believe that my father was a good man.

Chapter 8:
Preservation Devastation

I'm not much of a comic book guy. I'm not much of a reader in general, but I do enjoy some indie comics from time to time. When you spend most of your nights hanging out with people in masks and capes and getting into superpowered fistfights, you pretty much lose all interest in reading superhero comics in your free time. So I've been to a few comic book stores to pick up a non-superhero related comic or two, and seriously, Specialized Comics might be the worst place to buy comics in the known universe.

The store is poorly lit. There's one fluorescent light that works, and the rest of the light in the place leaks in through the cracks of the blinds covering the windows. As soon as I stepped into the store, my nose was blasted with the scents of decaying paper, musty, never vacuumed carpets, and cat piss. The culprit responsible for the cat piss, a morbidly obese black cat, sat on a long box of comics and stared at me like I couldn't be any less welcome in his territory. No one was behind the counter, which was a cluttered mess of superhero action figures posed as if they were fighting to the death. There were also toys still in their original boxes stacked on the glass counter, preserved in plastic and cardboard like prehistoric insects in amber.

Anhur had confided in me that Specialized Comics was a front for a black market super-tech dealer and ultra-engineer, "The Specialist," the same guy who regularly repaired his spear. After our long and enlightening conversation about my father, Anhur let me know that if anyone in the city knew about the sale of any of the stuff in my father's trophy room box, it was the Specialist. I walked around Specialized Comics and looked at the dusty shelves of superhero comics. There wasn't a single indie comic outside of the cape genre. It was very difficult to believe that this dump really concealed some supervillain's weapons trade operation.

One row of comics in particular stood out to me. It was an entire section of comics that were about superheroes that I actually knew. I was aware that The Millennials licensed out our team name and likenesses to a comic book company, and I had seen pictures of the cover artwork before, but I had never actually seen a copy in person. I picked up The Millenials #56, encased in a plastic bag with a rectangle of white cardboard keeping it rigid, and I was extremely amused by the cover. The cover depicted a much more kid friendly version of us, and we were fighting Captain Haiku who looked genuinely menacing, when in reality he was an ineffectual buffoon. The cover read, "Captain Haiku and his Syllabullies March to War!!!," and that triple exclamation point was seriously on the cover. I swear I didn't add that in there.

"That issue is actually kind of an investment. A major character dies in that one," someone said behind me in a nasally voice. I turned around and saw a short, skinny man in his mid 30's. He was balding, had a scraggly goatee that looked like the facial hair on his chin never really filled out, was wearing a t-shirt two sizes too big for him with a Beyond Man symbol on it, and he reeked of onions.

"Oh jeez…I didn't recognize you from behind. It's so cool to meet you Spectacle, so awesome that you're in my store. My name's Neil," he wiped his onion ring grease covered hand off on his cargo shorts, and he extended it to me to shake. I shook his hand and made a mental note to wash my gloves later.

"Thanks, nice to meet you Neil…you said someone dies in this issue? I actually remember this fight with Captain Haiku and you know, no one died…and also, his 'Syllabully Army' was like five henchman. Not that much of an army, really."

"Ah well, the sales on The Millennials have been pretty bad. I mean, no offense. They probably wanted to bump up their numbers a bit by killing off a character, make things a little more exciting you know?"

"Sure, I guess."

Neil was staring at me in a really weird way as I put The Millennials #56 back on the shelf and started looking at some of the other titles. It was really distracting. I tried to evaluate some of the other books like Doc Hyper #305, an issue featuring the original Doctor Delusion, and Ultra Lady #107, which showed the superheroine teaming up with Queen Quantum. I couldn't concentrate on the colorful covers with Neil's bulging eyes aimed at me.

"Can I help you find anything…anything in particular?"

"Actually, yeah, but I'm not really interested in comics."

"Well, we have a wide assortment of action figures, busts, maquettes, trade paper backs…I think maybe I've even got a couple old Spectacle action figures, they weren't really selling so I'd be happy to give you—"

"Cut the shit. I'm not here for any of that. You know exactly why I'm here," I snapped at him, and Neil nervously giggled.

"Okay, okay. This is a shakedown, right? You want some cash in exchange for not busting my little side business, am I wrong?"

"What? No, this isn't a shakedown. I'm a customer. I want to see whatever super-tech you've got in back, Neil. I want to talk to the Specialist."

"Well, you're talking to him already, but really, I prefer Neil. But okay, yeah. I'm a little surprised, I never figured the Spectacle for the kind of crimefighter who gets involved with black market type stuff, I sort of thought of you as a little lower tier than that, no offense." The Specialist led me through aisles of long boxes stuffed with yellowing comics and into a back room. I detected a little passive aggressiveness in his nasally voice, and I was a little insulted, but I tried to ignore it.

The back room of the store was even more cluttered and disgusting than the store itself. It was packed with boxes filled with comic books. They were stacked on top of each other and towered all the way up to the water spotted ceiling. Newspapers were strewn all over the floor. There was a litter box in the corner, and in the middle of the room, an 80 year old woman was sitting at a small table and eating a big bowl of oatmeal. The Specialist guided me past her and towards an empty section of space that looked out of place in the disorganized, hoarder mess of the rest of the room.

"Neil, who's your friend? It's so rare that you bring friends by, introduce me won't you?"

"...*Mother.* Please don't bother us, and finish your lunch. You haven't even touched your lunch. I thought we talked about this?" The Specialist practically yelled this at the poor woman, and if I thought he was distasteful before, now I completely hated his guts.

"So...what are you looking for? I got it all, except for SUHP. I heard a rumor that you're a bit of a souphead, so I hope that's not what you're here for," The Specialist took a small remote out of his pocket and clicked it. A couple of tables covered in super-tech shimmered into view in the empty section of space, and I was surprised to see that the merchandise was meticulously organized.

"Holographic cloak. I told you, I got it all."

As gross as he was, The Specialist did seem to have it all. The two tables that just appeared before me had enough super-tech to satisfy the needs of any major superhero team and then some. There were compact smoke bombs, jet packs and canisters of extremely expensive fuel, personal teleporter badges, a plethora of grappling hooks, both with and without extra spools of high tension nylon wire, miniature force field generators, teeny tiny homing devices that could be stuck to things like stickers, and that was just the tip of the iceberg as far as legal crimefighting tools went.

He also had a cornucopia of illegal devices; taser boots with a voltage level that was way above legal limits, proton accelerator pistols, a bunch of pairs of gamma ray gauntlets which I'm pretty sure are used exclusively by supervillains. I saw a couple of knock off reality rewriters that could warp the fabric of space and time to a limited and highly dangerous degree, and even more things that I'd rather not list because, frankly, I think it would frighten a lot of people to know that items as dangerous as these were for sale and not in a government vault somewhere. Something at the back of one of the tables behind some swatches of energy blast resistant fabrics in various colors caught my eye. It was one of my father's Golden Slings.

"Where did you get this?" I asked as I reached across the table and picked up the Golden Sling.

"You don't want that, that's a piece of garbage. Maybe I can interest you in this new flight belt I just made? I've been tinkering with it recently, and no offense, but flying might help your game quite a bit."

"No thanks, and actually I am a little offended by that, but whatever. Where'd you get this thing?"

The Specialist eyed me suspiciously, and he ignored my question again.

"Neil, can you take me to the pharmacy today? I have a few prescriptions I need to pick up," his elderly mother asked, and he glared at her with such a high level of disrespect that I wanted to slap that scraggly goatee off of his face, but again, I restrained myself.

"Look, Spectacle, I just put together this new utility belt, it's fully loaded, really, it's got the works, think you'd be into adding a utility belt to your ensemble? I'll let you have it for 20% off."

"...here's the thing, Neil. I'm a collector. I collect old, obscure superhero equipment, and right now, I'm on a big time Jack Titan kick. Do you have any other Jack Titan stuff, or do you know where I could get some more?"

The Specialist snatched the Golden Sling out of my hand, and he placed it back on the table. He scratched the top of his balding head, and he intently considered what he was going to say next.

"I might have something for you. Let me go check in my car, I just got some new stuff in, I'll be right back," he stammered, and he hastily grabbed the jet pack off of the table along with a handful of smoke bombs and one of the proton accelerator pistols.

"I forgot, this stuff, someone was real interested in buying it, they sort of reserved it, shouldn't even have it on the table," The Specialist muttered, and he slung the jet pack onto his back and fastened the straps as he rushed towards the door.

"Oh, Neil, you're leaving? Could you be a dear and pick up some cat litter while you're out? Cornelius is having tummy problems and we need some more," his mother called after him, and he suddenly broke into a sprint out of the back room without looking back.

"Shut up, mother! God damn it! Shit! Fuck!"

I ran after him and accidentally knocked over a pillar of comic book boxes in the process. Hundreds of comics mummified in their bags and boards spilled onto the floor and I stepped all over them as I pursued The Specialist. He had reached the door of Specialized Comics by the time I had made my way through the cluttered store, but he hesitated at the sound of his precious comic books being toppled out of their protective cardboard boxes and exposed to the elements.

"You…that was a complete run of Beyond Man! Issues 1 to 697, every issue from 1964 to today! Do you have any idea how much a collection in that condition would sell for? Now it's ruined! It's fucking ruined! You…you fuck!" The Specialist aimed his proton accelerator pistol at me and fired a blindingly bright, blue stream of protons at my head. I ducked out of the way of the high energy proton beam that could have punched a hole in the molecules of my skull, and a shelf of comics behind me exploded into a cloud of shredded multicolored paper.

Pulped comic pages filled the air. I couldn't see the Specialist exiting the store and making a break for it through the shredded paper raining down all around me. I heard the mingling of his poor old mother's screams and Cornelius's hissing as I struggled to make my way through the tables of comics and maquettes and collectible toys as the fog of disintegrated comic pages dissipated. By the time I finally got to the door, I had maybe a half a second to witness the Specialist on the street and powering up his jet pack. He barely even looked at me while his jet pack started glowing red hot at its exhaust ports. It was like I was a very annoying cost of doing business to him but not really anything to be overly concerned about. Then two blasts of scarlet energy shot out of the bottom of his jet pack and fired him into the air like a missile. A car swerved out of the way of the billowing mists of red energy that his jet pack left in its wake, and it crashed into a streetlight.

The Specialist was already about ten blocks away, and he was just a speck trailing plumes of red energy above the city. Since it was so useful in my fight with Anhur, I had started carrying around my father's Golden Sling along with three rubber lacrosse balls for ammunition (not everyone can take a piece of concrete hitting them in the dome at 200 meters per second). I whipped out the sling and fitted one of the rubber balls into it, swung the golden ropes around my head once, twice, three times, and then I let go and fired the ball at the tiny glint of metal in the sky that was The Specialist. If I could hit that jet pack of his and mess up his trajectory, it might slow him down and give me the edge I would need to chase him down on foot.

I didn't wait to see if the ball hit its target. I leapt from the street and onto the roof of Specialized Comics, and I ran as fast as I could across the rooftop of that abysmally bad comic book store and in the general direction of the Specialist. I hurled myself from that building and to the next one while tracking the Specialist in the sky, and I could tell from the perfect arc of red energy following his path like a comet's tail that I hadn't hit him with the throw. I was angry at myself for even trying to use the Golden Sling when I should have just started immediately chasing him, and that anger fueled my pursuit.

I furiously dashed across the next rooftop and then bounded off of it and towards a much taller building, landed on a fire escape, and used its metal railing as a starting block to rocket myself towards a flag pole jutting out of the side of a skyscraper, then swung on the flag pole and harnessed my momentum to fling myself towards the Specialist. I ripped through the air and flew at least a dozen city blocks before landing on yet another rooftop which I ran on like the devil was chasing me. The fact that the Specialist had run from me and the way that he did it convinced me that I was closer than ever to finding out who had stolen my father's trophy room. I couldn't let that comic collecting bastard slip away from me.

I was getting closer now to The Specialist, who had to be only a block or two ahead of me, and I was experiencing none of the thrill that I usually got from leaping above the city skyline. I was totally focused on the task, eyeballing angles of jumps that would save me only a few feet of travel distance, pushing through the burning in my lungs and my legs as I darted across rooftops to close the gap between me and the Specialist, and every second counted because that jet pack of his was carrying him at least 50 miles per hour, and I could only keep up this pace for so long.

The Specialist was only a few yards ahead of me now. He was soaring above the city streets way too fast for me to try to jump onto him, but he was definitely within throwing distance. I took out the Golden Sling again while clearing the gap between two buildings, put the second rubber ball into the leather patch in between two lengths of gold painted rope as I ran across a window ledge, whirled the sling around my head and let go. The rubber ball flew at The Specialist, and it sailed over his head.

I kept running after him, and I heard him scream a string of profanities in his sharp, nasally voice as he saw the ball shoot past him and he looked over his shoulder to see that I was still on his tail. He banked left hard, and I skidded to a stop on a rooftop just before I would have had to jump in the wrong direction. He pointed his proton accelerator pistol over his shoulder and fired three blind shots in my general direction. One of the blue blasts of highly charged protons would have torn most of the electrons from my molecules if I hadn't dived onto the ground. I stayed there and covered my head with my hands as the second shot disintegrated the aluminum panels of an air conditioning unit behind me, and the third shot scorched the ground only a few feet away from me.

I got up, and I was all out of juice. Couldn't possibly catch him on foot now as he pulled ahead of me and left me in his red plasma dust. I put the third and last rubber ball into the Golden Sling, swung it around my head and focused on the Specialist rocketing away from me and getting smaller and smaller by the second. I felt a desperate urge to take the shot as fast as I could but I resisted and I took my time, inhaled and exhaled as I tracked the Specialist's flight and tried to picture the throw in my mind, and then I let that ball fly. It was a hopeless Hail Mary throw, and I assumed that it had no chance of hitting him, much less actually doing any significant damage.

I stood on the roof and put my hands on my head to help me catch my breath, and I watched the Specialist fly farther and farther away from me. By this point, I had accepted that I had lost him. I was about to give up and go home when I saw a disruption in the trail of red energy that the Specialist's jet pack was leaving in its wake. Instead of a steady stream of smokey scarlet energy, it was shooting out of his jet pack's thrusters erratically like a dotted red line. The Specialist started careening all over the place, then the jet pack almost completely stopped sputtering its red energy propulsion, and he crashed through a billboard.

For a few seconds, I stood on that rooftop completely shocked. I honestly couldn't believe that worked. It took me a few minutes to make my way across the city skyline and to the building with the Extradimensional Fitness billboard that had a gaping hole in it, and the whole time I was hoping that I didn't just accidentally send the Specialist falling to his death. I landed on the ledge of the billboard with Beyond Man's smiling face plastered on it. Luckily, I looked through the hole in Beyond Man's normally impeccable teeth to see the Specialist lying on the roof below and still alive with relatively minor injuries. His jet pack was popping and crackling with little gasps of red energy coughing out of its exhaust, it had a big dent on it from the ball's impact that had almost entirely crushed its left tube-like side. The Specialist was groaning and trying to unbuckle the straps.

I climbed through the hole in the billboard, and I jumped down to the roof near the Specialist. He was making a pointless attempt to crawl away from me on his belly and towards his proton accelerator pistol, which he had dropped in the fall. I turned him over with my foot to face me like I was flipping a pancake. I still was riding high on the charge I got from actually hitting him with that desperate half court shot of a throw, and I was excited to pry whatever information he had out of his balding head.

"Where'd you get the Golden Sling, Specialist?"

"I...ordered it from this little website called...go fuck yourself Spectacle...dot org."

I crouched down next to the Specialist, who was scratched up pretty bad from crashing through the billboard and onto the gravel covered roof top, and honestly, I felt bad for the guy. He looked so small and pathetic lying there on that rooftop, strapped to a bulky metal jet pack that made his already skinny body look gaunt, wearing a Beyond Man symbol t-shirt when he was about the complete opposite in both character and appearance from Beyond Man.

"Specialist...Neil. Jack Titan was my dad, okay? Someone stole all of his superhero mementos, and I'm trying to—"

The Specialist started laughing before I could finish.

"Don't you think I know that? Why do you think I ran, dummy? I was contracted to steal that box of garbage from your apartment. Nice place, by the way," the Specialist sneered at me in between bursts of nasally giggles.

"Contracted by who? Who sent you to steal that stuff?"

The Specialist didn't answer me. He just kept giggling, and normally his laughter would just be annoying, but in this particular situation, it was infuriating. I grabbed him by the Beyond Man symbol on his chest and yanked his whole upper body towards me.

"Look, Spectacle, I can't tell you that. I've already jeopardized my career and reputation by telling you that much. Who's gonna hire the Specialist if they can't trust him not to blab all over town about who paid him to secure their contraband?"

"Okay, how about I throw you off of this roof, and we'll test to see if that nifty jet pack is still working?" The Specialist resumed giggling at this threat, and I shook him violently by his shirt, but that only made him laugh even more.

"You won't do that. You're a superhero. I've read every appearance you've ever made in any comic. I could practically recite your Wikipedia page and I've read more forum posts about you than any guy should in a lifetime. You're a goody two shoes, self-righteous, sanctimonious, bland crimefighter. You wouldn't kill me. You wouldn't even beat me up to get information, you're not like that," The Specialist rattled off with such confidence that I knew the smug little jerk was telling the truth. He really knew his shit. It wasn't hard to believe that this guy had spent years living on the internet and absorbing everything there was to know about the superhero community.

"You're right. I won't kill you. That's a little too fucked up for my tastes. But you know what I would do? I would be perfectly happy going back to Specialized Comics and taking a look at some of those boxes of comics I saw in your back room. You think stepping on some old issues of Beyond Man was bad?"

"You wouldn't," the Specialist quaked, and now it was my turn to laugh.

"Oh no? I would love to go back to that shithole you call a comic store, and I would love to make you watch while I slowly took your oldest and most treasured comic out of its plastic bag…"

"Stop it," the Specialist whispered.

"…and *sloooowwwllllyyy* rip the cover, just taking my sweet time with pulling apart the ancient fibers of that paper…"

"Shut up, I get it," The Specialist insisted.

"…oh, I can just hear it, the scratchy sound of that paper tearing. And it wouldn't end there. It would take hours to destroy all of your collection, and I'm a creative guy, I could come up with some fun ways to do this. Maybe I'd eat a bucket of barbecue wings and then read your, I dunno, Anhur #1 or whatever and just paint those pages with honey barbecue sauce. You like honey barbecue? Or maybe I'd use a few early issues of Superb 6 as toilet paper, might be a little uncomfortable but hilarious nonetheless—"

"Alright, okay, I'll tell you what you want to know. Just promise me you won't mess up my comics?" The Specialist looked at me with a sad, pleading expression in his eyes.

"I promise," I said, and I was overcome with pity that almost made me apologize for threatening his comics.

"I was hired by Mistress Gorgon to steal the box of your father's stuff…but it wasn't for her. I have a rule about clients, I need to know about the product that I'm securing, for my protection. So I asked her about this box of garbage you had in your apartment, and she didn't know anything about the stuff in it. All she would say is that she was doing this as a favor for someone else, she was like a middleman for, I don't know, someone who didn't want to expose themselves to crimefighting dicks like you. Someone who was smart enough to not leave a trail. And I couldn't help myself, I'm a collector...so I took one of your father's stupid slingshot things, okay? That's it. That's everything. Now can you help me down from this roof?"

I did help him down from that roof, and paid for a cab to send the guy back to his store, his elderly mother, his corpulent cat Cornelius, and his precious, pristinely preserved comic book collection. The Specialist was pretty embarrassed as I carried him on my shoulder and down to the street, and I was processing what he had just told me the whole time that I sent him on his way. Mistress Gorgon was a high level supervillain. She was not the sort of D-list criminal that I usually handled. She was an old school ultra-outlaw who had been fighting the Superb 6 since before I was born. She was exactly the type of superhuman that I would have avoided because of my one simple rule, my personal policy of never fighting villains that are more powerful than me.

I walked home instead of leaping from rooftop to rooftop so that I could think about this. I was oblivious to the people on the street gawking at me in my superhero costume, I was lost in a whirlwind of doubts and anxieties and confusion, and I was afraid. I was afraid of confronting a villain on the scale of Mistress Gorgon, I was afraid of whoever she was representing, I was afraid that I would give in to the powerful urge to just give up this stupid and increasingly dangerous search for my father's legacy, and those were just the fears that I was aware of at the time. There were also things nagging at my subconscious that I didn't realize until much later, like the fear that on some level, I was as immature as the Specialist, that I was so disgusted by him because I saw myself when I looked at that stunted man-child, that maybe my own obsession with regaining the physical remnants of my father's superhero career was the same thing as the Specialist's obsessive preservation of aging comics, that maybe I was falling apart while I tried to preserve the past.

Chapter 9:
Lady of the Past, Lady of the Future

The Z-Ray Lounge is the kind of establishment where you can throw away your money on lap dances from superhuman ladies, you can drown yourself in booze and sex and soup if you know the right people, and I was more than a little embarrassed to be there. I'd asked around about Mistress Gorgon, and I'd learned that she had gone legit and bought this "super-gentleman's club." I had been to the Z-Ray Lounge when I was younger and stupider, and on the night that I went there again for answers from Mistress Gorgon, I wasn't exactly as happy to be there as I was when I was nineteen and flush with cash to stuff into utility belts.

I paid the cover to get into the Z-Ray Lounge, and as I walked into the place, memories of being there in a drunken stupor bubbled up in my mind. I remembered the smells of bad perfume and cigarettes and sweat. I remembered the way that it was decorated like someone tried to imitate the look of a superhero team headquarters that they had seen on Hyper-Cribs, but it came across as a gaudy neon parody of a crimefighter's lair. I remembered the beautiful women peeling off capes and gloves and cowls and practically painted on spandex costumes on stages around the club, I remembered the leering men sitting on red felt chairs, and maybe most of all, I remembered the strange mixture of shame and excitement that accompanied being in that place.

I walked past one of the stages where a young stripper dressed as Queen Quantum was doing something that Queen Quantum would never do, and I sat down at the bar. The bartender was a young attractive lady dressed in a much skimpier version of Doc Hyper's costume, and she was whizzing around behind the bar like a hummingbird. She was mixing drinks, taking orders, masterfully flirting and feigning interest in men she clearly had no interest in, delivering drinks, and cashing out tabs, all at impressive super speeds that she could have used to be a crimefighter instead of tend bar in a place like this. I caught her eye, she darted up to me in a blur, and a few napkins blew up into the air in her wake. She snatched the napkins and put them back into their stacks on the bar before they could even start to fall back down.

"What can I get you, sweetie?"

"I want to talk to the owner," I said, and I was all business despite the considerable charm of her smile and beautiful green eyes. She looked familiar to me for some reason, but I just assumed it was my imagination.

"Oh, I'm sorry baby…is there something wrong? I can help you with any problems you've had here…"

"No, everything's fine. I have something to discuss with the owner, that's all. Can you get her?

"Well handsome, I can't just get the owner. She's a busy woman. Actually, she's not even here right now." She sped away from me and took another order at the other end of the bar, then she was back in front of me and pouring a beer before I had time to exhale.

"Then call her. Tell her The Spectacle wants to have a word with her."

"Oh, The Spectacle? I've heard of you," she chimed, and then she delivered the beer to the other end of the bar so fast that I couldn't even see it happen. One second she was standing in front of me with the beer, I blinked, and then the beer was gone and the guy at the other end of the bar was drinking it. I'm pretty sure she didn't spill a drop, either.

"Yeah, you're in that super-group The Millennials, right? You guys are cool, I've watched a bunch of your videos online."

"Listen, I appreciate it, but get Mistress Gorgon on the phone. Tell her to get down here—"

"Baby, I can call, but I can't promise that she'll show…she's a busy woman, you know?"

"…she'll show. Tell her The Spectacle is waiting."

"Okay, can I get you anything while you wait?"

"I'll have a beer," I said only because you can't just not order a drink in a place like that. It took a lot of willpower to not touch that beer in the Z-Ray Lounge, especially when it would have helped calm the storm in my stomach. I was extremely nervous about confronting Mistress Gorgon, but I wanted to have my wits about me, or as much as I could have my wits about me when gorgeous women were taking off their clothes all around me.

I sat there at that bar, on that bar stool designed to look like a chair at a superhero headquarters round table, and I waited for hours while loud music blared all around me. For a long time, I kept my head buried in my phone. I tried to focus on reading e-mails and checking various social media stuff while my beer sat there sweating. I exuded an aura of seriousness that was very out of place in the Z-Ray Lounge, I turned down several ladies who came up to me and asked if I wanted a lap dance, I imagined my conversation with Mistress Gorgon and I wrote out clever dialogue in my head...but after a while, my attention drifted and I swiveled in my chair to watch the dancers on the main stage. What can I say? I may be superhuman, but I'm still human.

The music, the gyrating naked women, the colorful flashing lights, it all had the effect of zoning me out. The super speed bartender dressed as Doc Hyper assured me that Mistress Gorgon was on her way, but I had my doubts after waiting for so long, and I drank the beer that had gone completely warm. I was about to order another beer from the bartender, and I still couldn't shake the strange feeling that I knew her from somewhere, when a soft hand graced my shoulder. I turned around expecting another lap dance request, but instead I saw Mistress Gorgon, and despite all that time preparing what I would say to her and how I would say it, I was speechless.

I had seen pictures and videos of Mistress Gorgon before, but there was clearly something about her that was hard to capture on film. She was both shockingly beautiful and terrifying. She had tan, flawless skin. She was tall and curvaceous in her tight cut red dress. She had a perfectly formed face with high cheekbones and full, pouting lips that curled at the corners like she knew exactly how easy handling me was going to be for her. I knew from her lengthy and storied career spanning from the 60's to modern day that she must have been pushing 60, but she looked 29 at most.

But her incredible beauty was mixed with superhuman features that were very unsettling. Her hair was a tangle of writhing black snakes, each of which had glowing red eyes like bloody rubies. The spaghetti-thin serpents squirmed around on the top of her head, and it was almost impossible to not stare at the shiny black mass of wriggling snakes. Her piercing, white eyes looked like they were carved marble orbs. I don't mean that she had white eyes. I mean that they literally looked like they were made out of rock. Her stony eyes connected with mine, and it almost looked like her irises and pupils were carved onto them with a chisel.

"Sorry to keep you waiting, Spectacle," Mistress Gorgon said in a smokey voice that sent chills through my spine and raised the hair on my neck.

"It's…alright?" I sputtered, and all of the brilliant opening lines that I put together at that bar suddenly disappeared from my brain.

"Let's go get a seat, and chat for a bit," Mistress Gorgon took my hand and led me over to a corner of the Z-Ray Lounge without waiting for me to answer. I followed as she held my gloved hand in hers, and tried to not look at the nest of slithering snakes that was her hair. She slinked into one of the tacky armchairs plastered in cheap upholstery, crossed her legs, and gestured for me to sit down in front of her. I sat down and tried to pull myself together as her marble eyes bored into mine.

"Can I get you something before we get started? On the house, of course. A drink? A lap dance? Or maybe some soup, I know your father had a taste for the soup—"

"No," I said, and her barbed comment about my father cleared my head in a way that was probably the opposite of what she had intended.

"Well, you're a formal sort of boy, aren't you? Let's get right down to it then," Mistress Gorgon hadn't broken eye contact with me yet, and the snakes on her head started hissing and flicking their forked pink tongues at me.

"I don't have any problem with you, Mistress Gorgon. I don't want to disrupt your business here—"

"I'm sure you don't. My ladies tell me you've been enjoying the sights here for quite some time," Mistress Gorgon smiled.

"I was just…waiting for you to show. I don't have any beef with you, Mistress Gorgon, I just want to know why you contracted the Specialist to steal my father's things. I want to know who you were arranging the buy for. I want to know who has the box that basically contains Jack Titan's soul," I said in my best attempt at a commanding tone, and as I'm writing this, I can't believe that I actually said that soul line out loud.

"Jack Titan's soul, huh? I don't know about that, but it was quite the collection. Honey, just calm down, take a deep breath. We can be reasonable adults about this, right?" Mistress Gorgon laid one of her small, perfectly tanned hands on my knee as she said this. I brushed it off.

"I don't want to play games, Mistress Gorgon. Just tell me what I want to know, and I'll leave."

Mistress Gorgon blinked and finally broke her marble glare. She took a cigarette out of her pocket book and put it between her lips. One of the snakes on her head slid down her forehead and towards the cigarette. It opened up its mouth wide as if it was going to swallow the cigarette like a mouse dinner, and a blue flame spurted out of its gaping maw and lit the cigarette. She took a long drag on the cigarette, and then she let the smoke flow out of her nose while she looked at me as if she was considering turning that blue flame on me next.

"Relax," she said, and she leaned over to the table between us and tapped her cigarette in the ashtray. She was exposing a lot of her cleavage to me, and the teasing look in her rock eyes made it clear that it was intentional. "What do you want, Spectacle? You want to know about your daddy? Because I could tell you quite a bit about him. Probably more than you want to know, actually."

"I know that you had a relationship with him, if that's what you mean."

"Oh, did you? Did you know that he was still with your mommy when we had our 'relationship'?"

"...no, I guess I didn't."

"Well, he was. You don't really know that much about your daddy, do you? Is that what this little hunt for that box of trinkets is about?"

I didn't say anything.

"It is, isn't it? Let me tell you something. Your father was a deeply fucked up individual. He was with me when your mom was pregnant with you. He was with me when I was at the height of my supervillain career, when I was regularly fighting that sell out Beyond Man and those egomaniacs in the Superb 6. Your father didn't care about saving people, he wasn't this comic book superhero that you've got in your head. He just wanted to get stoned on SUHP and get laid, and he was a superhero just for the crazy rush it gave him. And you know something?"

She took a final drag on her cigarette, and blew a cloud of smoke in front of her. A couple of the snakes on her head poked their heads into the smoke and breathed deeply.

"I think that you're just like him."

I was at a loss. She waved to the bartender, and she zipped over to us in her Doc Hyper costume.

"Two whiskeys on the rocks. I think Mr. Spectacle here needs something for his head," she said, and I wanted to refuse the drink, but I just couldn't. The bartender looked at me in an oddly concerned way before she blurred to the bar and back with the drinks. She handed the glass to me, I still couldn't shake the feeling that I knew her, and then she ran off again at super speed.

"Let me tell you how it is," Mistress Gorgon stated in a matter of fact way, and she took a sip from her glass of top notch whiskey.

"I'm not going to tell you who contacted me about stealing your daddy's box of junk. That's just not going to happen. Here's what is going to happen. I'm going to treat you to the best night of your life. All the drinks are on the house. Have as many lap dances as you want, no charge. You see any of these ladies that you like a little more than the others? She goes home with you tonight. Maybe I'll join her if you play your cards right. Forget about your dad. He's gone, you're not. Live in the moment, Spectacle. Have some fun."

I drank the whiskey, and it was very good. I looked around the Z-Ray Lounge at the lithe, nubile ladies in colorful spandex that clung to their bodies. I drank from the glass again, and I looked at Mistress Gorgon who had a seductive smile on her face that was growing with every moment that I thought about her offer. I went into that situation with my best poker face, and she looked right through it. I knew that she was right about me.

My entire superhero career had been about crimefighting for the sake of the thrill and the money, not for "truth and justice". It had been about getting fucked up with my teammates in the Millenials as much as possible, and being with beautiful superhuman women. I was the same as my father, and her offer was like the pinnacle of everything that I had ever wanted out of being a superhero…but I just had to see for myself what was in that box. I had to read what my father wrote about his decades of superheroism in those dozens of spiral notebooks. I just had to know, or I'd never be able to live with myself.

"Sorry, Mistress Gorgon. No deal."

"Well, that's a shame, Spectacle." Mistress Gorgon put out her cigarette in the ashtray, and she averted her stony gaze.

"You really do remind me of your father…now you're turning me down, just like he left me in the 90's for your hag of a mother."

A vicious glint surfaced in those marble eyes of hers. She popped up and out of her chair, she snapped her fingers, and three strippers rushed over to her and surrounded me. The snakes on Mistress Gorgon's head started twisting and hissing, their ruby eyes glowed intensely like a little halo of red suns, the strippers in revealing versions of various Superb 6 member's costumes closed in around me, and a few bouncers cleared all of the clientele out of the club. I downed my entire glass of whiskey in one quick motion, and I wished that I had taken her up on her offer of unlimited decadence and debauchery. The shiny black serpents on Mistress Gorgon's head flared towards me and each of their mouths lit up with blue flames.

"Get down!" I heard someone shout. Someone shoved me, and I fell over the chair I had been sitting on and onto the filthy purple carpet. When I looked up, I saw the bartender in the Doc Hyper costume standing in front of me and engulfed in the blazing blue fire shooting from the unhinged jaws of those snakes like projectile vomit. The inferno bent around her instead of burning her to a crisp, and her apparently invulnerable body saved me from being swallowed up by the blue fire.

"The fuck?" I said in complete shock, and then the bartender's blond wig and mask burned up and revealed her flowing brown hair. It was Ultra Lady, the new member of the Superb 6 and friend of my father who came to visit me all those months ago.

"Get my back," Ultra Lady said as she shielded me from the blue flaming death surging out of the snakes on Mistress Gorgon's head, and she didn't have to tell me twice. I sprung to my feet, and the three strippers launched at me like sexy superpowered assassins. I flipped backwards and away from them and landed on the mainstage.

I saw Ultra Lady unleash a red burst of heat vision at Mistress Gorgon's face, and the snake haired temptress screeched in pain. Her head whipped back and that blue flame spurted all over the place and lit the ceiling on fire.

One of the strippers dressed as Queen Quantum flew at me, and the blue flame started spreading on the ceiling and dripping onto chairs and tables. Stripper Queen Quantum tried to punch me, I ducked out of the way and her fist struck the stripper pole and bent it like a paper clip, and now a lot of the club was being consumed by an unnaturally blue bonfire. Then the other two strippers joined Queen Quantum on the mainstage, the sprinkler system turned on, and it started pouring on us as I danced around the three superhuman strippers hovering around me and trying to kill me. I never thought I'd be dodging soaking wet, beautiful women like my life depended on it.

A shockingly thin Beyond Girl threw a fist at me that was brimming with glowing energy. I bobbed out of the way, and stepped right into a puddle of water that was coursing with electricity. Sadly, Stripper Supra also stood in the pool of water, electricity flowing from her feet through the sprinkler water and into my body, and my whole body seized up as at least fifty thousand volts of electricity surged through me. Supra ran out of juice, the current stopped, and I collapsed to my knees in a splash of water. The other two floated above the ground next to her, careful not land in any electrified water, and they lined up in front of me like a voluptuous firing squad. I was trying to recover from the powerful shock, but I couldn't even stand up.

Behind the three strippers preparing to execute me on the mainstage, Ultra Lady and Mistress Gorgon were brawling in a blue sea of flames. Ultra Lady was not doing so well. Mistress Gorgon's marble eyes lit up like halogen headlights and Ultra Lady's shoulder was coated with supra-stone where the white light touched her skin. The supra-stone restricted her movement severely, and the Serpent Seductress kicked her with a six inch stiletto so hard that a shockwave throbbed throughout the burning club. Glasses shattered and blue flames flickered with the radiating force.

While Mistress Gorgon had Ultra Lady on the ropes, Beyond Girl raised a fist that crackled with plasmatic energy. Supra pointed a finger at my face that was spewing sparks. Queen Quantum tore the crooked pole out of the ground and held it like a huge metal beating stick that had been wiped down thoroughly in between dances. I did my best to prepare myself for death by superhuman stripper.

I started to close my eyes and think that there are worst last sights than three beautiful women, and Ultra Lady landed a lucky uppercut on Mistress Gorgon's chin that shattered the supra-stone encasing her arm. The blow threw the Serpent Seductress across the club like a rag doll, and the fire spitting serpents on her skull went limp as she was knocked out cold. The superhuman stripper firing squad in front of me vanished along with the rest of the club, and I found myself in the air above the Z-Ray Lounge with serious whiplash. I honestly didn't have any idea what just happened, and that's when I realized that I was in the arms of Ultra Lady as she flew me to safety at super speed.

"Nice work. Do you know how long it took me to get that deep undercover in there?" Ultra Lady scolded me, but I had no response. My mind was boggling at the fact that she had just whisked me out of that place so fast that even with my superhuman reflexes and perception, from my point of view it was like we had just teleported out of there.

"Uh…" I was bewildered by the bird's eye view of the Z-Ray Lounge going up in turquoise flames below us and the fire engines that were arriving outside of the seedy establishment.

"Seriously, Spectacle. Try to think like an adult for one second in your life. I was this close to busting Mistress Gorgon's human trafficking operation, and you just forced me to flush all of that time building a case down the toilet so I could save your ass. Thanks, seriously, thanks a lot," she said, and she flew so smoothly with me in her arms that it was like we were gliding on rails.

"Ultra Lady…I'm sorry, I didn't know, I was just…" I finally managed to make my mouth work as she coasted near the corner of a rooftop and gently dropped me onto it.

"You were just looking for Jack Titan's soul, right?" Ultra Lady said with a sly smirk on her face as she touched down on the roof in front of me.

"Heh…it sounded cooler in my head. But yeah, I'm trying to figure out who stole a box of everything my dad collected from his superhero career. A lifetime of pictures, countless mementos, thousands of pages documenting

Jack Titan's every adventure in his own words..." I stopped talking as I watched the fire fighters spray down the Z-Ray Lounge, and it occurred to me that I was literally watching my last hope of finding that trophy room box go up in grayish blue smoke.

"I know, Spectacle. I heard your conversation with Mistress Gorgon. Ultra-hearing, remember?" Ultra Lady touched my arm while I looked down at the smoldering strip club. It must have been obvious to her how hopeless I felt in that moment.

"Don't worry. Mistress Gorgon made it out...that immortal bitch always does, probably with a mini-teleporter because I can't see her with my Ultra-Vision anymore. I'm sure she'll be back at her superhuman trafficking ring in a matter of weeks, and when she surfaces, we'll be there, and you'll get what you're looking for from her."

"Yeah," I said as the firefighters ushered coughing strippers out of the Z-Ray Lounge, including the three deadly minxes who were just about to slaughter me. There was no sign of Mistress Gorgon.

"Even though you just ruined months of undercover work, and believe me, I'm gonna be pissed at you for that for a while, I gotta say...I'm still pretty impressed. When I came to talk to you, what was it, almost half a year ago? You were...not doing so great. Wallowing in self-pity, living at the bottom of a bottle, fighting legions of supervillain scrubs instead of dealing with your dad's death...and that deal Mistress Gorgon offered you?

Seriously, I'm proud of you for turning that down. That couldn't have been easy, especially for you."

"Especially for me? What's that supposed to mean?"

Ultra Lady laughed. She grasped a small golden locket she had around her neck, and she clicked it open. Her iconic red and white costume burst out of the tiny locket and expanded to full size. She became a super speed fog of colors, I blinked, and there she was, standing in her full Ultra Lady costume like she had just stepped out of a Superb 6 meeting on their satellite headquarters. Her seared, skimpy Doc Hyper stripper disguise was strewn on the rooftop like a discarded butterfly cocoon.

"There's this charity dinner at the Kirby Museum of Superhero History, I can get you in as my plus one. We can talk about this search for Jack Titan's legacy, discuss your next move," she said naturally, as if her transformation into Ultra Lady, the Indestructible Woman, the Lady of the Future, was the most mundane and normal thing in the world.

"You hungry, Spectacle?"

Chapter 10:
Museums and Prisons

Paparazzi swarmed around the Kirby Museum of Superhero History. There was a line of limousines leading back four blocks. Spot lights dotted the corners of the building and lit up the sky with beams of swaying light. Armies of fans assembled behind red velvet ropes with their glowing phones raised high above their heads. Many of them had signs saying things like "Marry me Anhur!" "#queenquantumforpresident," and "BringBackDocHyper.com". They were so loud, like giant ocean waves crashing against the rocks. I strained to keep my eyes open as the sea of cameras flashed endlessly. A steady stream of superheroes in costumes and obscenely expensive designer dresses and suits flowed into the museum while the feeding frenzy of fans hysterically screamed for their attention. These public superhero events are easy to watch on TV. In person, they're a full blown assault on the senses.

Ultra Lady flew with me in her arms right to the front of the red carpet and bypassed the line of limousines. As if that wasn't embarrassing enough, she then proceeded to gracefully strut down the red carpet radiating confidence while I walked with her and stumbled over my own feet. I was dumbstruck by the flashing cameras and the screaming and the overwhelming insanity of it all, and the contrast between the uncomfortable look on my face and her natural, charismatic smile must have been hilarious.

"Try to relax," she whispered to me as she linked her arm with mine and smiled for the cameras. She waved a white gloved hand, and I did my best to pretend like I wasn't having a panic attack.

The Kirby Museum of Superhero History is built like a fortress. It's a thick, sturdy block of a building, and it's isolated from the surrounding buildings with a space that used to be filled by a twenty foot high wall. It used to be the Wertham Superhuman Correctional Facility, a prison built in the late 60's to deal with the surge in the superhuman population from the creation and widespread use of SUHP. Back then, society looked at all superhumans like they were drug addicts. Hundreds of thousands of superhumans across America served out long prison sentences in places like this, whether they were addicted to SUHP or they had used it just once. A lot of these people were dangerous individuals who deserved to be behind bars, but the vast majority were guilty of nothing more than being born with superhuman potential. The world's changed a lot since then, and the government doesn't treat all superhumans like criminals anymore. Still, when I walked arm and arm with Ultra Lady towards that foreboding cube of a building, when we stepped through its massive metal doors, it felt like stepping into prison.

We passed through the three foot thick, titanium reinforced walls, and we waded into a flood of colors that instantly washed away my dread. The interior of the building was the complete opposite of its gray stronghold exterior. A legion of vibrantly colored costumes stood in glass cases around the entrance of the museum, as if the spirits of all the superheroes that had come before us were protecting this place. They posed proudly in their glass cases, with their flowing capes and gaudy logos and dazzling spandex, like they were just waiting for someone to put them on and pick up where their previous owners left off.

"I've never been here before," I said softly, and Ultra Lady chuckled at the obvious amazement in my voice.

"Yeah, it's pretty cool. I've been here a bunch of times…the Superb 6 throws these fundraiser banquets all the time," she said, and guided me through the aisles of superhero costumes standing guard over the entrance. The main hall of the museum was filled with a grid of tables, each of which was set with the finest plates and silverware, and I looked up as we walked to our table.

There were a dozen floors of exhibits that circled the walls of the building all the way up to its ceiling. The way that the floors of the building were like balconies around a cavernous main room was a feature left over from its days as a panopticon prison. It was designed that way so that the inmates would feel like they were always being observed in their prison cells, but this place didn't feel like a prison at all. It felt like a temple.

The Superb 6's original satellite headquarters hung on wires from that domed, cathedral-like ceiling where the prison guard's watchtower used to stand. The blue and chrome satellite was the sparkling crown jewel of the museum. It gently rotated as if it was still floating in orbit above the Earth, and there were still heroes up there, watching over us all. It was surrounded by the open floors of the building which overflowed with artifacts from throughout superhero history, and the way that they were open on the center of the building allowed you to look up and drink it all in.

There was a floor devoted to all the tools of the crimefighting trade. There was every type of utility belt imaginable; from the bulky pouch covered belts, to the sleek metallic belts, to the laughably impractical belts that strapped onto the bicep. There was a whole wall of grappling hooks, tasers and tranquilizer darts and tracking devices in the silly shape of superhero symbols, smoke grenades and night vision goggles and kevlar costume linings, there were beautiful, brightly colored shields gleaming under the fluorescent lights. There was anything and everything that crimefighters used in their life long mission to save as many lives as they could.

The floor above it was dedicated to all of the superheroes who had fallen in the line of duty. Every superhero who had sacrificed their life so that others could live, they were all up there. Some of them just had a small plaque with a picture and a little blurb detailing their lives, as if an entire life could ever be distilled into a few short paragraphs. Others had statues that immortalized them forever in cold bronze, and row after row of them looked down on us with eyes that silently wondered if we would do the same thing, if we would surrender our lives to stop the death and suffering of innocent people.

The whole history of superheroes was in that museum, and it was truly humbling. It's easy to get caught up in the thrill of being a superhero. It's easy to lose yourself in the money and the attention and the adrenaline rush and all the bullshit that comes with costumed crimefighting, but this place, this temple honoring all things superhero, it was wonderful. It was like a sacred shrine to that silly idea, that ridiculous but beautiful idea of putting on a colorful costume and saying "You know what? No more. If you want to hurt these people, you have to hurt me first. And if I have to, I'll die to stop you. I'd gladly die so that no one has to hurt anymore."

I sat down at the table for two with Ultra Lady. She looked at the little card with her name on it, and then she looked at me and laughed. She could see that I wasn't just amazed by the museum itself. I was also star struck by the superheroes seated all around us at their own tables. These were the greatest superheroes in the world, some of the most famous and powerful people alive. It was like sitting down to eat at a restaurant with all the mythological gods and heroes of every culture on earth.

Only a few feet away, Beyond Man and Queen Quantum were chatting at their table as their children, Beyond Girl and Prince Quantum, typed furiously on their Teen Superb smartphones. Sleight of Hand, dressed in a dark purple three piece suit, was charming his entourage of young supermodels. He gestured with his luminous magic wand to punctuate the punchline of an elaborate joke about The Immaterial Man's obsession with collecting commemorative coins. Doc Hyper, who had on his streamlined, aerodynamic costume even though he was retired, buzzed around the room at super speed like a hummingbird, snatching hor d'oeuvres and downing drinks. Anhur was sitting at the open bar with Supra and they were drinking what seemed like gallons of top of the line champagne. They traded stories about fighting The Abnormalite, and Anhur laughed that thunderous laugh of his that echoed throughout the main hall of the museum.

"Spectacle, get a hold of yourself, man," Ultra Lady joked as I gawked at everything and everyone around me.

"Sorry, sorry. You must be so used to all of this."

"I am, as much as anyone, but you never get totally used to it. It really is something, isn't it?"

"Yeah, yeah it is. And you're a part of it now, with joining the Superb 6."

"I guess I am, but it never really feels that way. It just feels like a job. Anyway," Ultra Lady paused for a moment while she looked through the menu. I opened mine and perused the list of gourmet items, half of which I couldn't pronounce.

"So you had a box of all the things your dad collected over his superhero career, and someone stole it? Do you have any idea who could be responsible?" Ultra Lady asked as she clapped her menu shut.

I told Ultra Lady about everything that I had been through in my search for my father's trophy room, except for the particularly embarrassing parts. I don't know if it was her Ultra-Hearing picking up on the tiny alterations in my heart rate, but somehow, she knew. She knew that I left out a lot of important details, details of how hard it had been for me to pursue this line of investigation when it would have been much easier to just forget about my father's death and move on with my life.

"I never would have thought that visiting you and talking some sense into you would start this crazy journey you've been on. On the other hand, you've clearly got a problem with your strategy."

"What do you mean?"

"Well, you're being led around by your nose. You just react, you know? You just follow one lead to the next. You go somewhere because of a tiny clue, someone gives you a tip, and then you blindly chase after it to the next tip. You've got to be more proactive."

"...fair enough," I replied. She had a point.

"What would you suggest, though? There are so many people who could have stolen that box. Jack Titan had a lot of enemies. The list is practically endless."

"You're right, your dad fought a lot of supervillains. Any one of them could be behind this. I want to say it's The Punster, but it couldn't be him. He's so old. And he doesn't have any superpowers, unless you count really annoying wordplay as a superpower."

"I thought The Punster was dead?"

"A lot of people think that, but he's actually on the Superb 6 watchlist...but he's been quiet for so long we're confident that he's retired. It could be The Shill, he hated Jack Titan, and he's still active. Or it really could just be as simple as some obsessed collector who wanted that stuff for his collection, who didn't want it ending up behind glass in a place like this."

"I was so close, Ultra Lady. Mistress Gorgon set up the buy for someone else, someone who didn't want to leave a trail. If I could have just got her to give me what she knew—"

"See, this is what I'm talking about. You're too passive about this thing. If you want to make it as a superhero, you're going to have to learn to stop relying on people to give you what you want. Nobody is going to give you anything." I raised my eyebrows at this little speech of hers.

"What?"

"Nothing. It's just...come on. Isn't that a little...self-helpy?"

"Maybe. What I'm trying to say is that you should have expected Mistress Gorgon to do what she did. That's the predictable move for her. That's the game. The question you have to ask yourself is what's your next move?"

I felt like Ultra Lady was being condescending, but I also knew that she was much better at this superhero thing than I was. She was only a few years older than me, but she was the youngest superhero to join the Superb 6 since they were founded. She was on her way to becoming one of the all time greatest superheroes, and it wouldn't surprise me if she had an exhibit in that museum one day all to herself. So I held back my admittedly immature urge to tell her she was being patronizing, and seriously considered her advice.

"I think it's like you said outside the Z-Ray Lounge. Mistress Gorgon will resurface eventually, and I'll find her. Maybe she'll slip away from me again, but then I'll find her again, and again, until I get the information I need from her to put this whole search to rest. I'm not going to give up. Not yet, anyway."

"You're on the right track, Spectacle, but you're forgetting something." Ultra Lady smiled. It was like the smile of a math teacher who could see that I was close to getting the right answer to the algebra problem, but I wasn't quite there yet.

"What's that? Let me guess, I should poke around the rubble of the Z-Ray Lounge for clues, right?"

"No—"

"Hold on, I can get this, I should interrogate Mistress Gorgon's known associates. I should hunt down her henchwomen, the Harpies. That's it?"

"No, Spectacle. No…what you're forgetting is that you're not alone. Not anymore. You just need to ask for help, and you've got the resources of the Superb 6 on your side."

"Seriously?"

"Of course. Your dad, he really was a mentor to me. I mean, we only teamed up a handful of times, but he helped me when I was starting out. He could have…taken advantage, you know how some of these older male superheroes are. But he didn't. He gave me a lot of real help and advice. I wouldn't be in the Superb 6 without Jack Titan, and I feel like…"

"You feel like I remind you of him. Right. Great."

"No, that's not what I was going to say. I feel like…looking at you, looking at the kind of superhero you are, I feel like you could use the same help that your dad gave me. He would have wanted that, I think."

"Oh," I said, and for the first time since my dad died, I felt some shadow of what closure must feel like fall over me. Ultra Lady put her white gloved hands on top of mine on the table.

"Seriously, Spectacle. You're not in this alone anymore. We're going to find Mistress Gorgon and the Superb 6 will get the identity of whoever stole your father's trophy room. Maybe Sleight of Hand will cast a confession spell on her, maybe Queen Quantum will extract the information on a subatomic level. One way or another, we'll return what was taken from you."

"Thank you," I answered, and I started to say some clever, smart ass response, but I stopped myself. Sometimes being a superhero can feel like a never ending war with costumed psychopaths with superpowers to back up their severe psychological disorders. But sometimes, very rarely, there are moments like in that museum with Ultra Lady, surrounded by half a century of superhero history and a roomful of people dedicated to the same life of costumed crimefighting, sometimes there are moments when you realize something important about being a superhero. We're all in this together.

Ultra Lady and I had our dinner, and we changed the subject to something a little less heavy. We talked about the normal things. We talked about movies we had seen recently, superhero gossip, TV shows we were catching up on, and eventually the charity event began. There was an auction to raise funds for the museum, and absurdly wealthy people bid on absurdly expensive things, like a signed pair of Doc Hyper's latest limited edition running shoes, a couple of weeks of training in superhuman MMA from Supra, and a date with Anhur who promised to answer any of the lucky winner's questions about "that spoiled little shit" King Tut.

After the auction, Queen Quantum played a few songs, and she was incredible. She played the guitar, drums, bass, and the piano, by manipulating their molecules all at once with her superpowers, like a quantum mechanical one woman band. Then Beyond Man talked about attending the opening of the museum in the early 70's, and how the kids there thought he was just an actor in a Beyond Man costume. He managed to drop a not so subtle plug for Extradimensional Fitness at the end of his speech. Sleight of Hand finished the event with a really touching story about how he actually served time in the building back when it was a prison. He spoke about having his freedom taken away in this place, being under constant surveillance, treated like he was less than human because of his addiction to SUHP and his superhuman abilities, how he lost all hope for humanity in this place. He spoke about coming to the opening with Beyond Man years after he served his sentence, and seeing it converted into a museum inspired him to overcome his addiction to SUHP. The fact that it still stood today filled him with hope that maybe humanity will make it through the darkness. Maybe, just maybe, everything really will be okay.

It was an amazing night, and at the end of it, Ultra Lady and I exchanged phone numbers, and we agreed to meet again soon. I walked home, something I had started to do more and more, and I was filled with a feeling of hope and optimism as I took in the night air. I felt like anything was possible. I should have known better.

I was about to cross the street outside my building when I tripped and almost fell on my face. My left foot wouldn't lift off of the ground, and when I looked down, I saw that my shoe was covered in a viscous, purple goo that rooted it to the asphalt. I looked behind me and saw a mob of men in white hazmat suits and black gas masks rushing towards me. There was at least fifty of them and they each carried a black hose that connected to a set of purple tanks on their backs, and I yanked at my stuck foot so hard that my shoe ripped off along with most of the hair on my ankle.

I bolted. I ran from that hazmat clad battalion and I leapt into the air, but their black hoses shot a shower of purple immobilizing goo at me that plastered my legs and shoulders and arms and pulled me back down to earth. I crashed onto the street in a pile of purple ooze, and the hazmat suit wearing bastards surrounded me. I struggled to pull myself out of the purple adhesive goo swallowing me up, I thrashed my legs and wrenched my arms which were tangled up in ropes of stretchy purple goo, but it was like fighting against quicksand. The more I struggled, the more that purple gunk sucked me back into it and devoured me whole. The hazmat horde slowly circled in as I flailed around in the dripping, sticky mass of purple goo. They looked like one giant animal with many arms and legs moving in for the kill on their wounded prey. One of them took the purple tanks off of his back, and he raised them high above his head.

"Goddamn it," I sighed, and then he brought them down on my skull.

The lights went out.

Chapter 11:
After Hours

I came to in complete darkness. A black hood was over my face. My head was pounding with pain, so much that it was hard to think about anything but the pulsating ache in my forehead. I tried to stand up, but I was tied to a chair and I couldn't move any part of my body. My mind was consumed with total panic, a panic so strong that all rational problem solving parts of my brain shut down, and I tried to rip free of the bonds restraining me to the chair almost completely on animal instinct. It took me a few minutes to recall what happened. I have never been more convinced that I was about to die than in that moment when it all came back to me.

"He's awake," I heard someone say behind me.

Someone pulled the hood off of my head in one quick motion like tearing off a band-aid. I couldn't see for a few seconds as my eyes adjusted from the darkness. I blinked a few times, and then I saw that I was in the Flasked Crusader. All the lights were on in the bar. The curtains were drawn over the windows. The hazmat thugs stood around the walls of the place like silent, judging witnesses at an execution. One of them had familiar eyes. It took me a moment to place them, partly hidden behind the clear plastic of the black gas mask. It was Jane, the bartender who told me exaggerated stories about my father and The Punster.

Thick steel cables were wrapped around my body and tied me to the chair, and blood had dripped down my forehead and onto my costume jacket. I tasted my blood in my mouth, and I spit it at those mute, purple sludge spraying bastards.

"It's so nice to finally meet you, Spectacle!" A cheery voice spoke behind me, and I tried to turn my head but I couldn't see who it was.

"Sorry about my Goons roughing you up. They're new recruits. Not too experienced with my goo formula and its sedative properties yet. Bashing you in the head was completely uncalled for, the goo would have knocked you out. No muss, no fuss." I still couldn't see who was talking to me, but he sounded very warm. He sounded sincere and friendly.

"I'd offer to shake your hand, but I'm sure you're *bound* to decline," the strangely pleasant man said. He walked in front of me then, and as soon as I saw him, I knew exactly who he was, and there was no doubt in my mind that he had arranged for my father's trophy room to be stolen.

"No pun intended," The Punster said. He stood in front of me with an air of overwhelming kindness. I was still panicked and afraid that I was about to be killed, but something about him started to put me at ease. There was something in his eyes, some sort of apologetic understanding as he looked at me, and it was oddly comforting.

"You're not much to look at, are you? You're not so much Jack Titan's heir as you are *Jack Titan's err*," The Punster slapped me lightly on the face as he threw out this new, even stupider pun.

He paced around me a bit and looked at me. The Punster had changed very little from what I saw of him in the clippings I found in my father's apartment. He was about six foot five and roughly 65 years old. He was mostly bald but he had white hair on the sides and back of his head. He had perky, almost jolly green eyes and a perpetually wry, crooked smile, like he always had a joke on the tip of his tongue but he was waiting for the perfect opportunity to use it. He wore a dark purple turtleneck with a small, quarter sized, "P!" symbol on the breast. He was a little flabby, but seemed surprisingly spry and energetic for a man of his age. The Punster stopped pacing and crossed his arms.

"Are you going to kill me?"

"Kill you? No, of course not, Spectacle. Killing you would attract a lot of unwanted superhero attention…I don't need the Superb 6 breathing down my neck. I know how this looks, but you've got the wrong idea about this whole situation."

"You had your henchmen ambush me...knock me out...and now I'm tied up. I'm pretty confident that I have the absolute right idea." Punster walked over to the bar and dragged a stool in front of me. He sat on the stool, and he scratched the top of his bald head.

"Look, Spectacle. Your father's death...it really rattled me. We were rivals for a long time. Over 40 years. What do I have to show for it? I'm pushing 70, and I wasted my entire life on a silly, petty rivalry. And how did it end? In the most anti-climactic way possible, with Jack Titan overdosing on soup like any ordinary souphead. It's a true tragedy, the way your father died." The Punster seemed genuinely mournful. He was quiet for a moment, and I was taken off guard by his sincerity. This was not the mad, egomaniacal Punster that I had imagined from all those clippings and from Anhur's stories.

"Anyway. Jack Titan's passing, it made me realize that it's time for me to move on. That's why I had the Specialist steal that box of your father's things from your apartment. You showed up to the Flasked Crusader...which I own, by the way. The pun name should have clued you in. But you showed up there, talking to Jane, who works for me, of course." The Punster nodded towards Jane who stood near him. Even through the gas mask, you could see her loyalty and devotion to The Punster shine as she nodded back at him.

"She told you I was dead, which was a lie, obviously. Most people assume I'm dead. Dead, or a weak, elderly man. And that's the way I like it. I like to be underestimated," The Punster said, and he smiled.

"Anyway. She called me right away…and I just had to have closure. I can't tell you how touched I was when the Specialist procured that box for me and it was practically an altar to our rivalry. There's so much history in that box," Punster got up from the stool, and he walked out of my line of sight. A few seconds later, he returned with that cardboard box marked "Trophy Room" that I had been searching for all this time. He sat back down on the stool with the box in his lap.

"But, as I said earlier, I'm trying to move on. I'm trying to let go of what I realize now was a shallow, childish feud with your father. So…I want to make you an offer."

"An offer?"

"An offer for this box you've been hunting for. What do you want for it, Spectacle?"

"Excuse me?"

"I'll give you a hundred thousand dollars cash, right now, in exchange for this box and your word that you'll never try to obtain it again. What do you say?"

I'd like to say that I didn't even consider it, but the truth is that I sat there for at least a solid minute. It was an extremely tempting offer, and of course, Punster and his Goons could just kill me if I said no. I really wanted to take the money, and maybe it was the mild concussion one of the Goons gave me with that crack on the skull, maybe it was the glass of whiskey that I had earlier at the Z-Ray Lounge, but I just shook my head no.

"Really. That's surprising, Spectacle. Your father would have taken a deal like that in a heartbeat."

"That's a lie."

"No, it's the truth. Your father and I...we were enemies since we met at the Harvard SUHP Project in '64. You have a conflict for that long, and it goes through cycles. Sometimes there were periods of intense hatred between us, and at other times...the war cooled down. There were times when I would just pay Jack Titan a hefty sum, a nice little 'truce package', and he would stay out of my way for a while."

"Bullshit."

"I'm afraid not. Can I be frank with you, Spectacle? I'm not interested in diverting my attention with this idea of the superhero/supervillain rivalry anymore. It's stupid, it's childish, and there are more important things to focus on." The Punster stood up from his stool again. He carried the box over to me, and he dropped it in my lap.

"Here. You can have it. I honestly don't care. All I want is for you to stay out of my affairs, can you do that for me?"

I looked down at the box as it rested on my steel cable wrapped legs. The Punster had meticulously organized its contents. All the photos were in neatly stacked piles, all the notebooks were arranged in chronological order, the countless mementos and super-tech trinkets had been filed in small tupperware containers with labels like "Superb 6 Misc" and "Team Up Souvenirs" rather than just thrown into the box, but it looked like nothing was out of place. It looked like The Punster was really offering me what I wanted. I didn't know what to say.

"I'll take that as a yes, Spectacle," The Punster said, and he drew in a breath to continue speaking, but something made him hesitate and reconsider. He paused for a moment, and I got the sense that he was considering what to say next very carefully.

"Your father's death…it really fucked me up, son. It made me realize that I have to do something more with my life, and believe it or not, there's a place for you in that. I don't want to be your enemy…we could work together, we could truly change the dynamic of the costumed community for the better." Punster hunched down in front of me so that we were eye to eye. There was a pleading look in his eyes.

"There are always going to be supervillains. As long as people unlock superhuman ability with SUHP, there will be people who will abuse that power. There will always be superpowered people who use that power to steal, to hurt people. And people *do* get hurt, Spectacle, innocent people get caught in the crossfire of these asinine, superpowered fistfights we have with each other. There's a better way to do this, and I'm already implementing it. I've been organizing all of the supervillains in this city, all of the most powerful and experienced superpowered criminals."

"Please. What makes you different from any other wannabe super-crimelord? You don't think others have tried this scheme before you, like The Immaterial Man for instance—"

"I don't think you quite grasp the scale of what I'm talking about, Spectacle. I already have The Immaterial Man, the sick, intangible sociopath that he is, working with me. As well as Mistress Gorgon, and The Abnormalite, Dragon General, Dr. Delusion, an up and coming young gentleman who calls himself The Whimsy, and a hundred more lower level players. We also have The Specialist providing us with enough super-weaponry to outfit an army." I was legitimately surprised by this list. Those were people who were notorious for not working well with others. If The Punster really got those superpowered psychos to cooperate with each other, he would have to be one incredibly dangerous and intimidating individual.

"I'm going to run all the super-crime in this city like an efficient machine. The most powerful supervillains will execute quiet, organized operations that will neither hurt a single person nor draw attention to crimefighters. Meanwhile, the legions of weaker and less professional idiots in costumes will cause as much of a scene as they can, with their museum robberies and jewelry heists and bids for global domination. They'll distract the superheroes with the pointless, hollow battles that they crave while the adults take care of the real business."

"The real business of being glorified thieves, right?"

"Is it stealing if we take back from the people who robbed billions of dollars from everyone else? I'm talking about stealing from the predatory lenders, the banks that tanked the economy with their irresponsible practices, yet they got trillions in bail out cash, the CEO's whose paychecks get fatter every year, the multi-billionaires who horde 40% of the wealth in this county while 99% of us scrounge for pennies, the people who stuffed their pockets while they threw the rest of us to the wolves. I'm talking about taking money from people who stole it in the first place." Some of the Goons standing around the walls of the Flasked Crusader bobbed their gas mask covered faces up and down in agreement. They were eating up The Punster's speech. There was an enthusiastic vibe spreading through the gang of hazmat suited henchmen.

"Whatever, Robin Hood."

"I wish you would listen to me, Spectacle. I want to use the money generated from this operation to fund scholarships for inner city kids. I want to donate millions to the run down schools, I want to give heavily to charities, I want to develop outreach programs for young superhumans, I want to create SUHP addiction treatment clinics. I want to establish institutions to help the underprivileged, instead of trod all over them like the wealthy people in this city do. There will always be supervillains. Fighting that truth with your fists is an endless, pointless war. Your father's death taught me that. I want to eliminate the societal conditions, the poverty and terrible quality of life, that produce dangerous and violent supervillains. You could save more people working with me than you ever could as a superhero."

"And I guess Mistress Gorgon is just going to give her money to charities. I'm real sure that The Immaterial Man's going to donate to a soup kitchen."

"Oh, don't get me wrong. They can do whatever they want with their take. I'm just talking about the millions that I'll make…and the millions you'll make, if you can play ball. Work with me. Be my mole within the superhero community. Feed me information on the activity of superheroes, like when and where The Millenials will be patrolling. Use your relationship with Ultra Lady, find out if the Superb 6 are onto my scent and let me know. Help me distract the superhero community with meaningless super-brawls and, if you'll excuse the term, spectacle. Think of all the lives that could be saved, and all the good that we can do, together, as friends. As partners, son." The way that The Punster was crouched in front of me and the desperate passion in his voice almost made it seem like he was begging me to see things from his perspective. He seemed completely earnest, and his proposal actually seemed to come from a genuine desire to make the world a better place. On top of that, he had a comforting, grandfatherly presence that made me want to help him. But I wasn't buying it.

"No thanks," I answered.

"You're sure? There's no way we can talk about this—"

"No, there's no way we can talk about this. You're full of shit, Punster. You're putting on a show for me right now. None of this is real. You never bribed my father. There's not going to be any charity, you're not going to give back to the community. You want the same thing every supervillain wants. You want everyone to appreciate your greatness, you want to be filthy rich. You want to be the king of everything. And I don't care if you give me this box of my dad's stuff, I'm not going to stop until you're in a prison cell."

The Punster furrowed his brow. He stood up, and his old knees cracked. He stretched a bit, and he rubbed the white stubble under his chin. Then The Punster looked back to me, and all of his kindness and warmth was gone.

"Listen to me, you little shit. I don't care if you believe me or not about the bribes, read your father's journals, it's all there. You'll see in his own words that I'm telling the truth. And here's another thing. If I even get a vague idea that you're trying to interfere with my operations…I command some of the most powerful superhumans on the planet. I will not hesitate for a second to kill you."

"Yeah, okay, but you just said you weren't going to kill me."

"No, I won't just *abduct you* and make you disappear, because that'll make people like Ultra Lady ask questions that I don't want asked. Then I've got the Superb 6 searching for you. No, I'll have you killed in the most explosive, extravagant way possible. No one will wonder what happened to you. I'll have The Abnormalite rip your arms and legs off in the middle of the street. I'll have Mistress Gorgon burn you up while crowds of pedestrians record it all on their phones so that the whole world can watch you screaming as you die."

"You're bluffing...you're just an old nerd who's obsessed with puns."

"Am I? Was I bluffing when I killed your mother?" The Punster shouted in my face at the top of his lungs.

"That's not true, my mother died in a car accident," I said, and The Punster smiled.

"Oh, is that what Jack Titan told you?" The Punster grinned in a way that contorted his entire wrinkled face. I saw the murderer that he hid behind the curtain of a soothing, kindly senior citizen. I saw the pure glee in those eyes. I saw the swirling madness that was The Punster, and I knew. I knew that he was telling the truth. I knew that this deranged bastard killed my mother.

"How old were you, Spectacle? Two? Three? That was my greatest victory over Jack. Sabotaging your mother's car by replacing the brake pads with pads of paper. She was a wonderful woman, by the way. I killed her just to hurt your father, just to spite him. He never quite got over that. If I'd do that to an innocent woman, you don't think I'll kill you? You don't think I'd put some idiotic kid with severe daddy issues out of his misery, if he stood in between me and cementing my legacy? Just. Fucking. Try me." Tears ran down my face. If I wasn't restrained with thick steel cables, I probably would have killed The Punster right then and there. The Punster waved over a few Goons, and they started spraying that cold, sedative goo all over me. I felt my eyelids getting heavy.

"When you wake up, you'll be home, Spectacle. Keep that box of your father's things, and move on with your childish life of squabbling with bottom of the rung, loser supervillains like the loser superhero that you are. Keep playing spandex dress up and crimefighter make believe in Never Never Land with your little friends while the adults handle the real adult business. Can you do that? Can you do that for me, Spectacle?"

Chapter 12:
Soup de Grâce

Armadillotron is easily one of the silliest supervillains in a long, storied history of ridiculous costumed criminals. Basically, he's a guy with a lot of free time who put together a bargain basement exoskeleton armor that looks like the gross, leathery segmented shell of an armadillo. You'd think if you were going to build a suit of weaponized armor, you'd come up with a cool name that has to do with knights, or metal alloys, or at the very least, something that sounds vaguely technological. But no, Armadillotron really committed to his whole armadillo theme. He even had a swarm of little robot armadillo drones for back up. One month after I met The Punster, this was the caliber of supervillain that I was fighting.

"Armadillo Army, attack formation alpha seven!"

It was 2 pm, I had just woken up, and I was watching online video of The Millennials fighting Armadillotron and his absurd armadillo robots. The armadillo drones skittered across the street and towards us with their taser tails spitting sparks, and I could only watch the video sober for thirty seconds before it was too much to take.

I got up from my couch, where I had passed out last night, and I walked across the garbage coated floor of my apartment to grab the first of that day's many beers. As I crossed my apartment, I heard Armadillotron ranting something about the "little armored ones inheriting the earth." I grabbed a beer out of the fridge, then I heard myself in the video drunkenly slur something about Armadillotron's reign being "armadillover before it started," and I grabbed the three more beers that I would need to deal with the fact that I actually said that out loud.

I walked back to the couch and continued watching the video that Joe Metal had recorded on his armor and uploaded to the internet. Mr. Mercurial started to snake his metallic tendrils into the seams of Armadillotron's exoskeleton, and I looked through the playlist of recent videos of Millennials fights. In the past month, we had fought Armadillotron twice, the Lacrosse Assassin (the less said about him the better), Master Boson and the Ninjatoms, Professor Dinosaur and his Henchasaurs, and a guy who called himself, no joke, Bob the Invincible.

I was two beers deep by the time Mr. Mercurial had taken apart Armadillotron's shoddily constructed exoskeleton and Insight telekinetically socked the shit out of his glass jaw. Even though he was beaten, it was obvious from the video of Armadillotron's smug face that he was completely satisfied. This is what The Punster paid him to do. This is what The Punster paid all the bottom feeders that the Millennials fought to do. They were paid a respectable fee to make as much noise as possible, to rant and rave like carnival barkers about taking over the world, to cause a spectacular distraction that would preoccupy superheroes like me while The Punster and his forces quietly pilfered untold millions of dollars. The game was rigged.

I had started on my third beer when I clicked on the video of our fight with Professor Dinosaur and his Henchasaurs. Professor Dinosaur was beginning his spiel about "the superiority of homo sapien dinosaurus," and my eyes started to glaze over as I watched myself and my teammates fighting the scaly skinned blowhard for the umpteenth time. My attention drifted to my father's box sitting on my messy coffee table. His so called 'trophy room,' which I had worked for months to obtain sat there, with the empty beer bottles and half eaten plates of food. I leaned over the coffee table, and I snatched one of my father's journals out of the box.

For the past month, I had been reading about my father's career as a superhero in his own words. That cardboard box was stuffed with mementos from his life as Jack Titan, but none of them provided me such a clear window into his world as those dozens of spiral notebooks. I never knew that my father was a superhero when he was alive, and I never had a chance to talk to him about it. Those journals revealed more to me than he ever would have.

I read about the first time that his superpowers manifested when he was just a kid participating in the Harvard SUHP Project. He said that he was sure that the psychoactive drug had killed him as his heart raced, he saw strange visual distortions and vivid colors, and his muscles grew strong enough to tear through a metal table like tissue paper.

I read about the day he met The Punster, a cripplingly shy linguistics student who was also in the study, and how The Punster never got over the fact that SUHP didn't give him any permanent superhuman ability. I read about that first night that my father put on that golden wreath and mask and called himself Jack Titan, and that amazing feeling he got when he saw that they were calling him "The Man of Myth" in the papers.

I read about his first confrontation with The Punster who almost pulled off the largest SUHP heist in history which he called "the soup drive", and how he never understood The Punster's all consuming fixation with Jack Titan that began that day. The Punster's unhealthy obsession with Jack Titan may have started their feud, but it was my father's pride and inability to just ignore that psychopath and his endless pun-themed schemes that turned it into a full fledged rivalry. If you read in between the lines, it was clear that he became infatuated with the idea that Jack Titan always beat The Punster at his own game.

He wrote about meeting my mom after almost getting killed by The Punster's giant rampaging ant robot, the

"Antdroid." He wrote about never believing in the idea of love at first sight before he met her. He wrote about the night that I was born, and how that changed everything about being a superhero. He held my tiny body in his hands, and wondered how he could go on risking his life every night in fights against costumed criminals when there was this little life that depended on him? How could he justify leaving a baby boy without a father because he got a thrill from slapping on a Titan-motif costume and beating up maniacs like The Punster? When I was born, being a superhero changed for him. It'd been something that he did purely for the charge, for the adrenaline rush, for the fun of it, but it had become something else. He couldn't put it into words, but he clearly knew that it wasn't about the super-brawls for the sake of super-brawls anymore. He had a responsibility to continue that he could not explain or understand.

I had read maybe half of all of my father's journals by this point, and as Professor Dinosaur went on and on about "the reign of the Dinosaur", I flipped to a random page in the notebook I just grabbed. I took a sip from beer number three, and I expected to read about another fistfight with The Abnormalite or maybe a particularly surreal confrontation with the original Dr. Delusion. What I actually read was so disturbing that it made me feel sick to my stomach. All I'll say about what I read on that page of that notebook is that The Punster killed my mother. You don't want to know what my father wrote on that day. There are some things that don't need to be repeated in these memoirs.

I dropped the notebook on the floor. Insight telepathically attacked Professor Dinosaur's reptile brain in the online footage, and the video ended with Mr. Mercurial making some joke about asteroid impacts and extinction. The room was silent now, and I sat there clutching a beer and wishing that I had never read what I just read in that notebook. I closed my eyes and pinched the bridge of my nose. Took a few deep breaths. It didn't help. I still felt like I had a bucket of ice in my stomach.

When I opened my eyes and got up from the couch, I happened to notice something out of place on my cluttered coffee table. It was a small gift wrapped box with a purple bow. Someone must have broken into my apartment and left it on the coffee table while I was passed out right there on the couch. I picked it up and ripped apart the wrapping paper. I opened the box, and there was a baggie of SUHP crystals inside of it. A little card attached to the baggie read, "Soup de Grâce." A bouillon cube mercy killing wrapped up in a neat little bow.

There was a tapping on the window behind me. It startled me, and I dropped the bag of SUHP crystals onto my laptop keyboard. I turned around and saw Ultra Lady hovering outside of my window.

"Open the window," she said.

"What do you want?"

"Just open the window, Spectacle."

I unlocked the window and opened it. Ultra Lady wafted into the room like she was carried in by a gentle breeze. She crunched an empty beer can under her red boot as she touched down on the carpet. Ultra Lady looked around at the mess that my apartment had devolved into over the course of the last month. She looked at the legions of empty beer bottles, the unwashed spandex littering the floor, and she scowled at the stench of half eaten food and mountains of unwashed dishes. She saw the cardboard box on my coffee table marked "Trophy Room," and she was confused.

"I…I came to tell you that I tracked down Mistress Gorgon. I wanted to warn you that…I can't prove it, but I know that she's working with The Punster. And maybe even a few more high profile villains are involved. This is…big. I wanted to let you know because I figured you'd need to know what you're getting into if you're going to confront Mistress Gorgon about your father's things…but obviously you've already found them. What happened, Spectacle?"

"Nothing. I'm fine," I said, and I opened another beer. I took a long sip. There was an awkward silence.

"After the museum, The Punster blindsided me. His henchmen, his Goons, ambushed me and brought me to talk to him. Turns out The Punster took my dad's stuff. He gave it back to me."

"He just gave it to you? Why would he do that? What did he get in return?"

"Nothing," I said, and I drank again. Ultra Lady leaned over the couch and shoved my shoulder.

"What the hell, Spectacle? What is wrong with you? What happened to you?"

"I'm fine. Thanks for the concern, but I'm fine."

"I don't know what to say...when I saw you at the Z-Ray Lounge and at the Kirby Museum...you had changed so much from the first time I met you. You were doing great. Now look at you. Jesus Christ, Spectacle, you look like shit."

"Whatever. I'm completely fine, thanks."

Ultra Lady gave me this look of skepticism mixed with disappointment.

"Spectacle...stop lying to me. Every time you say you're fine, your heartbeat tells me that you're losing your shit. Talk to me. Tell me what's wrong."

"Ultra Lady...I just...I got what I wanted, okay? I wanted to find my father's 'trophy room.' I wanted to know about his superhero career. Now I know. Everything I imagined about Jack Titan is bullshit. The truth is that my dad was a superhero because of his own fucked up addiction to the adrenaline rush. The truth is that he antagonized The Punster, he was just as responsible for their lifelong rivalry as The Punster was. The Punster killed my mother, Ultra Lady, did you know that? Did my dad tell you that my mother would still be alive if he hadn't played this stupid game with The Punster?"

"...No, no I didn't know that. I'm sorry...that's..."

"Yeah. Yeah, you're sorry. Look, I don't want to have anything to do with The Punster. I never want to see that man for the rest of my life, so you take this to the Superb 6. You...*people* deal with him. The Punster has organized all of the major league supervillains. Mistress Gorgon is working with him...so is The Abnormalite, The Immaterial Man, Dr. Delusion, Dragon General, and a goddamn legion of D-list supervillains too. The Punster is running the super-crime in this city. You take that to the Superb 6, I'm washing my hands of the whole thing."

"You knew about this? And you've been doing, what..." Ultra Lady gestured at my disgusting apartment.

"Drinking and doing nothing?"

"Not doing nothing. I took down the mighty Armadillotron, I defeated the fearsome Professor Dinosaur—"

"Spectacle, I just don't get you. I saw you survive a fight with Mistress Gorgon and her Harpies. Not many people can say that. Yet for some reason, you're playing in the minor leagues with jokes like Armadillotron. What the hell, man?"

"What do you want me to say, Ultra Lady? You don't know me. Don't *pretend* like you know me because you had some team ups with my old man. I mean, what is this? What the fuck is this? You're trying to be my mentor or something because you think my dad was your mentor? You are just completely full of shit. My dad didn't write a word about you. He wrote hundreds of pages about The Punster. But I haven't found a single sentence about you."

Ultra Lady was hurt. She didn't say anything, and I felt bad for lashing out at her almost instantly. She sat down on the couch next to me, and she saw the baggie of clear SUHP crystals on my laptop keyboard.

"Seriously, Spectacle? Seriously? You're doing crystal SUHP now? After what happened to your dad?" Ultra Lady snatched the baggie off of my keyboard and held it up in front of me.

"That's...that's not what you think. One of The Punster's Goons must have left it there while I was passed—while I was asleep last night. It's got a pun note on it."

"Oh. 'Soup de Grâce'?"

"It's a stupid pun on final blow, or—"

"I know what it means. What I don't understand is why The Punster gave you your father's things. And why is he even bothering to taunt you with this?" She shook the baggie of SUHP in my face.

"I don't know what to tell you..."

"Spectacle, enough. Stop lying to me."

"I don't know, okay?"

"This isn't just about you anymore. If The Punster is really working with all those villains...this is serious. You need to tell me what you know, right now."

"I told you what the Superb 6 needs to know already, just leave me alone—"

"What the Superb 6 'needs to know'? What's that supposed to mean? Spectacle, you've got to come clean—"

"Fine! Okay? Fine!" I threw the empty beer bottle I was holding at the wall and it shattered. Ultra Lady didn't even flinch. She just stared at me with those big, green X-Ray eyes.

"The Punster…he's deliberately distracting superheroes with big, extravagant superfights by paying off all the lower tier supervillains, your Armadillotrons, your Professor Dinosaurs. These guys attack jewelry stores and malls and coffee shops, they make a huge scene and attract all the crimefighters. Meanwhile, The Punster and the major players are committing a series of under the radar crimes. They're robbing the city blind while all the superheroes preoccupy themselves with pointless, superpowered pissing matches."

"Was that so hard? Why couldn't you just tell me that?" Ultra Lady asked sincerely. I almost didn't answer her, but I was a little drunk at this point. I just had to talk to someone about it.

"Because…maybe The Punster is right. He said he's going to use the fortune he makes from this to do some real good. You know…give millions to charities, fix up inner city schools, establish scholarships for underprivileged superhumans, create SUHP addiction treatment centers. Address the problems that create violent costumed criminals."

"You actually believe that?" Ultra Lady laughed.

"The Punster…I don't know. I just don't know. Maybe he's right. Maybe the only reason supervillains even exist is because our society is fucked every which way to begin with. Maybe what we do is a complete waste of time...we're just fighting an endless parade of supervillains while we completely ignore the problems with our society that creates them."

Ultra Lady took a deep breath. She leaned towards me and put both of her white gloved hands on my shoulders. She gripped my shoulders firmly with fingers that could stretch titanium like silly putty. She looked me right in the eyes, and I tried to look away, but she wouldn't let me turn from her.

"Spectacle...you have got to listen to me. *The Punster...is in...your head.* You've got to know that. He was obsessed with your dad. He'll say anything to fuck you up. And whatever he said worked."

"You weren't there."

"Okay, are you for real? I'm in the Superb 6, Spectacle. You don't think I've had my share of supervillains play mind games with me? The Punster planted the seed of doubt in your head. Forget everything he told you."

"You didn't hear what he said. You didn't hear how he said it."

"Spectacle...snap out of it man."

"...The Punster said he'd kill me if I interfered. And I believed him," I shrugged off Ultra Lady's hands as I said this, and she let me.

"You don't get it. I'm not like you, Ultra Lady."

"Don't give me that bullshit, I saw you fight Mistress Gorgon's Harpies. You've got serious potential—"

"No. That's not what I mean. I mean, I'm not fucking bulletproof. I can't survive an explosion like it's nothing. I can't lift a hundred tons, I can't outrun sound waves. The Punster…he killed my mother, Ultra Lady. He killed. My mother. And he's got some of the most powerful superhumans on the planet working for him. Maybe he's lying about trying to fix the issues that create supervillains, maybe he's not. But he's not lying about killing me. That's real."

"Okay, so, finally, it comes out. That's why you didn't want to say anything. You're scared of The Punster."

"You're goddamn right I'm scared. I don't care anymore, Ultra Lady. Honestly, I got what I wanted. I wanted my father's box of stuff. And I've got it. I'm perfectly happy fighting the C-list losers and collecting the respectable warrant money. Let the Superb 6 handle The Punster and his bullshit."

Ultra Lady stood up from the couch quickly. It was like a switch had flipped in her head, and she knew this debate was going nowhere. She walked away from the couch and around the coffee table. She peered into the cardboard box which contained everything that was left of my father, and she glanced at me with a look on her face that screamed 'I hope it was worth it'. She opened the window that she had floated in through, and she hesitated before climbing out of it.

"Spectacle…the Superb 6 can't solve all your problems. I came here today to tell you about Mistress Gorgon working with other powerful supervillains because I'm not gonna get another chance for a while. I'm going out of town, Spectacle. The Superb 6, we would normally handle The Punster, but we just can't. This crime spree you're talking about…it's extremely important, but we just can't spare the resources to manage it right now."

"How convenient."

"Seriously, you wouldn't believe me if I told you."

"Try me."

"Okay…the Superb 6, we recently discovered a network of terrorists in the Middle East that has got a hold of a massive supply of SUHP left over from the Cold War and the Russian invasion of Afghanistan. They've got thousands of oil drums filled with the stuff. They could fill up a dozen Olympic swimming pools with this shit, and they're giving themselves insanely dangerous superhuman abilities with it…and some of them are even unlocking permanent superhuman potential. I'm talking about terrorists who were already willing to blow themselves up *before* they had superpowers. Now some of them have indestructible skin and pores that sweat radiation. Now some of these fuckers are as powerful as members of the Superb 6. Millions of people will die if the Superb 6 doesn't focus all of our attention on stopping them."

"Right. Of course."

"I'm serious, Spectacle. The Superb 6 can't deal with The Punster. Saving millions, maybe billions of lives takes precedence over one little criminal conspiracy in one little city."

Ultra Lady gently floated through the window. She hovered outside of my apartment building for a moment, and I walked over to the window to close it.

"Spectacle..." She tossed the bag of SUHP crystals at me through the open window. It hit my chest, and I caught it as it fell.

"Grow up. Seriously, just fucking grow up. You can do this. You, and your friends in your team, The Millennials. You guys can stop The Punster and his thugs. You can't always rely on the Superb 6 to be your babysitters. You have to grow the fuck up and face this thing. What else are you going to do?"

Ultra Lady looked at the little baggie of SUHP in my hands.

"Get drunk all day and high on crystal SUHP? I think you can be better than that. I *hope* you can, anyway," Ultra Lady blasted away from me in a super speed blur before I could spit out the bitter, sarcastic response I had on the top of my head. I was left standing there, alone, in front of an open window and holding a baggie of SUHP. I felt the rough crystals in between my fingers through the plastic of the baggie. It would have been so easy...but I threw the baggie out of the window, and I closed it.

Chapter 13:
There's No "I" in Superhero Team-Up

I never expected a fight with a loser like Captain Haiku to radically alter the course of my life. I was just 19 years old, and I had been a superhero for only a year. When I first put on a costume, The Whimsy beat the shit out of me. That taught me to pick my battles a little more carefully. So I did some research, and I decided that I could beat Captain Haiku without even breaking a sweat. I read every article ever written about that ex-poet laureate turned supervillain, I watched the online videos of him robbing the audience of a poetry slam, and I even read every post on his blog which was written entirely in haiku. That's why I found myself fighting Captain Haiku on that particular night.

"All of your money
Give it to my henchmen now.
Or face destruction!"

I was on the ledge of a building across the street from the restaurant that Captain Haiku was holding up. Even from that far away, I could hear him screaming his terrible poetry at the top of his lungs. In those days, I listened to a police band scanner app on my phone a lot and I was doing my homework (for a poetry class I was taking in college, believe it or not) when I heard dispatch call in a robbery in progress and described the suspect as "a lanky, Caucasian male dressed as a pirate with a big H on his chest, talking strangely, possibly under the influence of SUHP." I threw my costume on and made my way across the rooftops of the city to the address as fast as I could. Dispatch didn't mention anything about henchmen though, and I could see through the window of the supervillain themed restaurant "The Lair" that Captain Haiku had brought over a dozen of his lackeys with him.

I leapt off the ledge, grabbed onto the metal bar of a stop light, and swung down to the sidewalk outside of the restaurant. The Lair was one of these gimmicky tourist attractions that was decorated to look like a supervillain's underground bunker. The outside of the place had a facade of plaster painted up to look like thick titanium walls, and through the windows, I could see Captain Haiku with a musket terrorizing the patrons of The Lair.

He sauntered around the restaurant that looked like a laboratory that was straight out of a cartoon with its bubbling tubes of brightly colored liquid and giant, paper mâché death machines dangling from the ceiling on wires. It was actually kind of funny to see Captain Haiku strutting around The Lair like he owned the place in his cheap, probably Halloween store bought pirate costume with a big letter "H" hastily taped onto his chest.

A maître d' dressed up in a generic supervillain costume, which was still somehow better than Captain Haiku's crappy costume, cowered on the floor while several of his henchmen stood around her. His henchmen were dressed up in pirate outfits similar to Captain Haiku's that made them look like his crew. They each had "H" patches with skull and crossbones on their shoulders, as if it was the official insignia of some absurd, haiku-focused pirate ship. They watched the maître d' and customers to make sure that no one tried to call the police. They weren't doing a great job, or I wouldn't be there.

I walked through the door of The Lair. Several henchmen whirled around and looked at me.

"Excuse me...is there any wait for one?"

For a full second, the restaurant was quiet and for once, Captain Haiku was speechless. Then, his gang of henchmen were after me like a school of ravenous piranha. One of them lunged at me, I spread my legs and jumped over him like I was playing leap frog. Another threw a punch at me as I landed, I grabbed his fist as it flew towards my face and I thrust it into the face of another henchman. People burst into laughter at their tables as one henchman accidentally knocked out the other.

"Hey...is there any wait for three?"

I didn't know who he was at the time, but Mr. Mercurial said this as his liquid metal form spilled through the cracks of the closed glass doors of The Lair. Two more superheroes piled in after him, and I was pissed. I got there first, and I had the situation under control. Who were these assholes to just insert themselves into my win?

"I already made that joke," I said as I clunked two henchmen's heads together and they both fell over on top of each other.

"Yo, bro, we got this," Joe Metal said as he clanked into The Lair in his exoskeleton armor.

"You got this? Go fuck yourself, I was here first," I leaned out of the way of one of the henchmen as he slashed at me with a butterfly knife. I brought my elbow down hard on his wrist and the knife flew out of his hand and stuck to a menu on the wall. It stabbed into the "World Domination Bacon Burger" like a dart hitting a bullseye.

"There's three of us, and just one of you. You don't have to be so unprofessional about this. We're all on the same team, man," Insight said as she telekinetically caught one of the henchmen's punches and bent his arm back in a direction it was definitely not supposed to go. She realized that a teenage girl at one of the tables was filming her with her phone, and she smiled for the camera as she broke the henchman's arm with her mind.

"Whatever. You just want the warrant money from catching Captain Haiku. You're swooping in like goddamn vultures here," I said as I sidestepped a henchman that was trying to tackle me. He flew by me and crashed into a fake control panel with flashing buttons and unnecessarily large levers.

"Don't forget about the publicity, we really want the publicity too!" Mr. Mercurial chimed in as he stretched one of his metallic legs over three tables and roundhouse kicked one of the henchmen from across the room. People at their tables screamed and gasped as his thigh muscle elongated several yards over their mediocre, tourist trap food. Mr. Mercurial also looked at people filming him, but he crossed his eyes and stuck out his silver tongue at the camera.

"Mr. Mercurial, you're not helping bro, just shut up for once," Joe Metal sighed, and the motors in his exoskeleton armor whirred while he punched one of the henchmen in the jaw. His armored knuckles probably broke the poor guy's jaw.

"Listen to yourselves.

Bickering like little kids.

Unbelievable."

Captain Haiku said this from the back of the restaurant, and it was clear from his desperate, caged animal eyes that he knew that it was time for him to make his exit. At the same time, almost all of the tourists seated at their tables collectively snapped out of their shock and erupted into a frenzied panic. They practically stampeded for the front door and blocked our view of Captain Haiku who was making a break for the kitchen. His henchmen, like most henchmen are prone to do, just gave up as soon as they saw that their employer was running away and probably wouldn't be paying them in the near future.

"My Syllabullies...

Don't surrender! Kill them all!

Leave no survivors!"

Captain Haiku yelled as he pushed through the swinging doors of the kitchen, and stopped for a second to raise his musket at us and the charging mob of terrified tourists.

"Syllabullies? You call your henchmen 'Syllabullies'? Come on, man. I thought you were a writer," Insight said, and she pinched the barrel of his gun shut with her telekinesis from across the room. She wasn't scared of the gun even a little...she was having fun.

"Form of...a wedgie! Shape of...public embarrassment!" Mr. Mercurial shouted as he stretched a spindly metallic arm across the room and through the throngs of pushing and shoving people exiting The Lair in a disorderly fashion. He snaked his arm around and behind Captain Haiku, and gave the verse spouting villain a wedgie so severe that it probably scarred him for life.

"Seriously bro, we saw him first, we're on top of this," Joe Metal said, and he pointed a finger at Captain Haiku. Captain Haiku winced and dropped his useless gun, Joe Metal flicked his wrist...and vodka sputtered out of his index finger and drizzled onto the floor.

"Apparently," I said, and Captain Haiku, who looked like he wouldn't sit right for a month because of the superhuman wedgie, shuffled into the kitchen of The Lair.

"Ah shit, this thing's always lagging, hold on, I got him now, I got him," Joe Metal said and he tracked Captain Haiku with his index finger as the kitchen doors swung back and forth. A packed herd of tourists bottlenecked at the doors of the restaurant while Joe Metal's exoskeleton hummed, the octagon shaped ports in its stainless steel surface glowed, and he followed the bolting Captain Haiku with his finger.

A father shepherding his family out of the restaurant accidentally bumped into Joe Metal's shoulder right as he fired a concentrated stream of sound waves from the tip of his armored finger. There was a deafening blast like the thrum of a hundred thousand bass guitars rocking the same deep power chord all at once. Joe Metal's arm was jerked to the left and the powerful sonic blast that would have knocked Captain Haiku out and probably damaged his hearing permanently fired wild and shattered one of the glass tubes filled with bubbling colored water. Shards of glass flew everywhere. Hands flew up to cover ears, and women screamed. Green water burst out of the tube and rained down all over everyone in The Lair.

"Fucking amateurs," I muttered under my breath, and I wiped colored water out of my eyes. I jumped onto a table, then onto the shoulders of one of the Syllabullies, and I launched myself off of him and towards the still swinging kitchen doors. I rocketed through the air and just narrowly missed a papier mâché death ray hanging from the ceiling. I landed in front of the kitchen doors and, not sure what was waiting for me behind them, I slowly pushed through the swinging doors.

"Superheroes. Hah.

More like some super-lushes.

You kids fight like drunks."

Captain Haiku stood at the far end of the kitchen near a back door. He had a knife to the throat of one of The Lair's chefs.

"Captain Haiku...don't do this." I had only been a superhero for a year. I didn't have any training whatsoever. It suddenly hit me that I was totally unprepared for a situation like this where one wrong word could cost someone their life. Also, Captain Haiku was right. I had been drinking a little bit before going out on patrol.

"Here's how this will go:

Back off. Walk away slowly.

Do it. Or he dies."

Captain Haiku pressed the knife against the throat of the young chef who couldn't have been more than a year older than me. The kid looked at me from across the room, and I'll never forget the terror in those eyes. I backed up a few steps.

"I'll do it. I will.

I'm leaving. Don't follow me.

I swear, I'll kill him."

Captain Haiku kept his eyes locked with mine as he walked backwards with the kid towards the exit. Metallic liquid dripped out of the ceiling behind Captain Haiku. He didn't seem to notice. A few drops of the chrome liquid even dropped onto his pirate hat and rolled down onto his costume in glistening beads. Mr. Mercurial's strange, silvery body formed out of the droplets of metallic liquid falling from the ceiling like it had been poured into a mold, and he raised a finger to his shiny smile and gave me the "shhh" signal.

"Teen superhero.

A two word contradiction.

You're no hero, kid."

Mr. Mercurial waited through this entire last haiku and mockingly counted the 5-7-5 syllables on his fingers behind Captain Haiku's back, then his left arm dissolved into a morphing mass of metallic tendrils that surged onto Captain Haiku's body. The knife in his hand was plucked away by a little strand of living liquid metal, the metal flowed over his entire body like a net of thin silver wires enveloping him, and Mr. Mercurial pushed the now free chef aside with his other arm.

"You know, haikus are really supposed to be about, like, the seasons and nature and rose petals and stuff. This is supposed to be your schtick, and you're not even doing it right, you clown," Mr. Mercurial laughed as the metal of his dissolved arm trickled around Captain Haiku's mouth and formed an improvised gag that prevented him from saying another one of his improvised poems. Joe Metal and Insight waltzed into the kitchen. Joe's eyes flickered as he read tweets about Captain Haiku's failed robbery of The Lair, and his hand danced as he typed on an invisible keyboard.

"So looks like Mr. Mercurial took down Captain Haiku, that means The Obscure Crew beat him, bro. We get the warrant money…I'm already tweeting about it."

"Obscure Crew? That is easily the worst superhero team name I've ever heard," I said, and I watched Mr. Mercurial's flowing liquid form move from Captain Haiku's mouth to envelop his nose. The ex-poet laureate struggled for a few seconds before passing out.

"It's too late bro, it's official. 'Obscure Crew just beat Captain Haiku at The Lair, video available later.' Just blasted that out to the internet on all social media platforms," Joe was really rubbing it in as his eyes rapidly scanned invisible websites that fed directly into his visual cortex from his exoskeleton armor. I had just met him, but I hated this guy.

"Boys, boys, there's no need for a pissing match," Insight said as she levitated a bottle of champagne off of a shelf and into her hand. She put her arm around Mr. Mercurial, who was beaming from metal ear to metal ear, and she popped the cork out of the bottle of champagne with a little puff of purple telekinetic energy.

"What'd you say your name was again, man? Spectator? Spectator, come over here, pose for a picture," Insight insisted in a teasing way. She knew what my name was, and I was annoyed that she was fucking with me, but I stood with the two of them with Captain Haiku's unconscious body anyway.

"Joe, take a picture for the website," Insight laughed, and arcs of her purple telekinetic energy guided champagne up and out of the bottle and into her mouth like the bubbling liquid was weightless. Octagon shaped ports on Joe Metal's armor flashed as he took a few pictures of us standing together, and for the last picture, Insight telekinetically sprayed champagne all over the four of us until the bottle was empty.

"We just had a team-up, gentlemen!"

I went to the Domino Mask bar for the first time with Insight, Mr. Mercurial, and Joe Metal to celebrate the capture of the ever elusive Captain Haiku. I didn't even want to go with them, but Insight persuaded me to join them in the "Obscure Crew" ritual of celebratory drinks. I think she may have even used a little telepathic peer pressure, but I've never asked her, and I don't think I really want to know the answer. We were all under 21, but we got into the Domino Mask with no trouble at all. How do you check ID's at a bar that caters exclusively to superheroes that have secret identities to protect?

"I don't know what your problem is, Spectacle. You're lucky that we showed up. The Obscure Crew is the shit. We're gonna be the next superteam on the cover of Teen Spandex. You're lucky to even be connected with us at all, bro," Joe Metal boasted as he poured vodka from a tube jutting out of his armor and into my glass.

"I wish you'd stop saying that, Joe. We shouldn't care about being on the front of some corporately owned, corrupt super-rag. That's all an artificial social construct, man, it's all illusion. We should want to be invited to be on that podcast Superhumanity, or to like, speak at TED or something," Insight interjected, and then she went back to haggling over the price of SUHP from Silver Scribe, who was bartending at the Domino Mask and dealing a little SUHP on the side in those days.

"Again, I've really got to stress this, Obscure Crew is a terrible name. And also, again, you guys cherrypicked the shit out of that fight with Captain Haiku. I had that locked down," I said, and I choked down the vodka Joe poured for me.

"I told you, Joe! I told you Obscure Crew was stupid. We should have gone with my team name idea, The Funny Bone Three. That's much better," Mr. Mercurial said enthusiastically with a massive metal smile stretching across his face. You could never tell when Mr. Mercurial was serious. He was pretty much always fucking with people to amuse himself.

"Whatever, Spectacle. Maybe you had Captain Haiku beat, maybe you didn't," Joe Metal said without dignifying Mr. Mercurial's interruption with a response beyond glaring at him for half a second. He poured vodka from the spigot in his armor directly into his mouth.

"I totally did. You're serious about your team though? You, Insight, and Mr. Mercurial?" I didn't want to admit it, even to myself, but I was a little impressed by Joe's ambition.

"Yeah, bro. Look, it used to be that if you were a member of the Teen Superbs, you were pretty much on deck to join the Superb 6 when spots opened up. Now look at the Teen Superbs: they're a total joke. Supra was never even a member of the Teen Superbs, and she was the last person to join the Superb 6. They don't even think about Teen Superbs anymore for membership. That's not the way the world works anymore...with the internet, anyone can get themselves noticed by the Superb 6," Joe was getting excited, and he took a breath and another sip of his drink before continuing.

"I'm trying to make the Obscure Crew like our generation's Teen Superbs, you know? The way it used to be back in the day, pre-internet, when the Teen Superbs was the only way to break into the Superb 6. If we hustle now, if we really go crazy on social media and consistently produce content and relatable online personas, we got a shot at making the Superb 6 before we're 30. Being a superhero is all about marketing, bro," Joe was a little drunk, but he was passionate. He even briefly stopped scanning the invisible social media feeds that his armor streamed into his optic nerves while he made this pitch.

"Our generation's Teen Superbs. That's interesting...the Teen Superbs of the Millennial Generation," I took another drink of the vodka Joe poured for me. I remember thinking, even though I still disliked the three of them, that the concept was intriguing.

"That's what we should call ourselves...The Millennials. That's much cooler than the Obscure Crew," Mr. Mercurial chimed in. He stretched his lips into his beer like a long, living metal straw made out of his face, and I gagged while he glanced at me mischievously.

"I don't know about you, Spectacle, but I don't want to spend the rest of my life fighting the Captain Haikus of this world. I want to be in the Superb 6. That's where the money is, bro, not in getting cats out of trees and archenemies and all that bullshit. I want to get paid big to save the world while I'm still young," Joe said, and then his eyes started flickering once again as he immersed himself in the stream of social media.

"Amen to that, Joe. I mean, I dunno about all that internet stuff, but I want this team to be something special, man. I want it to be, like, a piece of art," Insight smiled.

"Like a fucking awesome band that blows everybody's minds and changes their perspective about what music can be. I want us to be, like, a force for expanding consciousness in the crimefighting community. I want to get stoned out of my mind on SUHP with Sleight of Hand and talk to him about the 60's, hippy era of superheroes, man. I want to party on the deck of the Superb 6 headquarters before I'm too old to make it look good," Insight said, and her eyes lit up with sparkling purple telepathic energy.

"To partying on the deck of the Superb 6 headquarters before we're bald, and our knees hurt, and we complain a lot about people speeding, and our music preferences are decades out of date, and we wear velcro shoes with really high black socks!" Mr. Mercurial practically shouted in my ear, he raised his glass of beer high, and even Joe Metal couldn't help but laugh. The four of us clinked our glasses together, and that's how it all started.

We drank the way that only the underage drink, with the feverish excitement that came with the chances of getting caught, and the reckless abandon of young people who had not yet learned that they won't live forever. We danced for hours in the Domino Mask. I can still picture Joe Metal drunkenly doing the robot on the dance floor in his booze stained exoskeleton armor with Mr. Mercurial as they both laughed their asses off. I still think about the long, philosophical but slightly pretentious conversation I had with Insight about the nature of being a superhero in the 21st century. I remember how idealistic we were about superheroism, and how half of our talk took place telepathically in our intoxicated brains.

To this day, I can still see Mr. Mercurial making me laugh until I couldn't breathe while he morphed his silvery face into a perfect impression of Captain Haiku. I can still hear him coming up with haikus about porn stars off of the top of his silly, shiny head. I can see it all, as hazy as the pictures might be. I can see us drinking all night in the Domino Mask until they closed, I can see us drunkenly jumping and flying and stretching above the city streets, and I almost made an ambulance crash with a sloppy leap through an intersection. I can see us taking drops of SUHP in Joe Metal's apartment. I distinctly remember the moment that I was sitting there, drunk and high out of my mind on SUHP while we watched old Superb 6 cartoons in Joe Metal's place, when I realized that these people are awesome, and I loved being around them.

Chapter 14:
No Archenemies

Master Boson is one of those supervillains who is distinguished not by his talent, of which he has none, but by the fact that he has an extraordinarily gifted lawyer. Only a little less than a year ago, The Millennials stopped Master Boson from robbing a liquor store and sent him on his way to jail. This was the same night that I found out my father died of a SUHP overdose, and it was also the same night that Master Boson's lawyer got his client out of police custody on a technicality.

Apparently, Master Boson's electromagnetic powers disabled all the security cameras. There was no actual evidence of his participation in any crime, other than his terrible ninja mashed up with molecules costume, for which I have no doubt the fashion police would prosecute him to the fullest extent of sartorial law. A little less than a year later, The Millennials beat up Master Boson and his henchmen the Ninjatoms again, and sent them all on their merry way to jail, again. Afterwards, we had the obligatory drinks at the Domino Mask, again, and really, stopping Master Boson from robbing a pawn shop was just the thinnest of excuses to drink to absurd excess. This sort of thing is cute when you're 19. Not so much when you're 29.

"I'm actually happy that he got out of jail so easy. It was just a matter of time before he went back to his small time robberies, and we got to catch him again and double our warrant money," Joe Metal said to no one in particular as he sat at the bar of the Domino Mask and looked into his bottle of cheap beer. I sat there next to him looking into my own beer and feeling a strong sense of déja vu.

"Fuck, I actually hope that lawyer of his gets him out of prison time so easy again. Catching Master Boson over and over again establishes a brand identity for our team that I can work with online. Maybe we can catch him next week, if we're lucky," Joe looked up from his beer, and his eyes scanned back and forth while he read through endless, invisible tweets that his armor leaked directly into his brain like a morphine drip.

"Yeah. If we're lucky."

The Domino Mask was packed that night. I hadn't been there in the month since I met The Punster, and it seemed like a completely different place to me even though they had changed nothing about the cultivated look of dirtiness there. Young superheroes drank and talked and danced on the dance floor, and I could barely hear myself think. The dance floor was a gyrating mess of brightly colored spandex, and they all seemed so...relentlessly happy. There was an overwhelming air of satisfaction, like everyone there knew that they were fighting the good fight in their day jobs and they had earned a little time to blow off some steam. I remembered feeling that way once, but I didn't anymore. Not while I knew that punning bastard was out there making every single person in the Domino Mask dance his hollow two-dimensional dance when they fought C-list supervillains, like shadow puppets fighting on the wall.

"Joe, I've gotta talk to you about something."

"Yeah, I've been meaning to talk to you as well. About our social media strategy for The Millennials, I really think we should go with my idea to wire us all up with streaming video. 24/7 live streaming, POV video of each member of the team. It's like I said bro, privacy is dead, and after it goes viral and gets insanely popular, we throw some ads in and just start fucking printing money. And you really need to step up your posting game—"

"No, not that. I've gotta talk to you about something else, something really important. Outside."

The Domino Mask has an area outside that's enclosed by a small fence, and on a good night it's packed with superheroes smoking cigarettes and talking over the blaring music and each other. I've spent a lot of nights in that back area. I've wasted a lot of hours looking at the wooden fence plastered in graffiti and hastily scribbled drawings of silly things like Beyond Man's head on Queen Quantum's body and The Abnormalite riding a golden unicorn through a ring of fire. I've made a lot of happy memories in that dirty, cigarette butt littered back area.

There were a few clusters of superheroes outside smoking as I stood in front of Insight, Mr. Mercurial, and Joe Metal. The three of them sat in front of me on this cheap wooden bench built into the graffiti coated fence. They were talking to each other about this article about Sleight of Hand's third divorce in Spandex, and they were already deep in pregame mode for a party over at Crystallor's new apartment.

"Okay, I'm gonna go ahead and say no, no you can't get a bigger cut of our profits, Spectacle," Joe Metal said, and he freshened up his drink with a double shot of vodka from the spigot jutting out of his stainless steel armor.

"...No, no I don't want a bigger cut of The Millennials' profits, Joe. That's not what this is about..."

"Okay, my turn to guess...you're starting a twelve step program? Because seriously, I'm no teetotaler or anything, but you've been hitting it *hard* this past month," Mr. Mercurial joked, and his perpetual smile wrinkled the tiniest bit into an expression that was very rare for him. It was the smallest hint of concern.

"...No, no, nothing like that. It's actually...this is gonna be hard to explain..."

Insight looked up at me from her drink. Her eyes radiated purple, telepathic energy and pierced into mine for a split second. I could feel her on the borders of my mind, and that was all it took. Her normally care free, fun loving expression dissolved into a look of intense worry.

"Oh my god, Spectacle. What's wrong?"

"Wait what? What is he thinking, Insight?" Joe Metal snapped out of scanning the various social media feeds.

"I don't really know how to say this…I don't really like talking about private stuff like this…here's the thing. My dad died, almost a year ago now. He didn't like talking about private stuff either, apparently, because it turns out he was a superhero too. He was Jack Titan, you probably haven't heard of him."

"…man, I'm so sorry. I had no idea," Joe Metal said, and he put a heavy armored hand on my shoulder.

"It's alright."

"How did he die?" Mr. Mercurial asked.

"SUHP overdose."

Insight gave me a hug. I could smell crystal SUHP smoke on her clothes. Joe Metal and Mr. Mercurial were quiet.

"Are you okay?" Insight asked as she broke the hug. Her SUHP dilated eyes glittered with purple telepathic energy again, and I could feel her gauging my emotions.

"I'm okay, actually. I mean, it fucked me up, in a big way, for a long time…but I'm getting better, I think."

"You should have talked to us, man," Mr. Mercurial said this, and I could have sworn that I saw metallic tears welling up in his eyes…but his whole face was made of liquid metal, including his eyes, and it was really hard to tell if it was just my imagination or not.

"Yeah…I didn't really deal with it that well…I was sort of working through it in my own way, you know? And I had this box of all his superhero stuff, I was trying to learn about his life as Jack Titan and then it got stolen, and well…that's what I wanted to talk to you guys about."

I took a deep breath, and then I continued.

"This supervillain, The Punster…he was my dad's archenemy. He's this pun obsessed psychopath. My dad's death, it sorta snapped him out of semi-retirement, and now he's back in a big way. He's organized all of the heavy hitter villains. I mean, all of them. The Abnormalite, The Immaterial Man, Dragon General, Dr. Delusion, Mistress Gorgon…and an army of other small time assholes."

"No," Insight said adamantly.

"I haven't even said—"

"I can feel what you're gonna say, and you know that's not the, like, kind of thing The Millennials does, so you can just stop, man. Just stop, seriously," Insight demanded.

"Whoa whoa slow down, Insight, I want to hear this from him…" Joe Metal was intrigued, but Insight wasn't having any of it. She crossed her arms, and looked away. A little storm cloud of purple telepathic energy raged above her short brown hair. I lowered my voice so that the other superheroes on the other side of the back area wouldn't overhear this next part, and I continued.

"Here's the thing, Joe. The Punster, he confronted me, he tried to get me to be his mole in the superhero community…I turned him down, obviously. But when we fight guys like Master Boson, we are doing exactly what The Punster wants. Guys like that get paid off by The

Punster to put on a show, to take a dive while The Punster and the major league supervillains get away with the real crimes. I'm talking about hundreds of millions of dollars that just quietly disappear while we have superpowered brawls with clowns like Master Boson or Professor Dinosaur or Captain fucking Haiku for the millionth time. The Punster is deliberately distracting us with that bullshit."

"Wow. And, what, you're saying we should try to stop him?" Joe asked incredulously.

"Well, yeah. Yeah, I am."

"Why? Bro, I hate to say this, but I'm kinda with Insight on this one—"

"Thank you!" Insight practically shouted.

"I mean, she's right, Spectacle, that's not really what we do. We've always gone after the small time guys like Master Boson. *On purpose.* It's always been our strategy to catch ten losers and collect ten small warrant checks, rather than go after one incredibly dangerous guy like The Abnormalite with a huge warrant on his head. Ten small checks is better than one huge check that comes with the possibility of getting your head ripped off by that four armed psycho."

"I'll tell you this much, Joe, I wouldn't be surprised at all if Master Boson got paid more tonight for putting on a show than we did for catching him. Hell, The Punster probably paid him more than we make in a year."

"Seriously? So you're basically saying that supervillains now have sweet union perks? Man, I should become a supervillain," Mr. Mercurial kidded, and his trademark silver smile had returned.

"It's not about the money, Spectacle," Joe insisted.

"Speak for yourself. I'm already trying to come up with a cool villain name. How's this look for a villain face?" Mr. Mercurial asked, and his gleaming face morphed into a maniacal, crazy eyed version of his normally friendly face. His villain caricature even had a pencil thin mustache that he twirled while he looked at us with menacing eyes.

"It's not about the money, Joe? What is it about, then?"

"It's...look, Spectacle, I'm sorry about your dad. I really want to make that clear...but you want us to try to fuck with The Abnormalite? The Immaterial Man? The goddamn Dragon General? These are dudes that the Superb 6 fight! Those guys, they're some of the most powerful superhumans alive. They're not the kind of people you want to mess with, you know?"

"I can't believe this. You're the guy who always used to go on and on about how we were gonna be members of the Superb 6 before we were 30. What happened to that?"

Joe didn't say anything. He looked away from me, and then his eyes resumed poring through the endless streams of social media.

"Oh, whatever man, just go back to sucking on your digital baby bottle, that's just great. What happened to us, Joe? We were gonna be next in line to join the Superb 6...instead, we spend night after night fist fighting with jackasses like Captain Haiku, the same guys we've been fighting since we were teenagers. We act like we're better than dudes like Captain Haiku...but from a distance, we all look like a bunch of idiots in costumes fighting each other, Joe. You gotta see that."

"Spectacle, that's enough," Insight said.

"No, no I'm tired...of this fucking cartoon show!" I raised my voice, maybe a little too loudly, and the superheroes across the back area walked back inside with uncomfortable expressions on their masked faces. Joe stopped browsing the constant flow of tweets and feeds and tumblr posts.

"I can't keep fighting these C-list losers, Joe. Not while The Punster is laughing all the way to the bank."

"Spectacle...the Superb 6 will deal with this. This is their, what's the word...this is their jurisdiction, you know? This won't help our brand, bro. This isn't something we're equipped to handle," Joe said.

"You're right. But I've sort of become friends with Ultra Lady—"

"You've become friends with Ultra Lady? Since when? Oh man, you gotta introduce me to her..." Mr. Mercurial said, and his eyes contorted into big heart shapes and his silver tongue dropped out of his mouth like a dog's tongue flopping around on a hot day. He slobbered little beads of mercury on my shoulder, and I pushed him away.

"The Superb 6 isn't available to take care of this right now, Joe. They're too busy, oh, I don't know, *saving the world* while we fuck around with Master Boson and his goddamn Ninjatoms."

"So? They'll be back. I'm sorry, I just don't see what the big deal is."

"I did some research, Joe. Did you know that in the past month, there's been a series of kidnappings from orphanages? Dozens and dozens of teenagers just disappeared into thin air...I think The Punster is abducting them. I think he's building a child slave army of henchmen."

Joe raised an eyebrow, and he started to say something, but he stopped.

"Here's another thing. The Abnormalite and Mistress Gorgon raided several gun stores and even police armories. They're stealing guns straight out of police stations now, Joe. They gotta be selling them, probably through The Specialist. And surprise, surprise, gun violence has risen a lot in the past month. There's also been several high powered CEOs and multimillionaire investment bankers who vanished from their homes, and their entire bank accounts emptied out...The Punster and his little buddies stuffing their pockets, no doubt, and murdering everyone in their path. These are people with families, Joe, despite whatever irresponsible things they've done. Oh, and SUHP sales? They're through the roof...Dr. Delusion's got the full power of The Punster's resources supporting his drug trade. He probably slaughtered all of his competitors. People are dying, Joe, while we have yet another rousing fight with a wannabe ninja with lame energy powers."

"Spectacle…what makes you think this is any different from the way things normally are?" Insight asked, and the telepathic storm cloud above her head dissipated into purple mist.

"Excuse me?"

"That stuff is terrible…no one's gonna argue with you about that. And maybe it's a little more extreme than the normal level of costumed criminal activity. But come on, Spectacle. You can't be this naive. This is the way it's always been. There's always been costumed criminals who try to be the big boss of supervillains. Let's say we do take on The Punster, and let's say we actually beat him…which we won't by the way, but let's just say that we do, for the sake of the argument. It'll be a week until another asshole replaces The Punster, if that. What's the point?" Insight's eyes radiated purple telepathic energy as she said this, and I could feel her trying to calm me down.

"Stop that. I mean it," I said, and the purple light in Insight's eyes blinked out.

"Okay. I'll stop. But you know I have a point."

"Spectacle, again, I want to stress that I'm extremely sorry for your loss. And I hate to have to say this, but I don't know what else to say, you're kind of forcing my hand here. What was the one rule that we built The Millennials around?" Joe locked eyes with mine. I knew what he was going to say, but I wasn't going to give him the satisfaction of saying it myself.

"No archenemies. Remember? No archenemies, because making it personal with extremely powerful, sociopathic superhumans is what gets you killed. If you want to survive in this business, you don't want to have someone like Mistress Gorgon infatuated with the idea of murdering you or your loved ones. There's a reason we fight low level supervillains...because it's easy, and easier is always better. I can't even believe I have to be the one to tell *you* this, of all people. This is practically your life philosophy. And this thing with The Punster, I dunno about you guys, but it sounds a hell of a lot like an archenemy situation to me."

"That's true, you totally say that shit all the time. You're all like, 'No archenemies, archenemies are for dummies who wanna get killed'," Mr. Mercurial transformed his face into a mocking, exaggerated version of my own, and he did his best impression of me. He was uncomfortable with all the tension. He was just trying to inject a little levity into the situation, but I just couldn't take it.

"Shut the fuck up, Mr. Mercurial," I said, and I slapped my face off of his metal face. I instantly felt bad, like I just kicked a puppy or something, and Mr. Mercurial nervously smiled. Joe Metal and Insight were stunned.

"I...I'm sorry. That was out of line. It's just...I know that's what I said. I know that. But The Punster...he's out there, and what are we doing? We're wasting our lives having pointless fights with bottom of the barrel losers. I don't know...maybe you're right, Insight. Maybe The Punster will just be replaced by someone else. All I know is that every day that we do nothing, people get hurt in the hundreds, maybe the thousands. People are dying because we're afraid to grow up and face this."

"I'm sorry too, Spectacle. But I'm done talking about this, bro. I can't go along with you on this death wish of yours," Joe Metal said, and he turned away from me. He flicked open a compartment in the forearm of his armor and pulled out a cigarette. He stuck it in his mouth, a little stream of fire flowed from his armored thumb, and he lit the cigarette. Joe couldn't even look at me as he smoked and retreated to browsing social media feeds.

"Spectacle, for what it's worth, I totally see where you're coming from, man. I just think…the Superb 6 will be back soon. There's no reason to risk our lives over this," Insight said, and she seemed completely unaware of the irony of that statement coming from a so called superhero.

"The superhero industry has always been an elaborate game, man. I guess with my mental abilities, it's easier for me to see, but it's always been an illusion, a push and pull of competing interests and political maneuverings—"

"Insight, spare me the half baked hippy philosophy. I've had enough of your whole enlightened, pseudo-mystical bullshit…you're a hypocrite. Why don't you take another hit of crystal SUHP and tell me all about expanding your consciousness and the true meaning of superheroism," I said, and I poured out my beer onto the gravel covered ground. I turned to leave, and in my mind, that was it. I was done with The Millennials.

"I'm with you," Mr. Mercurial said, and I stopped. I turned and looked at Mr. Mercurial. He extended a silver hand to me. I shook his cold, liquid metal hand, and he looked at me with those ball bearing eyes of his. For the first time since I had known him, Mr. Mercurial was being totally and completely serious.

"Thank you. Sorry, I uh, slapped you."

"It's cool. I'm just gonna wait, I'm gonna bide my time, and when you least expect it, I'm gonna slap the shit out of you. Probably when you're sleeping," Mr. Mercurial said, and that shit eating silver grin of his was back as if that moment of seriousness had never happened.

Insight and Joe Metal weren't talking. Insight's SUHP dilated eyes were glowing purple, and so were Joe's. They were having a private telepathic conversation about what just happened.

"Look…guys…I didn't mention this before. I don't know why. I guess I'm still wrapping my head around it, to be totally honest, but…The Punster killed my mother. When I was about three."

The purple light in Insight and Joe Metal's eyes went out.

"I thought she died in a car crash. My whole life, that's what I thought, because that's what my dad let me think. The Punster, he killed my mom, just to hurt my dad. That's the kind of insane murderer that we're letting run rampant…I've got to stop him. I've just…okay, maybe I do have a death wish, Joe. Maybe you're right. Maybe I'd rather die than do nothing while The Punster hurts more innocent people. People like my mother."

I started walking towards the back door of The Domino Mask, and Mr. Mercurial walked with me.

"Wait," Joe said, and I stopped.

"Okay, Spectacle. I'm in. You can't do this on your own, bro," Joe said, and I leaped over to him and slapped him on his exoskeleton covered back hard enough to make him stumble. His armor rang like a bell, and I hugged him.

"Thank you, Joe. You have no idea what this means to me."

"Yeah yeah, get off me man, it's gonna mean a lot to you when Mistress Gorgon turns all four of us into a goddamn pile of ashes."

"What about you, Insight? Will you do this with us?" I asked Insight, and she smiled.

"Okay. I can't believe I'm agreeing to this, but okay," Insight said, and purple telekinetic energy sparked and spasmed around her head. She was more than a little worried about this.

"Alright! Everybody! Hands in the center...The Millennials for life, on three! One, two, thr—"

"Shut up, Mr. Mercurial," Insight, Joe Metal, and I said simultaneously.

Chapter 15: Too Much

Fighting The Immaterial Man is like trying to have a fist fight with a swarm of bees. There's nothing to punch. He's everywhere and nowhere. But unlike a cloud of raging bees, The Immaterial Man can do a lot more than sting you. The Immaterial Man can slip between the molecules of your throat and pull out your esophagus. He can become a fog, wrap around you like a damp blanket, and suffocate you to death within his moist, amorphous form. Or The Immaterial Man can transform his smokey body into the shape of a man, and he can pummel you to death with fists as hard as iron while the rest of his body is as intangible as a ghost. I don't like to think about how many superheroes have died while The Immaterial Man's disembodied laughs echoed around them as he watched them die with those burning, molten hot eyes of his.

Insight's telepathic abilities allow her to see things within her mind's eye. In a deep, meditative state, she can remote view events happening around the world, and when she's really in the zone, sometimes things that haven't happened yet. That's how we were able to track The Immaterial Man to the world headquarters of a particular tech company that I won't mention by name because I don't want to get sued. Insight envisioned a high security lab within the facility where they kept the prototype for a certain company's next generation smartphone. She also very clearly saw The Immaterial Man moving his way through the downtown building's ventilation system like a fine, murderous mist.

"Alright guys. As soon as he steps out of that door…we go at him with everything we've got, okay? It's that easy," Joe Metal said as we stood outside the skyscraper headquarters of the tech company.

"Something's not right," Insight said. She furrowed her brow. Purple telepathic energy steamed off of her head.

"Yeah, something's not right. We should be doing, oh, I don't know, *anything but this,*" Mr. Mercurial said. Drops of chrome sweat poured down his face.

"What do you mean, Insight?" I asked, tasting stomach acid in my mouth. I was so scared to face The Immaterial Man that I had violently thrown up before we rushed across town to stop him from stealing the prototype smartphone.

"I mean, I don't think we're making the right move here…The Immaterial Man's got the phone, and he's dropping down, fast. He's falling, like, a rock through the building, man. He can go through walls…why would he come out the front door?" Insight looked to me.

Telepathic energy bubbled around her head now like a crown of boiling purple water.

"Hey, I'm just putting this out there…Crystallor is having a costume party at his place, and we already have costumes, right? Maybe we could head over that way?" Mr. Mercurial asked.

"The subway," Joe said.

"No, it's cool, don't listen to me, seriously that's awesome," Mr. Mercurial grumbled as we ran to the staircase leading into the subway tunnels. Terrified people were already running up and out of the subway, and we could hear screaming reverberating from down near the platforms. We had to push against the current of panicked, horrified civilians rushing up the stairs and onto the city streets.

When we got to the platform, I saw something that I never wanted to see. The Immaterial Man was seeping through the cracks of the subway tunnel ceiling like a sickly, greenish gray gas. The train left the station and barreled through the clouds billowing down from the roof of the tunnel, and I caught a glimpse of the train operator's petrified face as she got the hell out of there. There was an overpowering smell of rotten milk as the pale green fumes bled down from the ceiling. The smokey form of The Immaterial Man flowed down from above us, and solidified into the rough approximation of a man standing below us on the tracks, a man with horrible red eyes like bloody suns, a man with a swirling smog smile. And his laugh, that squealing laugh that came from nowhere and everywhere, it was like the disembodied voice of a mad god.

The Immaterial Man gave us one sideways glance with those smoldering red eyes, and then he ran down the tracks and into the tunnel. I could see the phone suspended in the middle of his hazy, translucent chest as he made a break for it. Against every reasonable instinct of self preservation that I have, I bolted towards the edge of the platform. I leapt towards The Immaterial Man and snatched that phone right out of his chest as I lunged through his foul smelling body.

"Get down!" I heard Joe Metal shout as I crashed onto the tracks with the phone clutched in my gloved hand. Joe fired a blast of sonic waves from the forearm of his armor and towards us both, specially configured to disrupt The Immaterial Man's gaseous anatomy. My teeth chattered like a jackhammer and my ear drums popped as Joe doused us in ultra high amplitude waves.

The Immaterial Man let out a piercing screech that rebounded off the walls of the tunnel, and his smokey body pulsed with the vibrations…but he was still standing, and now he was furious. He staggered towards me, like he was wading through thigh high water, and he pointed a smokey finger at me.

"Joe, flank him! Mr. Mercurial, seal the tunnel!" Insight said as she hovered behind The Immaterial Man, but it was too late. The Immaterial Man let loose a stream of foul smelling gas from his finger at me, and it was like he shot me in the face with a fire hose.

I tumbled across the ground and missed landing on the third rail by inches. Thick, suffocating gas shrouded my head, snaked into my nostrils, and forced itself down my throat. I coughed and wretched and my eyes bulged out of my head, and I tasted death filling up my lungs. I convulsed on the tracks, and I could hear him, I could hear The Immaterial Man's howls of laughter, his shrill cackles ringing off of the narrow walls of the subway tunnel.

"Spectacle!" Insight screamed, and I felt her telekinetic energy manipulating The Immaterial Man's choking gas back out of my lungs. It felt like someone was wringing out my lungs like dirty wash clothes.

"Spectacle?" The Immaterial Man's disembodied voice said, and he instantly allowed Insight to mentally squeeze his gaseous reach out of my lungs.

"Punster said you're off limits. Can't kill you, sadly…but the rest of you…" The Immaterial Man giggled, and his entire body exploded into a vortex of swirling gas and we were suddenly in the eye of a pale green hurricane. Mr. Mercurial melted into a shiny puddle and formed flowing, silver walls that blocked both ends of the tunnel. He coated all the surfaces of the confined space with his mirror-like liquid form and prevented The Immaterial Man from escaping, but now we were all hermetically sealed in here with this psychotic tempest. Insight burned with purple telekinetic energy as she struggled to stay airborne, but she was like a butterfly trying to fly inside of a tornado. She slammed into the mirrored wall of the tunnel and collapsed to the ground.

Joe Metal had fallen to his armored knees. He could just barely lift his gauntlet to fire an extremely powerful laser beam at the seething storm that was The Immaterial Man. The Immaterial Man laughed uncontrollably as the laser harmlessly sliced the cyclone that he had become, and a surge of smokey green tendrils thrust towards Joe Metal, grasped his exoskeleton like a child gripping an action figure, and the segments of his armor tore off of his body with the sound of sheering metal like fingernails on a chalkboard. Joe screamed in agony. I managed to get to my feet, but what could I do?

The walls started closing in around us, and for a brief moment, I was absolutely certain that I had lost my mind. The vortex that was The Immaterial Man started spinning tighter and faster in the shrinking tunnel, and then it hit me. Mr. Mercurial, that silly son of a bitch, was contracting his entire silver body which coated all the surfaces of the tunnel. He was like a giant, metal bubble shrinking down, and I won't even pretend to understand the science of it, but The Immaterial Man couldn't pass through Mr. Mercurial's liquid metal body. The Immaterial Man's squealing laughter was replaced by sounds of his frustration as he hurled rivers of gray vapor at the silver orb tightening in around us all.

Now Insight, Joe Metal and I were crowded inside the mirrored ball that was getting smaller by the second. The Immaterial Man solidified into his faceless, foggy humanoid shape. He beat his wispy fists against the chrome walls of Mr. Mercurial's body as it tightened more and more. The reflective walls rippled with each of The Immaterial Man's desperate punches. Then Insight, Joe and I slid through the shiny, reflective walls and popped out into the dark subway tunnel.

Mr. Mercurial stood there with a sheepish grin on his glistening face. His whole silver body was bulging like a water balloon that had been filled up with way too much water.

"I'm okay, I got him...but guys. I've got crazy bad heart burn right—"

And then Mr. Mercurial exploded. Silver liquid flew everywhere as The Immaterial Man burst out of his body with a deafening pop. There was desperation in The Immaterial Man's burning red eyes, and then he evaporated into coiling clouds that gushed by us and through the tunnel. He was gone before we could even react, and we were left standing in the dark tunnel, stunned and soaking in silvery liquid.

"Man, this is awesome. This is like going to my own funeral," Mr. Mercurial said from behind us. The shiny liquid that was his body was flowing down the walls, across the tracks, and off of our bodies to assemble into his sarcastic self behind us where he stood sneering. I've never been happier to see that goofy son of a bitch in one piece.

"Well...that could have gone worse," Insight said. Joe Metal laughed hysterically as he sat in a pile of his torn up, metal armor segments.

"Check it out," I said. I opened a gloved hand and showed them the smartphone prototype that I had been clutching like my life depended on it throughout that horrifying ordeal. Then I coughed up a copious amount of blood into my other glove.

–

"Be careful with those," The Specialist said as he watched The Punster's Goons carry heavy crates filled with machine guns. A few days after The Immaterial Man almost slaughtered us, Insight picked up strong mental vibes that The Specialist was moving millions of dollars worth of machine guns and super-tech down at the docks to be shipped off to god knows where.

"Okay. We gotta do this clean, and quick," I said to Joe, Insight, and Mr. Mercurial. We were crouched on top of a towering stack of metal shipping containers, and we were looking down at The Specialist and the dozen or so Goons in their white hazmat suits. The Specialist nervously scratched his scraggly goatee and kept checking his vintage Doc Hyper watch. The Goons carried wooden crates over a ramp and onto a small boat. In the dim moonlight, they looked like a colony of industrious albino ants with their black, insect-like gas masks over their faces. Some of them looked like they couldn't have been a day older than sixteen.

"Bro, this is gonna be nothing compared to The Immaterial Man," Joe said. He flexed the gauntlet joints of his new, straight out of the box exoskeleton armor, and I could smell a hint of liquor on his breath even though we had all agreed to be sober on these busts.

"Don't get cocky," I said, and before I could finish the rest of my thought, Mr. Mercurial jumped off of the top of the shipping crates.

"Don't mind me kids, this is just your regularly scheduled superhero ass kicking!" Mr. Mercurial shouted as he landed right in the middle of the gang of Goons. He stretched one of his arms and punched a silver fist into the face of the nearest Goon.

"God damn it, Mr. Mercurial," I said, and we followed him down to the now panicking Goons. A few of them dropped their wooden crates right where they stood. The Specialist took advantage of the commotion to get out of there while he still could. He ran through the aisles of the stacked shipping crates.

"Seriously guys, you're not even trying. I'm embarrassed for you here," Mr. Mercurial said as he stretched his whole torso around one of the Goon's sloppy haymakers. While he was busy not taking this seriously at all, a Goon to his left tripped over a wooden crate and knocked it over. A handful of The Specialist's weapons grade smoke bombs spilled out of the crate and went off right there on the dock. Blinding black smoke discharged all around us.

"Fuck, Mr. Mercurial! This isn't a joke man," I said, and a Goon jumped out of the darkness and tried to tackle me. I stepped out of his way, grabbed him by the metal tank strapped to his back, and tossed him into three other Goons who were trying to flank me.

"Watch out for their tanks of goo, it's a sedative and it'll put you to sleep—" I said to Joe Metal as I knocked out a Goon with a single punch before he could open up another of those wooden crates and take out more of The Specialist's super-weaponry.

"Gotcha," Joe said. He fired electromagnetic pulses at the Goons and knocked them unconscious, one by one, with little blasts of radiation to their brains. A Goon behind him raised his hose at Joe and sprayed a jet of purple goo at him. Joe saw him, he tried to stumble out of the way, but he was too drunk, and his exposed face was slathered in the purple tranquilizing gunk. He passed out instantly. He was snoring and frozen upright in his exoskeleton armor.

"Spectacle, I'm hearing Specialist's thoughts loud and clear. He's making a move for his jet pack," Insight said as she lifted the arm of a Goon with her mind. She made him point his spray nozzle at the black smoke and fire purple goo at the Goons charging out of the clouds. They stepped in the ankle deep goo and got rooted to the floor of the dock, but she accidentally sprayed Mr. Mercurial too. Mr. Mercurial, who was still focused on trying to be funny, wasn't paying attention, and he was painted with the purple goo. He slept like a baby.

I jumped on top of a tower of shipping crates. I couldn't see The Specialist in all the smoke bomb clouds. All I could see was the bright white shapes of the hazmat suited Goons in the black clouds as they circled in on Insight. There were still a dozen of them standing, despite the fact that they were practically children and we were supposed to be experienced, adult crimefighters.

"Insight, blow away this smoke!"

A shockwave of telekinetic energy radiated from Insight's head and washed away the blackness. I could see The Specialist at the end of an aisle of shipping crates and strapping that dented jet pack to his back as the smoke cleared. I ran across the tops of the shipping crates and towards him. That comic book collecting bastard was messing with buttons on the jet pack and the thrusters started to burn with scarlet energy. I sprinted across the shipping crates as fast as I could, and The Specialist started to lift off. Plumes of scarlet energy shot out of the jet pack's thrusters. The Specialist winked at me as he took off like a rocket…and then he froze in mid-air like someone had paused the video of his dramatic escape.

"Spectacle, now! Can't hold him go now jump now!" Insight shouted to me from the ground. Her eyes were lit up like spotlights with telekinetic energy as she mentally suspended The Specialist in the air. Angry scarlet energy spewed out of his jet pack, and The Specialist didn't look so smug anymore. The Goons rushed Insight, and she was focusing so hard on The Specialist that she was barely able to keep them at bay with blasts of telekinesis.

I dove at The Specialist and knocked him right out of the air. We crashed into the doors of a shipping crate, broke them open, and fell together inside the dark metal container filled with boxes of rotten apples. The crate filled up with scarlet energy while his jet pack belched up the last of its payload.

"Where is The Punster?!" I held The Specialist up by his limited edition, retro-style Superb 6 t-shirt. He wouldn't even look me in the eye.

"I don't know!" he said. I slammed him against the wall of the crate and his metal jet pack pounded against it with a sound like wailing on a gong.

"Don't fucking lie to me, Neil," I screamed in his scraggly bearded face. He squirmed against the corrugated metal of the crate.

"I'm not lying! Jesus don't you people learn anything? We went through this the last time you manhandled me, you superheroes are just glorified bullies who—"

"Stop stalling!"

"Look I'm telling you! I don't know! I just follow orders man, I have no idea where The Punster is holed up..."

I threw him aside and let him land on some soggy boxes filled with rotten apples. I ripped the jet pack off of his back, and I slapped some plastic ties onto his wrists and ankles so he wouldn't try to run again. He whined about me being a fascist throughout the whole ordeal. Then I walked out of the shipping crate and towards Insight. There were some Goons stuck to the floor of the docks and struggling to pull their feet out of their own purple goo, but most of them were laying unconscious all around her. Mr. Mercurial and Joe Metal were both sleeping the sleep of the unprofessional.

"Should we draw on their faces with sharpies?" Insight asked, looking around her with obvious embarrassment at the evidence of how poorly this was handled.

–

"Guys, I really hope you're hearing me. We can't afford to mess around on this one," I practically begged my teammates to listen to me as we stood on the roof of Dr. Delusion's upscale apartment building.

A few floors below us, Dr. Delusion was running what was probably the largest and most sophisticated SUHP lab in the world. Working with The Punster provided him with enough money and resources to set up a drug operation that had flooded the streets with cheap, high quality SUHP. SUHP use was way up, particularly in high schools where Dr. Delusion had his henchmen The Figments aggressively move his product.

Every week there was a new story about some poor kid who overdosed on crystal SUHP, or fell out of the sky like a bag of bricks when his high wore off and his drug induced superpowers gave out. Every day there were more dangerous, temporarily superpowered soupheads running rampant all over the city. A tiny percentage of these maniacs would permanently unlock dormant superhuman abilities in their DNA, which meant new supervillains were being born every day. And The Punster was raking in millions of dollars from his cut of Dr. Delusion's drug trade profits.

"Okay, we get it. We have to take this seriously," Joe Metal said.

"No, no I don't think you do. This Dr. Delusion guy looks like a scrawny little kid, but he's dangerous. We could get killed if we're as sloppy as we were with The Specialist."

"Come on, nobody's gonna get killed. We learned our lesson…let's try to tone down the melodrama buddy," Mr. Mercurial said with a silvery smirk.

"Mr. Mercurial, just shut up and listen to him. I've got a mental fix on this Dr. Delusion kid, and The Spectacle's right…he's young, but you should see the messed up shit rattling around in this kid's head. He's a killer for sure," Insight said.

"Yeah, yeah he is," I said, remembering when Dr. Delusion almost suffocated me to death with a plastic bag. I walked over to the door to the staircase that would take us down to his floor, and I hesitated before opening it. I looked back to my teammates.

"Guys…just remember: we're not doing this because of some stupid video we're gonna put online. We're not trying to get as many hits and shares as possible. Don't be a show off in there, okay? I'm looking at you, Mr. Mercurial. And Joe…we're not trying to squeeze every dollar out of this, and we're not trying to advance our careers. Just stay focused in there. Remember the plan. Okay…are we ready?"

I took the stairs with Mr. Mercurial down to Dr. Delusion's floor. Insight and Joe Metal flew outside of the building and hovered outside of the apartment, like we planned, so that we could come at him from every direction and do this thing right. For once.

"Hey man…listen, about that thing with The Specialist…" Mr. Mercurial started to say as we ran down the stairs. I slapped the chrome goofball on the back before he could finish.

"Don't worry about it…it's cool, Mr. Mercurial," I said, and opened the door to Dr. Delusion's floor. We walked down the decadent hallway lined with apartments that neither of us could even imagine affording.

Then I stood in front of Dr. Delusion's door. I took a deep breath, and I thought, "*It's on,*" to Insight.

I kicked the door right out of the frame. It shot into the apartment and bashed into a Figment, one of Dr. Delusion's hoodie wearing henchmen, and the drug peddling scumbag yelped an incoherent cry for help. He reached into the back of his jeans for a gun, and Mr. Mercurial stretched out a silver hand, wrapped it around his neck in an elastic sleeper hold, and The Figment was out in five seconds flat.

The door skidded across the nice wooden floors and stopped in front of 10 tables set up in a grid in the center of Dr. Delusion's huge apartment. Young women wearing surgical masks and rubber gloves were chopping up chunks of crystal SUHP and portioning them out into big plastic baggies. They turned and looked at me as I stepped into the room with Mr. Mercurial, and a lot of them just dropped their measuring cups and scattered. Dr. Delusion was sitting on his tacky golden couch and playing video games, and he swiveled his head in his tennis ball green hoodie to look at me. The pimple faced son of a bitch jumped up and reached for a machine gun on his glass coffee table, but Insight was floating outside of his massive glass windows and she telekinetically disassembled the gun. She rearranged all the parts into a nice little black flower and set it down on his coffee table on top of an issue of Spandex Magazine.

Then Joe Metal shattered those huge, floor to ceiling windows with a great view of the park with one swipe of his exoskeleton gauntlet. Insight and Joe Metal flew into the room, and Dr. Delusion's look of sheer panic as they drifted above his tables covered in hundreds of pounds of crystal SUHP was absolutely priceless.

"Fuck, I give up okay? You win," Dr. Delusion said, and he raised his hands above his head. I saw the small, black remote in his tattooed hand, the same one that he used to release the vaporized SUHP compound that he dosed me with the last time I was there.

"Watch his hand," I called to Insight, and Dr. Delusion pushed a button on the remote. I held my breath in anticipation of the release of the modified, highly hallucinogenic SUHP compound through the air conditioning.

"On it," Insight said, and everything turned purple. She had encased my head, and Joe and Mr. Mercurial's heads, with bubbles of purple telekinetic energy. Just like we planned, her thought construct was designed to let clean air in but nothing else.

"FUCK! You won't get away with this!" Dr. Delusion screamed, and he threw the remote at Insight. It broke against the purple bubble of energy around her head.

"Pretty sure that's our line, kid," Mr. Mercurial said, and his arms melted into long silver ropes that bound Dr. Delusion.

"You idiots couldn't just stick to fighting bush league supervillains, could you? That's what you fuckers are good at, not this shit. Not the fucking *business.* I'm telling you right now, The Punster will make you fucks disappear. It'll be like you never even existed," Dr. Delusion snarled at us while Mr. Mercurial tightened his silvery grip on him.

"We'll see," I said.

–

"To the New Millennials!"

Joe Metal raised his glass of champagne to toast our month of success against The Punster's highly organized crime spree. Insight, Mr. Mercurial and I raised our own glasses. It felt good to take a night off after weeks of hard work to obstruct The Punster's machinations. It felt good to just hang out like we used to in Joe Metal's apartment.

"I dunno about 'New' Millennials. I think we've still got a lot of work to do, but fuck it, I'll toast anyway," I said. We clinked our glasses together. Joe downed his glass of champagne in one quick motion. When he came up for air, the look on his face had changed from celebration to worry.

"Uh...I think there's something you should see, Spectacle," he said. He was frantically scanning the social media feeds that his armor leaked into his nervous system.

"You should sit down. Fuck me, I think maybe I should sit down," Joe said. We walked over to his couch and plopped down on it. A metal plate on the shoulder of Joe's armor pivoted to reveal an opening where a small projector flipped up out of his exoskeleton. A Youtube video projected onto the blank wall of Joe's apartment where a TV normally would be. The Punster appeared with a warm, friendly smile on his face.

"God damn it," I said before Joe had even started playing the video.

"Hi there, folks. I'm The Punster, or rather, I was in another life. You probably haven't heard of me, but I used to be a supervillain many years ago. The key phrase there is 'used to be'," The Punster said. He was wearing a purple wool cardigan and khaki pants, and he was sitting in a regular office chair with a black wall behind him. There was nothing that could give away his location.

"For some time now, a young, confused superhero named The Spectacle has been obsessed with me. Back when I was still working, I had something of a rivalry with his father, a superhero who called himself Jack Titan. Well, I'm afraid to say that Jack Titan passed away due to a tragic overdose of SUHP, and The Spectacle seems to blame me for that," The Punster said with an extremely sympathetic look on his wrinkled face.

He looked away from the camera and paused, and his gray eyebrows arched in concern. His tone of voice, his body language, his facial expression, even his purple wool sweater...everything about him screamed sympathetic grandpa, not psychotic, murderous supervillain. The Punster was a hell of a performer.

"I understand that this is a very hard time for the young man. I feel for him...I remember what I went through when I lost my own father. But I had nothing to do with Jack Titan's death, that I can promise you. I've been retired for years, and not a day goes by that I don't regret my life as a costumed criminal. I was a weak, pathetic man who broke the law to feel bigger than I was. I was sick, and I hurt people, and I can't begin to express how deeply sorry I am for my actions in that time of my life," The Punster said.

"Thank god I had just enough sense to quit before I got myself killed or worse, got someone else killed. And I've been an honest businessman ever since. I've been extremely fortunate. I've made more money as a legitimate businessman than I ever did as a ridiculous costumed criminal...but The Spectacle, he's infatuated with me. He thinks I killed his father, and I'm not ashamed to say that he's scaring me. I'm afraid for my life," The Punster said.

"This is complete bullshit," I said.

"That's why I'm offering one million dollars for the capture of The Spectacle. I don't want to see the boy hurt or killed, I just want him to get the help that he needs," The Punster said. Despite his convincing performance, I noticed the smallest hint of the same demented smile I saw when he had me tied up in the Flasked Crusader.

"Everyone deserves a second chance. I'm willing to spare no expense to help The Spectacle. Every day that he runs free, threatening myself and my family, I'll add one hundred thousand dollars to the million. Please, help me save the son of an old friend who passed away. Help me make it up to Jack Titan, who I never got a chance to repay for helping me when I was a dangerous, misguided young man. Thank you so much for your time, and God bless," The Punster said, and the video stopped. It already had over a million hits.

"Wow. You gotta hand it to him…this Punster guy has got massive balls," Mr. Mercurial said.

"Yeah…I know you guys don't want to hear this right now, but this video, it's all over the internet. People are going batshit about it…you're trending, bro," Joe Metal said.

"Yeah, great. I'm trending."

"This is not good, man. Any time you show your face, you're gonna be mobbed by people trying to get that reward money," Insight said.

"Yeah, yeah I am."

"Maybe we should take a break for a while? You know, lay low for a little bit," Joe Metal said. His eyes darted back and forth as he pored through a sea of articles, video responses, tumblr posts, and tweets all about The Punster's farce of a video.

"No. This doesn't change anything. This just proves that The Punster is getting desperate. He'll try anything to slow us down. We have to keep at it. We're gonna nail The Punster to the wall, it's only a matter of time," I said. I gulped down some champagne and tried to convince myself that I was right.

–

Insight didn't know what was inside the eighteen wheeler, but she saw enough for us to assume that The Punster was going to make an outrageous amount of money from whatever it was carrying. She tried to peer inside the trailer that the truck was towing, but there was overwhelming psychic pain connected to whatever was in there. She said that it was like trying to stare at the sun to count the flames. All she could tell us was that Mistress Gorgon and her Harpies were escorting the freight to the airport, and if The Punster put her, one of the most dangerous superhumans alive, in charge of this, it had to be of utmost importance to him.

"Fleece Shipping. He's not even trying to be subtle with the puns anymore," I said as we looked down at the eighteen wheeler from the rooftop of a ten story building. The truck was marked "Fleece Shipping" with a cartoon sheep winking above the name of the fake company, and it was stuck in bumper to bumper traffic. Fleece, as in to steal. The old bastard just couldn't help himself.

"My armor's got a visual on Mistress Gorgon. She's in the cab with three of her Harpies," Joe Metal said.

"Can you see what they're carrying in the back? I'm sorry guys, every time I try to look in there, I'm getting telepathic feedback like crazy," Insight said.

"No, no they've got it heavily shielded. I'm picking up some vague heat signatures but still, they've just got so much thick metal on that thing that it's hard to say what it could be," Joe Metal said, squinting as he tried to decipher the readings his armor's cameras supplied him.

"What's the play here, Spectacle?" Mr. Mercurial asked me, and I waited for a punchline that never came.

"Uh, what?" I said after a few seconds of anticipating his inevitable joke.

"I mean, how do you want to approach this?" Mr. Mercurial asked. My three teammates stared at me while I paused. The look of focus that they had, and in particular Mr. Mercurial's seriousness, surprised me. I had an abrupt moment of clarity. For the first time, I felt like I was a part of a team of competent, responsible adults. For the first time, I felt like an honest to god grown up.

"We could just have Joe and Insight lift that trailer right off the cab...but if it has something dangerous, some sort of supertech inside, it could blow and cause a lot of damage," I said.

"I could slip down there and melt through the cracks of the trailer door, try to do a little recon and figure out what's inside," Mr. Mercurial offered.

"No, that's no good. I read on Mistress Gorgon's wiki that those snakes on her head, their tongues have really great senses of smell. She'd smell your metallic body odor before you even touched that trailer," Joe Metal said.

"Metallic body odor? Yeah, you smell great stewing inside that sweat factory you call armor," Mr. Mercurial said with a smile. Joe elbowed him in his liquid metal shoulder which rippled with the playful nudge.

"I wish there was another way to do it...but I think we're gonna have to go down there and tackle Mistress Gorgon head on," I said, watching the truck plod through the rush hour traffic.

"Look...I know she's powerful, and dangerous, and honestly, pretty scary. But we can do this. I know we can. We survived The Immaterial Man, and she's on the same level as him. And I wouldn't want to go down there with anyone but you guys backing me up. I mean that," I said. I looked back down at the truck and its winking sheep logo.

"Enough of the corny pep talks man. Let's do this thing," Mr. Mercurial said and his silver smile widened.

The stoplight in front of the Fleece Shipping truck turned green as I jumped down into the middle of the intersection. One of the Harpies that tried to murder me in the Z Ray Lounge was behind the wheel of the vehicle, and Mistress Gorgon was sitting in the passenger seat of the truck next to her. Mistress Gorgon did look stunning in her elegantly designed, black cocktail dress, but she did not look happy to see me. Her marble eyes filled with anger, and the tangle of spaghetti-thin, black snakes that was her hair convulsed and writhed on top of her head.

The Harpy threw her door open and hopped out of the cab with her fists glowing red hot with superhuman power, but it wasn't her that concerned me. Mistress Gorgon stepped out of the passenger side of the cab, her black stiletto heels click clacking on the asphalt, and the snakes above her beautiful but enraged face arched toward me with their jaws unhinged. The rush hour traffic behind the truck shed any pretense of civility at the sight of her. Drivers frantically gunned their engines and raced through the light. Cars swerved in front of each other and cut each other off and tires squealed and horns beeped erratically like Morse code and I was almost run over by a freaked out soccer mom in a minivan, and Mistress Gorgon...she just stood there in the crosswalk seething.

"Your father would be so disappointed in you," Mistress Gorgon spit at me. Her reptilian tresses hissed, and then they spewed blue flames at me.

"Spectacle, I've got this Harpy covered," Joe called out to me as I jumped up and over the blue inferno. Joe jumped in front of the Harpy's blast of searing red energy and saved me from being incinerated by the rose colored plasma as I dodged Mistress Gorgon's fire. Two more Harpies piled out of the back of the truck cab, and Insight and Mr. Mercurial landed on the street prepared for them.

More sky blue flames gushed at me from the open mouths of Mistress Gorgon's snakes, and I jumped out of the way. I felt some of the stubble on my face singe down to my cheek as I charged at Mistress Gorgon and threw a punch at her tan, dimpled cheek. She caught my gloved fist in her hand like catching a wiffle ball. Two of my knuckles broke in her hand as she squeezed her finely manicured, black fingernails into my fist.

"You idiot man-child. We gave you every chance to stay out of this and save yourself, and you still couldn't do the right thing," Mistress Gorgon said, her marble eyes lighting up like white headlights.

"You, of all people, don't get to tell me about doing 'the right thing'," I shouted. I grabbed her wrist with my free hand. I pivoted on the balls of my feet, yanked her by the arm, and chucked Mistress Gorgon over my shoulder and into oncoming traffic as hard as I could, like I was pitching a fastball. She smashed into a sports car that was racing through the intersection and no doubt trying to get as far as possible from the superhuman street fight in progress. The entire front end of the car was demolished as she flew into it, the airbags inside the car went off and the middle aged driver was knocked out from the impact, and Mistress Gorgon, she stood up from the totaled car with not so much as a broken nail.

"Really. That was your best, Spectacle? You're not even close to the man that your father was," Mistress Gorgon jeered. She stalked toward me, those black high heels click clacking on the street, the snakes on her head squirming and drooling blue fire off of their forked tongues, and behind her, I saw that my teammates were preoccupied with fighting her three superpowered Harpies.

"Punster doesn't want us to kill you…but he didn't say I couldn't give you third degree burns over your entire body," Mistress Gorgon said, and those serpents gushed a blue bonfire right at my face. I fell backwards onto the street and lay there as the blue fire blazed over me. The heat was unbearable, my eyes teared up, my face was drenched in sweat, and I rolled across the ground and sprung to my feet. I heaved my fist right between her marble eyes with everything I had, and the impact cracked louder than thunder. A little hairline fracture was on her forehead when I pulled my fist back, like her beautiful, ageless flesh was made of rock, and she laughed as the fracture fused back together almost instantly.

"You know you could have made millions, right? If you had just listened to reason. If you had just made the mature decision and taken The Punster's, honestly, his overly generous offer to work with us, all of this could have been avoided. I may have even kept you as a pet," Mistress Gorgon's eyes glowed like spotlights, and my feet and legs felt ice cold. I glanced down and saw that they were encased in her supra-stone and rooted to the ground. I was a marble statue below the knees. I wrenched at my legs, but I couldn't move an inch.

"Your father would have taken that offer without blinking, Spectacle. He would have been so disappointed in you. Speaking of blinking, you'll want to keep your eyes closed for this next part. Punster wouldn't want you blinded with melted corneas for whatever games he's got planned for you," Mistress Gorgon said, and the gaping maws of those snakes salivated with blue embers. I closed my eyes, and thought, "*Well, at least I tried.*"

I heard a bang. When I opened my eyes, I saw that a pick up truck had driven into Mistress Gorgon at full speed and knocked her out of the intersection and onto the sidewalk. The driver, a thirty something construction worker, wasted no time pointing a shotgun at my face through his window. Dumbfounded, I raised my hands in the air. Several more construction workers hopped out of the back of his pick up carrying shovels and hammers and wrenches and screwdrivers. They surrounded me and went to work on the stone.

"Get him in the truck, let's go, chip away that rock. Let's go boys, there's almost 2 mil on the line here," the driver said.

"Don't move or I'll blow your head off," the driver added as the men hit the supra-stone as hard as they could with their tools.

I saw Mistress Gorgon was stunned on the sidewalk where she landed, but she was slowly getting up. Glowing white rock chipped off of me, and I felt every blow pound in my legs as the men desperately hammered and chiseled away at the stone. I saw my teammates above the Fleece Shipping truck fighting the superpowered Harpy henchwomen in the air. They were gaining the upper hand, they were doing a very good job of protecting the people trapped in traffic, but they were too engaged with the Harpies to divert attention to the recovering Mistress Gorgon.

"I'm serious, kid, I'll shoot," the driver said. I had started laughing and I hadn't even realized it. I felt the supra-stone loosening while the men worked hard for money The Punster would never give them. Mistress Gorgon was up now, and she was stalking into the street and towards me. Her hair of serpents spit up a crown of blue flame, and the click clack, click clack of her heels got louder with every step.

I grabbed two hammers so fast that the men couldn't even see it happening, and I brought them down on the supra-stone crusted over my legs. The stone and the hammers shattered like panes of glass, the driver pulled the trigger, but I was already gone. I was already leaping in the air above him and arcing down at the Serpent Seductress. Mistress Gorgon's marble eyes barely had time to flutter wide with shock as my fist clashed with her face.

She reeled from the blow, but those snakes didn't even flinch. Blue fire roared by me as I bounced to her side and bombarded Mistress Gorgon with punches, as many blows as I could throw and as fast as I could throw them. My knuckles screamed in pain, my shins that I had just hit tremendously hard with hammers felt like they were going to buckle under the pressure of my rapid bobbing and bounding around her flaming snake locks, and my right forearm blistered with burning heat as blue fire caught on my costume jacket sleeve.

"Please, this is childish. Just give up. You couldn't hurt me if your life depended on it, and it does. I've had more of a work out having sex with your father," Mistress Gorgon said as dozens of branching cracks in her tan face sealed up almost instantly. Fire spread down my arm, and she smiled. Those snakes on her head hiccuped tiny blue mushroom clouds as they prepared for one last blast of fire. I ripped off my costume jacket and threw it on her head right as the fire came pouring out of their mouths.

My jacket trapped the flood of fire on top of her head, and her entire skull went up in flames. Mistress Gorgon's shrill shrieks of pain are branded in my memory, and by the time she finally got the blinding, burning jacket off of her scorched face, Insight, Joe Metal, and Mr. Mercurial were standing behind me with unconscious Harpies at their feet. I still can't believe it as I'm writing it now, but Mistress Gorgon, a supervillain with half a century of experience, a superhuman thought to be one of the most dangerous women alive, the infamous Serpent Seductress, turned and ran.

She bolted into thick crowds of pedestrians on the sidewalk, knocking them to the ground and freezing them in their tracks with her supra-stone glare, and we were right behind her. She was fast, but not fast enough to lose us. We almost had her.

A swarm of people with dollar signs in their eyes herded around me. They grabbed onto my costume shirt, they clutched at my arms, they got in my face and screamed at me to leave that nice, old Punster man alone, and one woman even tried to pepper spray me but thankfully Insight telekinetically took away her mace. My teammates tried to pry them off of me, they held back flying fists and below the belt kicks, and I couldn't risk using my super strength without hurting these stupid but innocent people. I couldn't do anything but watch Mistress Gorgon get away.

"Don't help me, I'll be fine, go after Gorgon," I tried to tell my teammates, but they couldn't hear me over the drone of these locusts trying their best to beat the shit out of me and collect their two million. By the time we got them off of me, Mistress Gorgon was gone. She probably used the same teleport device that she had used to get away from Ultra Lady at the Z-Ray Lounge.

"This is unbelievable. We were so close."

"...You're kidding, right? We're alive! We just fought Mistress Gorgon, and we're not charred corpses. Maybe I'm just a glass half full kind of guy, but in my mind, that's a big win," Mr. Mercurial said as we all walked back to the Fleece Shipping truck. It was parked in front of the streetlight and holding up traffic.

"Yeah, I guess..."

"Also, we stopped them from moving whatever product they've got in this truck. That should put a big dent in Punster's bottom line," Joe Metal said.

"I really don't like the energy around that truck. It reeks of hardcore bad vibes," Insight said. The back doors of the eighteen wheeler had another cartoon sheep winking in an almost mocking way. It loomed over me as I cautiously unlatched the doors and opened them, ready for anything that could be inside. Light poured into the dark trailer, and the stench of urine and vomit and sweat poured out.

There were over a hundred young women and children packed into the back of the trailer like sardines. They were shackled to the floor, and they had black bags over their heads. Many of them were emaciated. Mistress Gorgon was running a human trafficking ring of monstrous proportions.

"Oh my god," Insight gasped. Her eyes strobed with purple telepathic energy, and the mental suffering that burst through those doors and washed over her was so powerful, so profound that she passed out. Joe Metal caught her as she fell.

I climbed up into the trailer. I tore apart the chains of the first person I came to, a young boy who looked like he couldn't have been older than ten. I pulled the black bag off of his head, and he screamed. He screamed the hopeless, desperate scream of an animal that's realized it's going to the slaughterhouse.

"It's okay…it's going to be okay," I said, and the kid looked up at me, his huge eyes blinking and streaming tears. The kid hugged me.

"It's okay…I've got you," I said, and I looked to Joe Metal behind me. His face was contorted in anger and disgust. Mr. Mercurial had a hand over his mouth, and he just kept shaking his head.

We waited with the truck until the authorities came. We watched police officers help over one hundred women and children out of the truck trailer and out of their restraints. It was clear that Mistress Gorgon had been holding them captive for weeks. The wounds on their wrists and ankles from tight handcuffs, their starved and dehydrated condition, and most of all the look in their eyes, that stare that said everything I didn't want to know, it was all evidence of the appalling, inhuman way that Mistress Gorgon had treated them.

"This is too much," I said to Joe Metal while children Mistress Gorgon and The Punster were going to sell into slavery were led into police vans that would take them all to child services.

"Yeah…I know what you mean, man. I was still thinking The Punster was sort of a joke, but this," Joe trailed off.

"No, you don't understand. *This is too much*," I said.

"What do you mean?" Mr. Mercurial asked.

"I'm going to kill him for this," I answered.

–

It took Insight almost a week to recover from the overload of psychic suffering that spilled out of that trailer. It wasn't a fun week. I was trapped in my apartment because any time I showed my masked face in public, people attacked me for the warrant that The Punster had promised them. Without Insight's telepathic abilities, we had no way of predicting where The Punster and his cabal of supervillains would strike next. It was a week of waiting, waiting while Mr. Mercurial took care of Insight who gradually got better, waiting to see what fresh hell The Punster would unleash next, and waiting for hordes of armed maniacs to storm my front door for money The Punster would never give them.

The Punster's bullshit warrant was up to almost four million dollars by the time Insight was feeling better. When she had finally recovered from the overdose of human suffering that had left her practically catatonic, she had good news. Insight had a vision. She saw The Punster breaking into the Kirby Museum of Superhero History. She saw him in the "Supervillain Weaponry" exhibit. She saw him stealing the motorized mandibles of his Antdroid, the same Antdroid that he had tried to kill my father with decades ago. She had a vision of The Punster, just a demented old man with no superpowers, breaking into that museum alone and unarmed. It was too good to be true.

"This place used to be a prison for superhumans before they converted it into a museum. It's designed to keep superpowered psychos in…it's pretty much a fortress. All we have to do is keep our guard up on the entrance, and he'll be trapped in here with us," I said to my teammates as we stood in the main room of the museum.

The old Superb 6 satellite headquarters was above us, suspended from the ceiling on wires and gently spinning as if it was still in geosynchronous orbit. The museum had been closed and evacuated, and it was so quiet in there. My voice echoed off of its walls. We were surrounded by the largest collection of superhero artifacts in the world. Floors that used to be lined with prison cells circled the walls of the building all the way up to the ceiling, and each of them was packed full of superhero history.

One of the floors above us showcased the costumes of superheroes that had died fighting to protect innocent people from psychopaths just like The Punster, superheroes who had made the ultimate sacrifice. Their uniforms, brightly colored and pristinely displayed under glass, looked down at us as we waited for The Punster. And the emptiness, the eerie silence of that shrine to costumed crimefighting history, it was almost like we were alone in a church. It felt like we were defending hallowed ground.

"Why would he do this? It seems so stupid to try to come in here all by himself to steal this stupid pun themed piece of garbage. Especially when he's been so careful to keep himself hidden so far," Joe Metal said. His eyes rapidly moved back and forth as he watched security camera footage that his armor was tapped into.

"Because he's crazy," I said.

"Are you sure about this, Insight?" Mr. Mercurial asked.

"Yeah, I'm sure," Insight replied. You could still hear in her voice how angry she was at The Punster. What he and Mistress Gorgon did to those people was a crime against humanity, and Insight had felt every moment of their trauma as if it was her chained up in the back of that eighteen wheeler for weeks on end.

"What's to stop him from using The Specialist's tech to teleport in, and teleport out? I mean, that's what I'd do. If I were a diabolical archcriminal. Which I'm totally not," Mr. Mercurial said with that infuriating yet somehow lovable silver grin of his.

"I've got my armor set up to detect teleporter signals…if he teleports in, my armor will broadcast the exact opposite teleport signature which should cancel out their teleport tech. Still nothing on the security cams, by the way," Joe said.

"That all sounds great, but I still don't feel good about this. Why would The Punster attack this place all by himself for some old toy he used back in his glory days? Seems like, I don't know, beneath him. Doesn't feel right," Mr. Mercurial said.

"You don't get it. You're thinking about this like a rational person, Mr. Mercurial. We're not dealing with a rational person. The Punster is obsessed with the idea of the superhero/supervillain rivalry. He's romanticized it. He's built it up in his head to be this glorious game between two opponents. He wants to steal back his Antdroid parts because he wants a trophy that symbolizes his victory over my father, and over me. That's what started all of this. The Punster needs his trophy," I said.

"No one's ever accused me of being a rational person before, but I think I get your point," Mr. Mercurial said, and his silver smile stretched even wider.

"He should be here any second. I can feel it, man. Everything looked just like this in my vision," Insight said anxiously.

"There's no way you could be wrong about this?" Mr. Mercurial asked again, his smile weakening a little.

"No. I mean, sometimes my telepathic premonitions are off by little details, but nothing big enough to give us any trouble. It is possible to trick my telepathy, but you'd need a, like, impossibly powerful will to pull that off," Insight said skeptically.

"Whoa…what? Trick your telepathy? I don't like the sound of that," Mr. Mercurial said, and his chrome smile shrank even more.

"It's not an issue. The Punster would have to meditate for days nonstop, literally over twenty four hours of uninterrupted concentration to transmit a false vision this vivid, and I just don't think we have to worry about that sort of—" Insight was interrupted by the glow of teleportation energy all around the museum. Even before they had started to materialize out of the soft white teleportation mist, I knew. I knew that we had done exactly what The Punster wanted. We underestimated him.

The Punster appeared in front of me. The expression on his wrinkled face was the height of smugness. The Immaterial Man blinked into existence to his right, and you could almost make out a smile on his hazy head as his whiny disembodied howls of laughter scraped the air. The rotten egg smell of his foggy body was choking. Mistress

Gorgon materialized to The Punster's left, the snakes on her head hissing and salivating with dribbling blue fire. I made eye contact with those marble eyes of hers, and they screamed "*I told you so.*" The Abnormalite appeared behind us, and now we were surrounded as that eight foot tall, neon pink skinned, four armed, eight eyed behemoth of a man towered over us, breathing heavily out of his fanged mouth.

And as if the three most powerful superhumans alive wasn't overkill enough, dozens of lower tier costumed criminals flickered into the room through the soft white glow of the teleportation energy. Captain Haiku, Professor Dinosaur and his Henchasaurs, The Lacrosse Assassin, Master Boson and his Ninjatoms, Armadillotron and his armadillodrones, Dragon General in full military regalia with his huge scaly wings beating gusts of wind throughout the room and accompanied by his Reptilian Guard, even The Whimsy, the first supervillain I ever fought, they were all there along with a horde of C-list supervillains. And then came The Punster's Goons, at least a hundred of those white hazmat suit wearing, gas masked thugs marched in through the entrance with their goo spray nozzles raised high like rifles at a firing squad. When the glow of the teleportation energy faded, the museum hall was crowded from wall to wall with an army of supervillains and henchmen.

"Kill them all," The Punster ordered.

Chapter 16:
Nobody Can Go to Jupiter

One night when I was four years old, I couldn't sleep. My mom used to read me stories or make me a snack when I couldn't fall asleep. I used to get out of bed late at night and wander around our dark house until I found her. She was never mad at me for getting up out of bed, even though it was way past my bed time. She said she had trouble sleeping sometimes too. One night when I was four years old, I couldn't sleep, but my mom died when I was three, and I didn't know what to do.

I haven't thought about that night for a long time. I'm pretty sure I blocked it out. It came back to me crystal clear when I started writing these memoirs, like it was always there, tucked away in some locked drawer in my mind, just waiting for someone to find the key and open it up. I remember walking in the dark hallways of our house and passing framed photos of my family on the walls. I remember passing the kitchen and the mountain of dirty dishes in the sink which my father would let build up and then aggressively clean them all in one crazed session of scrubbing. In hindsight, it's easy to say he was probably going through periods of manic depression, but at the time, all I understood was that the kitchen stunk.

I remember, most of all, being afraid as I tip toed through our quiet house. It wasn't that I was afraid of the dark, or the scariness of a big empty house late at night, although those fears were a part of it. It was really this fear that no one was looking for me. I wasn't getting away with being up past my bed time…no one knew that I was out of bed when I wasn't supposed to be, and no one cared. It was this gut wrenching idea that the person who loved me the most was gone, and the rest of the universe didn't care if I was alive or dead. I was on my own, and no help was on the way.

"Hey…hey buddy, what are you doing out of bed?"

My dad noticed me wandering around the house just as he opened the door of his study. He was a big man, a lumbering, broad shouldered guy with a thick, curly brown beard who really did look like a Titan straight out of Greek mythology…but I remember that on that night, he looked small. He was propped up against the frame of the doorway as light flooded out of his study and into the shadowy hallways of our home. His shoulders were slumped, his head sagged downward toward his chest, and he looked like he could barely stand.

"I can't sleep," I said.

"Yeah…me too."

We stood there looking at each other for a few seconds. Then he straightened up, as if he just realized how unusually tired and weak he looked slouched against the door frame.

"Come in here for a second...I want to talk to you," he said, and turned to walk back into his dimly lit office with its mahogany paneled walls without waiting for me to respond. I walked into the study. It was a room I was never allowed to be in before, and although I didn't know what it was then, the smell of scotch washed over me.

"What do you want to be when you grow up, buddy?" he asked as he poured more scotch from a decanter into his glass.

"I don't know."

"You don't know? When I was your age, I wanted to be an astronaut. I wanted to be the first man on Jupiter. I wanted it so bad. I wanted to be the first guy walking around on that big red spot on Jupiter, I wanted my face on cereal boxes. A few years later, I said that in science class. The teacher, she laughed at me, and she explained to me that Jupiter isn't like an enormous chunk of rock out there in space. It's this big ball of gas floating out there," he said. I just stared at him.

"What I'm trying to say is that nobody can go to Jupiter, buddy," he said, and drank the scotch and grimaced. Little beads of glistening yellow liquid clung to his beard and hung there like alcoholic Christmas ornaments. He didn't say anything for a while. He just swirled the scotch around in his glass, and I remember being profoundly confused by the whole situation.

"Do you miss mom?" he asked. I didn't say anything.

"Yeah. Me too," he said, and then he drank the rest of the scotch in his glass. He poured himself some more before crouching down in front of me.

"I want you to promise me something. Will you promise me something, buddy?"

"Okay…"

"Remember how…remember your mother and me, we used to say you're special. You can do anything, you can be anything because, because you're special you know? Do you remember?" He was slurring a lot. I thought maybe he was sick.

"Yes."

"Here's the thing, son. You're not special. No one is. I want you to promise me that you'll remember that, because it's the truth, and I don't want to lie to you," he said, and I started to say something, but he interrupted me before I could.

"I lie to you all the time, and I just, I just can't about this. Because I thought I was special. I was arrogant and stupid and, and, and I thought I could just keep *antagonizing* him. I kept pushing and pushing and *pushing* him and I thought there was nothing a little nerd like him could do to me, and I was wrong and now she's…she's—" and he turned away from me because he was crying, and I started crying too. I never saw my dad cry before or since, not even at my mom's funeral. I know what he was trying to tell me now, but when I was four years old, I thought he was talking about God.

He turned back to me, letting his half empty glass slip out of his meaty hand and spill scotch all over the nice Persian carpet that I was never allowed to walk on before that night. He put both of his huge hands on my tiny shoulders.

"I want you to promise me...promise me you won't trick yourself into thinking you're special. Always take the easy way. Don't take the hard way because the hard way gets you hurt, and I never want to see you hurt. Have fun...have as much fun as possible and don't worry about being special. Play by the rules. Always play their game and have as much fun as you can. Don't try to break the rules. Do you understand?" he asked with tears swelling in his eyes, and I had no idea what he was talking about or what he wanted me to say to him.

"I know this is hard, buddy, I know. I'm only saying this because I love you so much and I don't want to see you hurt, okay? Nobody can go to Jupiter, son, so don't even try. Promise me."

Chapter 17: The Museum Massacre or: The Last Stand of The Millennials

The main hall of the museum exploded into a chaotic swirl of crisscrossing energy blasts of all different colors. The eardrum rattling noise was so overpowering that I couldn't hear anything but a deafening buzz filling my skull. Insight threw up a purple telekinetic bubble around the four of us just before Mistress Gorgon's hellfire could incinerate us along with a rainbow of searing energy blasts. The sea of fire roared around us like we were inside of a sky blue sun. Insight screamed and her ears and nose gushed blood as her telekinetic field crackled and warped under the strain of enough heat to liquefy granite. I looked at Joe Metal, and then at Mr. Mercurial, and we didn't need to say anything. We knew Insight couldn't hold the field up for much longer. We knew that this was it.

Insight's telekinetic bubble burst. We broke formation the instant her field crumbled under the weight of all that power, and we scattered to avoid Mistress Gorgon's blue inferno. Insight shot into the air glowing with a purple telekinetic aura that saved her from the fire gnawing at her entire body. Mr. Mercurial snapped like a rubber band into spindly, silver tendrils that coiled throughout the room and wrapped around dozens of those goddamn ooze spraying Goons. Joe Metal's armor encased him in a force field that just barely held as he dove out of the way of the fire. And me? I sprung up into the air and was instantly pounded in the head by The Immaterial Man's smoggy fist.

I was flung across the room and onto the second floor where I bounced like a stone skipping across water until I crashed into a glass case containing Beyond Man's original costume. His blue cape fell over my face and shards of glass shred through my costume and lacerated my skin. As soon as I got to my feet and pulled that heavy blue shroud off of my head, I saw three out of four of The Abnormalite's fists tearing at me like pink cinder blocks launched out of a catapult.

I ducked and The Abnormalite punched craters in the wall that Beyond Man's original costume used to guard, and I ran. I ran as fast as I could past Queen Quantum's Cosmic Crown displayed in a little glass box that shattered as one of Master Boson's nuclear blasts just narrowly missed me. I ran through an aisle of Doc Hyper's aerodynamic friction proof running boots, each of them flopping to the floor as armadillodrones bumped into their platforms while they skittered after me with humming buzzsaws and sparking tasers, and I heard The

Abnormalite's plodding steps somewhere behind me making the entire second floor tremble like it was being rocked by an earthquake.

All I could think was *keep moving, got to keep moving,* and I made it to the railing of the second floor where I was about to leap across the main hall, anything to get some distance between me and the pink skinned horror that was The Abnormalite. I put one foot on the metal railing to propel myself off of it, and I had a fraction of a second to witness the battle below.

It was a clusterfuck of indescribable proportions. There was a blue bonfire growing on the floor of the museum. There was a kaleidoscope of multicolored energy blasts flying in every direction and piercing billowing clouds of smoke before causing miniature explosions wherever they connected. There were battalions of henchmen, Goons and Henchasaurs and Harpies and Ninjatoms and the Reptilian Guard and even Captain Haiku's Syllabullies, and they charged together on the burning marble floors and screamed with one voice like they were storming the beaches of Normandy. It was sheer chaos, and I had no idea if my teammates were alive or dead.

I pushed off of the railing and flew into the air with nothing even resembling a plan, and The Whimsy fired up from the floor of the main hall and collided with me. We tumbled together through the blinding smoke filling the museum, just me and the first supervillain I ever fought immersed in a gray smokey limbo, and then we plummeted out of the smoke cloud and back down onto the second floor. I got to my feet, out of breath and dripping blood from the deep cuts carved into me by glass that used to encase Beyond Man's original costume, and again, I ran. I ran right into The Abnormalite's pink fist.

I lost consciousness for an eternity of a full second, and when I woke up, I was sailing through the air like a baseball that The Abnormalite had just hit out of the stadium. I flailed my arms and legs in a useless attempt to control my descent, and I smashed through the observation window of the Superb 6 satellite dangling from the ceiling of the museum. I landed on my back on a round table with a big blue and silver S6 symbol on it and skidded across it, grinding even more glass into my body before I slid to a stop. The anarchy of the battle below was muted inside that space station, and it was like I had been punched into a quiet, quaint memory of the 60's space age. The inside of the satellite was all smooth, curved surfaces and chrome, like the Mad Men offices mixed with the Star Trek bridge.

I crawled across broken glass to the edge of the table. I staggered off of it and lurched towards the nearest control panel, which was an endless array of metal switches and knobs and dials, and I just started pushing things. I ran my hands all over the panel and frantically flicked switches and jammed buttons and twisted dials, just hoping that one of them was some kind of emergency signal that was still functional and would get the attention of the Superb 6, but there were no blinking lights, there were no readings on the dead, dust caked computer screens. I was on my own, and no help was on the way.

And then came the laughter, that squealing laughter of The Immaterial Man as he seeped in through the seams of the once air tight satellite. Sickly green gas trickled into the room from every direction, and before I could even think about bolting, The Immaterial Man's hand was at my throat like a vise crushing my larynx. His eyes, those burning rubies floating in his foggy head, they bored into mine as he choked the life out of me.

"No more running, Spectacle. You gave us a run for our money, you really did. I'm having more fun than I've had in years, but enough's enough. It's over, kid," The Immaterial Man said, and he carried me by my throat to the shattered observation window. He held me out of the window and over the seven story drop from the satellite to the main hall floor.

"Say hi to your pops for me," The Immaterial Man said in between shrill giggles. I couldn't breathe or talk, but I did the one thing I could do. I spit in his face. It flew right through his intangible forehead, and then he dropped me.

"I got you," Mr. Mercurial said as he caught me in one of his silvery hands that was expanded into the shape of a big metallic catcher's mitt. He caught me after I fell at least four stories. He was standing dozens of feet tall on stretched out stilt legs, the fingers of his other hand were elongated into five silver ropes, each of which were whipping all around the room and knocking down henchmen so fast that he was actually making a dent in their numbers. Despite everything, he still had that huge smile on his shiny face.

The Immaterial Man spilled down at Mr. Mercurial from the Superb 6 satellite like a pale green waterfall. Mr. Mercurial teetered on his silver stilt legs as the current of his gaseous body surged around him, and I was knocked out of his hand. I was bounced close enough to the fourth floor that I was able to grab the railing and pull myself up.

Mr. Mercurial and The Immaterial Man became a terrible yin-yang of flowing liquid metal and raging green gas, swirling around each other and attacking in ways that only shapeshifters can. The Immaterial Man was a hail storm of fuming fists striking out at Mr. Mercurial, who was a frothing, boiling multitude of balloons trying and failing to contain the raging green tempest, and that was just the first of many morphing, rapid fire reactions and adaptations which hurt my eyes to look at. And throughout it all, The Immaterial Man's sharp laughter punctured the air.

I wrenched myself away from their hypnotic fight, and I continued my strategy of running like hell when I was faced with a sign. It said, "Tools of the Trade." I realized that this floor showcased crimefighting equipment, and I darted into the exhibit to grab something, anything that could help us fight back. Just as I entered a section of the floor dedicated entirely to utility belts, Captain Haiku swung over the railing on a grappling hook rope like he was boarding an enemy ship and planted himself in front of me.

"Avast, Spectacle!

I always knew that I'd win.

That I'd destroy—"

I coldcocked him before he could get out the last syllable of his haiku, and I stepped over his unconscious body and into a hallway of utility belts. Every kind of utility belt was mounted on the wall in glass frames. I grabbed the first frame I came to which contained Supra's utility belt, and I bashed it against the wall. Her sleek utility belt composed of interlocking compartments fell out of the frame, and that's when I heard her.

"Oh, Spectacle...Spectaaacccleeee..." Mistress Gorgon called out in a sing song voice. I tried to ignore her while I clicked open the compartments of Supra's utility belt, and stuffed pellet flash bang grenades, smoke bombs, tranquilizer darts, and titanium hand cuffs into my jacket pockets.

"There you are, sweetheart," Mistress Gorgon said as she turned a corner and saw me with a fistful of flash bang grenades and Supra's emptied out utility belt at my feet.

"Sweetheart this," I said, and I chucked the flash bang grenades at the nest of snakes writhing on Mistress Gorgon's head. They bounced off of her like useless marbles, and she smiled.

"Spectacle...come on. This is a museum. Did you really think they'd have live ammo in here?" Mistress Gorgon strutted towards me, her serpents unhinged their jaws, and they let loose multiple streams of burning blue death.

I jumped away from her and took cover behind a suit of Anhur's bronze Egyptian armor, but I wasn't fast enough. Flesh sizzled on my left shin. I patted out the flames clawing up my leg as blue fire curled around Anhur's suit of armor, and I pulled the titanium handcuffs out of my pocket. Anhur's Breastplate of Ra melted and dripped molten metal with Mistress Gorgon's fire raging all around it. It wouldn't withstand the fire for much longer.

I sprung straight up and over Anhur's drooping armor, over the sweltering heat of Mistress Gorgon's fiery wrath, and I landed behind her. She whirled around with those wriggling black snakes still vomiting blue fire, I slapped the titanium handcuffs on her wrist and skipped out of the way before she could burn me alive.

"Honey, please. Don't insult me," she said, and now blue fire was spreading all throughout the fourth floor as those squirming serpents sprayed flame everywhere. Utility belts fell off the wall as their frames were consumed by fire. A cabinet of grappling hooks lit up and their neatly displayed nylon ropes burned like candle wicks. I kept moving, leaping and dodging and dancing around the displays until the entire floor was burning up and there was nowhere left to run, and Mistress Gorgon slinked through the fire towards me, her eyes glowing white like spotlights.

"You should've taken the money," she said, and I felt her supra-stone solidifying around my badly burned leg and weighing me down. Her snakes hissed and flicked their forked tongues like they were anticipating a delightful mouse dessert. She was moving in for the kill, and I knew it.

I sprinted at her as fast as I could. I pushed myself through the fire devouring the entire floor, my leg was getting heavier and heavier as her supra-stone advanced up around my knee, I ignored it and kept driving at her with everything I had, and I snatched her handcuffed wrist. I yanked her arm down to her leg and handcuffed her wrist to her opposite ankle, leaving her body contorted and bent over. She toppled onto the burning carpet, straining to rip the titanium chains binding her arm to her leg, and I shuffled back against the railing with half of my burnt leg covered in supra-stone like I was wearing a concrete cast.

"This is a joke, Spectacle...you're already dead. You can't beat us all you stupid fuck," Mistress Gorgon seethed at me, and really, I couldn't argue with her. The fourth floor was almost completely on fire, and I let myself fall back over the railing.

I plunged towards the main floor, watching the fourth floor rise away from me and go up in flames, and I heard a voice in my head.

"*Go limp*," Insight telepathically whispered to me.

My body began to glow with a weak purple light as the marble floor rushed at me, I started to fall slower than I should have but not nearly slow enough, not slow enough to make the ground look like anything other than a giant wall racing towards me, *Brace yourself,* Insight murmured in between my ears, and I slammed into the scorched marble floor so hard that the supra-stone on my leg smashed into splinters.

Shards of supra-stone stabbed my leg as I got to my feet. Insight was next to me telekinetically tossing back incoming herds of henchmen like rag dolls, but there were countless waves of them closing in on us, and there were ten more thugs for every one she threw back. Joe Metal was screaming as henchmen dogpiled on him and he fought to shake them off his armor, his exoskeleton torn like tissue paper all over and its damaged hydraulics system groaning with his every move.

"*We have to use their numbers against them,*" I thought to Insight as I grabbed a Ninjatom swinging a pair of irradiated nunchuks at me, and chucked him into the mob of henchmen, knocking a bunch of them over like bowling pins.

She nodded to me while keeping the hordes of henchmen at bay with radiating bursts of purple telekinesis. I glanced up and saw Dragon General gliding towards me with his scaly wings outstretched, and above him I saw Mr. Mercurial and The Immaterial Man swirling all around the Superb 6 satellite in a blob of morphing, contorting green gas and silver fluid.

"*Patch my thoughts into Mr. Mercurial's head,*" I thought to Insight as Dragon General swooped down at me, the razor sharp talons on his bare feet soaring right at my face.

I stumbled out of his way, but I still felt those bone claws clipping my shoulder and tearing into my skin. Dragon General flew straight into a cluster of his own Reptilian Guard, and they broke his fall along with more than a few of their bones. Dragon General didn't waste any time worrying about his snake skinned henchmen, and he slashed at me with his talon tipped fingers. I jumped back out of the way of his swiping claws, grabbed a nearby Goon by his hazmat suit and held him in front of me, and Dragon General accidentally hacked at the high pressure tank of goo strapped to his back. The tank erupted purple goo from the gashes Dragon General just sliced into it, I aimed the Goon's back at him and the mobs of henchmen, and drenched them in globs of purple sedative gunk.

Dragon General and a mass of henchmen passed out...but as they fell away from us onto a bed of purple goo, they revealed a wall to wall legion of henchmen still standing and marching toward us. Professor Dinosaur, flanked by his Henchasaurs, smirked as his rival Dragon General took a nap. Mistress Gorgon jumped down from the fourth floor and landed on her feet like the fall was nothing, and she waved at me with a broken titanium handcuff chain dangling from her slender wrist. The Abnormalite kicked henchmen out of his way as he stomped towards us with Anhur's spear grasped in all four of his hands. Fire was spreading from the fourth floor and climbing up the walls. You could hear the building creaking and straining under the pressure as its support structure began to break down. Henchmen stepped over the unconscious bodies of the few villains my teammates had taken down, like Dragon General, Armadillotron, and the poor, feeble Lacrosse Assassin. Behind them all, The Punster stood by the entrance of the museum, leaning against the big metal door frame and smiling at me like he was having the time of his life.

"*Bring down the satellite, Mr. Mercurial,*" I thought.

Insight cast a weak bubble of telekinetic energy around us, and we both looked up. Through her dim purple field, we saw Mr. Mercurial's amorphous, silver body mingled with The Immaterial Man's raging green clouds. Metallic tendrils lashed out at the wires suspending the Superb 6 satellite. Two snapped, then a third, a shudder ran through the building as the several tons of metal above us jerked hard on the ceiling, all the supervillains and henchmen stopped closing in around us and they looked up too, I saw through the purple tint of Insight's field that The Punster's smile had faded, and then it fell.

Supervillains and henchmen scattered in every direction. There wasn't even a pretense of teamwork anymore. It was every man for himself. Henchmen pushed and shoved and knocked each other to the ground and trampled over the fallen to get out of the way of the massive satellite. It dropped from the ceiling, spinning in the air like a giant blue and silver top, and Insight clenched her eyes shut and poured every last bit of telekinetic power into the purple bubble surrounding us. It glowed so intensely that I couldn't even see the falling satellite anymore. All I could see was blinding purple light, and I closed my eyes too. There was a thunderous crash, it was so loud that I couldn't hear my own screaming, and it seemed to go on forever, like the whole world was tearing itself apart around us.

Finally, silence. I opened my eyes, and Insight, both eyes bloodshot with ruptured blood vessels, let her telekinetic field drop. We were standing in a clean, empty circle of marble…but outside of that circle was a field of metal and plastic, of broken solar panels and crumbled satellite walls and crushed spacecraft modules, of a silly space age dream gone to shit and dismantled all around us in a soup of rubble.

Everything stopped. My ears were ringing. I couldn't hear it, but I could see the trembling, convulsing walls of the museum, and I knew that the whole place was coming down. I stepped out into the field of debris that coated the floor of the main hall, crunching metal and plastic under my shoes, and I looked for The Punster. Most of the henchmen got out from under the falling satellite and they were scrambling out of the museum entrance, but not all of them were so lucky. A Goon wandered by me clutching a bleeding stump where his hand used to be, his white hazmat suit spattered red with blood. There were mounds of wreckage that stood taller than the rest. I knew that henchmen and supervillains were buried beneath them. I couldn't see The Punster anywhere.

Mr. Mercurial drizzled down to me in a mist of silver, and when he had reformed his glistening body, he could barely stand. He slumped towards me, and I slung his arm around my shoulder.

Joe Metal was shouting something at me and gesturing towards the exit of the museum. I couldn't hear him. I limped towards the exit with Mr. Mercurial hobbling next to me. Insight and Joe were ahead of us and forcing the last of the henchmen through the door and out of our way.

We made it out of the museum and onto the street, but it didn't really matter. They were already there waiting for us.

Funny things go through your head when you realize that you're living your last moments.

"*They'll probably call this the Museum Massacre,*" I thought as one of Master Boson's irradiated throwing stars lodged in my shoulder.

"*Or maybe The Last Stand of The Millennials,*" I thought, and The Immaterial Man surged out of the collapsing building behind us. His furious, disembodied howls echoed everywhere like the wrath of god. The hurricane winds of his body forced me down to my hands and knees.

I looked up, and The Punster was standing over me. I glanced to my left and saw my teammates fighting for their lives, but they weren't going to win.

"*Nobody can go to Jupiter,*" I thought.

I looked back to The Punster. He raised one of the Specialist's proton accelerator pistols towards me, and his look of frustration, it was almost like he was disappointed that it was this easy.

"I had a really great pun prepared for this but…my heart's not in it," he sighed, and tried to make eye contact with me, but I was distracted by something up above him. A glint of light in the sky caught my eye.

"What?" The Punster asked, and he looked behind him and up at the growing flashes of color descending from the bright noon day sun. It took me a few seconds to register what they were, but once I did, I started laughing, and I couldn't stop.

"Oh, fuck me," The Punster said. It was the Superb 6.

They were flying in triangular formation straight at us with the sun behind them. It was hard to look directly at them with the glare of the sun silhouetting them, and I almost convinced myself that they were a mirage, a spandex-clad oasis in the desert conjured up by my soon to be dead brain. But no, they reached the peaks of the buildings around us and peeled away from their arrow shaped formation in individual directions like trained fighter pilots executing a dog fighting strategy that they'd rehearsed thousands of times, and they couldn't have been more real.

Beyond Man soared by The Punster and me, his blue and white cape close enough that I could have reached out and tugged on it, and the wake of his flight threw The Punster to his feet. He dropped his gun, it slid away from him, and he lay there dazed and twisting in pain on the ground. Queen Quantum hovered above the street and bottled up The Immaterial Man in fluctuating uncertainty fields. She chained The Whimsy to the street by entangling the molecules of his feet with the asphalt, and she disabled the chemical process that Mistress Gorgon's snakes used to generate fire with a flick of her index finger.

Supra was all over the place, moving fluidly through the crowds of henchmen so quickly that my superhuman eyes were barely quick enough to track her, and she was just beating the shit out of henchmen with martial arts so sophisticated that I don't even have names for half of the complex moves she was executing. Anhur and Sleight of Hand were standing back to back and working together like a well oiled machine. Sleight of Hand covered Anhur, sweeping his wand back and forth like a conductor masterfully leading an orchestra. Weapons disappeared from henchmen's hands, and blasts of energy transmuted into butterflies and snowflakes. Anhur, the Egyptian God of War, the Slayer of Enemies, he was pummeling The Abnormalite with blows that unleashed shockwaves and shattered all the windows for blocks around. And as Anhur knocked out that pink skinned, four armed, eight eyed son of a bitch, I couldn't help but cheer.

The way that the Superb 6 worked, turning the tide of the battle in less than a minute, fighting so well together that the six of them were like the parts of one big machine, the relentless efficiency of their attacks, such perfect form and accuracy, such elegance and grace while in complete control of boundless power…it was beautiful.

"We got your call," Ultra Lady said as she touched down in front of me and extended a white gloved hand. I took it, and she helped me to my feet.

"Call?" I asked, disoriented and exhausted and badly wounded.

"The emergency signal. From the satellite," Ultra Lady said. She turned away from me, pursed her lips, and blew a gust of Ultra-Breath at a mob of henchmen stupid enough to think that this just might be their chance to rush us. They lifted up and away from us like they were lighter than feathers.

"The signal. In the satellite. That actually worked," I said, and I started cracking up again, overcome with relief as I watched the Superb 6 handle the army of henchmen and supervillains like they were a bunch of unruly children.

"Don't go into shock, Spectacle. We're not out of the woods yet," Ultra Lady said, and she flew away from me as she noticed Mistress Gorgon jumping onto a rooftop and trying to make her getaway. I looked back to where The Punster fell. He was gone.

"We're gonna make it, I can't believe this, we're actually gonna fucking do this," Joe Metal said mostly to himself as his heavily damaged armor carried him to my side. His exoskeleton was dripping hydraulic fluid and leaking smoke at the seams and making awful grinding noises with every shift in position.

"Where'd The Punster go?" Insight asked me as she floated to my other side. She telekinetically flipped over a parked car in front of us to provide cover from the stray energy blasts flying everywhere.

"He couldn't have gotten far, he's like a thousand years old," Mr. Mercurial said. He was starting to recover from his amorphous brawl with The Immaterial Man, and he shakily got to his metallic feet.

"Let's finish this," I said to my teammates.

We moved out from behind the flipped over car. The streets were overflowing with panicked henchmen running in every direction. The Superb 6 were an unstoppable force of nature. They were effortlessly keeping the throngs of henchmen confined to the block around the demolished Kirby Museum of Superhero History. The Abnormalite was comatose on the street with half of his fangs knocked out of his mouth. The Immaterial Man was swirling inside of Queen Quantum's uncertainty fields and shrieking as he struggled to free himself. Ultra Lady carried Mistress Gorgon by the limp black snakes on her head back to the street, dropped her into a dumpster, and welded it shut with a glare of her heat vision. And The Millennials, we tore through those last henchmen, and it was a pleasure. While it lasted.

Joe Metal forced his grumbling, failing armor to its limits as he thrashed henchmen by the dozen. He waded through the swarms of Henchasaurs, Syllabullies, Harpies and Goons and just emptied out everything in his arsenal, tiny tranquilizer darts and EMP pulses and ricocheting rubber bullets and taser wires and blasts of propulsive energy from octagon shaped ports in his armor. Insight was zipping around the air like a purple firefly, telepathically putting henchmen into trances, and leaving them standing dull eyed and drooling. I hunted for The Punster. I knocked out Goons with tired, sloppy punches, and I roamed the battle torn street, searching for any sign of that pun obsessed motherfucker in the chaos.

"Spectacle," he said. I turned around, and The Punster was pointing that pistol at me again and breathing heavily. I tried to reach for his weapon, but I was too weak and sluggish.

"Set phasers to...pun!" The Punster cried, and he pulled the trigger.

It all happened so quickly. I heard Mr. Mercurial shout. I saw my own reflection, my dopey, surprised face gaping back at me. Mr. Mercurial had stretched his mirror-like body in front of me as a shield. Silvery liquid exploded everywhere like chrome fireworks. There was a gaping hole in Mr. Mercurial's elongated torso, and through it I saw The Punster's psychotic smile and the smoking tip of his pistol.

Mr. Mercurial belly flopped onto the asphalt. He was shaking violently. His stretched out body shriveled down until he was his normal height. He tried to get up, he started retching, and then he threw up blood mingled with silvery fluid. The Punster ran and watched this over his shoulder with delight. I dropped to my knees and cradled Mr. Mercurial's head.

"Come on, buddy. Pull yourself together."

"Not…not…naughh," Mr. Mercurial said. His metallic head was dripping through my fingers as I held him.

"Pull yourself together, Mr. Mercurial. Come on, goddamn it," I said, and now his entire body was melting like an ice cube on a hot sidewalk. Shiny metallic fluid poured through my hands. I could barely hold onto him as he slipped away.

"You always pull yourself together," I said.

Mr. Mercurial looked up at me, and his eyes were big, so big. I put a hand on his forehead. He was so afraid, and then he was gone. Completely dissolved into puddles of silver draining away into the gutters.

I stood up, dripping with silver and my own blood, and I saw The Punster across the street. The old man had managed to keep his head down and avoid the attention of the Superb 6 as they cleaned up the last of the costumed criminals. An old guy in a purple turtleneck isn't exactly a high priority compared to all those powerful superhumans. He was fleeing through the super-battle devastated street and about to duck into a little toy store called Amaze Toys.

I couldn't believe that he was getting away. After all of this. After all the senseless destruction, after all the needless loss of life, after he slaughtered one of my best friends, I couldn't believe he was just fucking walking away, and I was filled with rage. I've never been angrier in my life. I ran after him, all of the pain and exhaustion evaporated under the heat of my anger, and I saw red.

Chapter 18:
Into the Labyrinth

"Punster!" I yelled, and I ripped the front door of Amaze Toys out of its frame and tossed it aside.

"Sorry about your friend, Spectacle. That was a bad way to go…poor, pouring Mr. Mercurial," The Punster laughed at his own stupid pun as he ran through an aisle of Superb 6 action figures and towards the back of the store. I chased after him, pushing my way through the bikes and shelves that he had knocked over to slow me down.

"I guess you could say I really tested his metal!" The Punster shouted. He had reached a door at the back of the store that looked like the entrance of a storage room. He opened it with a key, and charged down a flight of stairs. He was just a few yards ahead of me, and I followed him down, gaining on him with every step, until he reached the bottom and opened another door with another key. He opened it and slammed it behind him before I could grab him.

The door was locked. I yanked on the doorknob and it came off in my hands. It wasn't a normal door. It was a thick, metal hatch, clearly built with superhuman intruders in mind. I threw myself against the door, ramming my shoulder into it over and over until it felt like I would dislocate it, but it didn't budge. Then it swung open for me like The Punster had built some kind of remote motorized opening device into it. I fell forward into a dark room with all the extra momentum of my ramming, and then the door slammed shut behind me.

"Amaze Toys? Get it, Spectacle? '*A maze*'!?" The Punster said over a speaker system. Dim lights in the ceiling came on, and I found myself in a long dark hallway with no doors.

"That toy store upstairs is yet another little business that I've purchased with all the money you watched me steal while you drank yourself into oblivion. It was a perfect front for constructing this, my greatest achievement. My masterpiece," The Punster said. I started slowly walking down the hallway, cautiously and unsure of what might be at the end of it.

"Pun's Labyrinth," The Punster said with obvious amusement at his wordplay, his obnoxious voice echoing out from speakers I couldn't see. I reached the end of the hallway. It opened up into a new hallway that forced me to make a choice between left or right.

"You know, I could always tell that your father was at least mildly entertained by my puns. You don't even seem like you get them. Then again, you're not your father, are you?" The Punster said. I turned left, and I smelled something funny. Fine mist was drifting up out of air conditioning vents in the floor.

"We have the young Dr. Delusion to thank for this feature of my labyrinth. It's a modification of his special SUHP compound mixed up with some other drugs of my own choosing into a nice hallucinogenic cocktail. It won't enhance your superhuman abilities like regular SUHP, but it also won't leave you a drooling vegetable like Dr. Delusion's brand of weaponized SUHP vapor. You'll love it, son," The Punster said, and already I could feel it hitting my system. The hallway in front of me stretched out a thousand miles. The gloves on my hands started leaving little trails of neon light. The fog of drugs blanketing the floor pulsated and throbbed as I passed through it.

"It's just a little party favor, Spectacle," The Punster said, and now his voice didn't seem to be coming from speakers, but from out of the fog on the floor, and out of the walls, and shining down from the dim lights in the ceiling, and even from inside myself. I tried to shake it off, and kept moving.

"You've got no idea how much work I put into this maze, son. I've been designing it for decades. Before you could read, I had entire notebooks filled with ideas for my labyrinth. I even had The Specialist outfit it with top of the line, super-sensory deprivation technology...if any of your friends, or even the Superb 6, look at it with their super-senses, they'll just see a storage space filled with toys.

This was supposed to be for your father. It was supposed to be the setting for our final battle. Jack Titan descends into The Labyrinth to face The Punster, one last time. Winner take all. It was supposed to be the big finish, Spectacle. It was supposed to be the climax of a lifetime rivalry between Jack Titan and The Punster, it was supposed to be what my *whole fucking life* was leading up to. It was supposed to be…" The Punster trailed off. He was starting to let his bitterness and anger out, but he caught himself.

"But your father took that from me," The Punster said, and now his pleasant, grandfatherly tone had returned. I had reached the end of the hallway with the SUHP tainted fog coating the floor, and there was a corner that forced me to turn right. I turned the corner, and what I saw made me trip over my own feet.

It was another hallway, but every surface was a screen that displayed moving black and white mazes. The floor, the ceiling, the walls, they were covered with flat screens that were seamlessly connected, and endless networks of black and white mazes rotated around the corridor in unison. Combined with the drugs, it was extremely disorienting.

I stumbled into the hallway, bracing myself against the walls as I walked, and the spiraling, snaking corners and bends and pathways spinning around me made me sick to my stomach. The tangles of geometric shapes organically split and divided into more and more branching pathways, into jungles of growing twists and turns and dead ends, and I could no longer distinguish between the effects of the drugs and what was the insane reality that The Punster had built here.

"Another word for pun is 'paronomasia'. Parono*masia.* Maze...get it?" The Punster said. I made it to the end of the hallway of gyrating mazes, and my head was swimming. I saw interconnected grids of black and white mazes when I closed my eyes. I had the option of going left, right, or forward. I took a deep breath, and pushed forward.

"Did you know the word 'clue' comes from 'clew', spelled c, l, e, w? A clew is a ball of thread, which is how Theseus found his way out of the labyrinth in classical Greek mythology. Not quite a pun, but still. Interesting word," The Punster said in a whisper that was soothing and almost hypnotic.

I moved through the next hallway which had detailed paintings of a beach landscape on every surface. The forced perspective of the photorealistic paintings was done in a way that created an optical illusion that made it feel like I had stepped onto the beach. There was blue, cloud freckled sky above me, there was an ocean horizon in front of me stretching out to infinity, there was sand on the floor that made walking even harder. I even felt, or thought I felt, a gentle breeze and smelled the sea and heard the crashing of the waves.

"See, that's what it was all about, Spectacle. Words. Everything the Punster did. Words were at the root of everything," The Punster said, and a chasm opened up in the little sand dunes. I stopped before I fell in, waving my arms and wobbling on the edge of the void, and inside there were these little plastic birds looking up at me quizzically. They were like miniature penguins but with longer, pointier beaks and fluorescent blue webbed feet. For a brief moment, I thought that the funny birds were conjured up by my drug soaked mind, and I hesitated.

The birds fired at me like little winged missiles. I spun out of the way, and most of them shot past me and stabbed into the wall. They stuck there in the painted wall, messing up the immersive effect of the photorealistic ocean horizon, their black beaks buried deep in the dry wall, their fluorescent blue webbed feet pointing out behind them, and I looked down at my leg and saw that not all of them missed. One of them buried its sharp beak in my thigh. It looked up at me and waggled its eyebrows up and down. I yanked it out of my leg and blood spurted out of the wound.

"Booby traps. Booby is a type of sea bird," The Punster murmured over the speaker system. I ripped up part of my costume jacket and tied it around my leg to stop the bleeding, and I stepped over the pit in the artificial beach.

"Are you even paying attention, Spectacle?" The Punster asked. I said nothing, and I staggered forward to the end of his simulated beach. The sand and the paintings and the smell of the ocean ended, and the hallway forced me around a 180 degree bend.

"Words are important, Spectacle. Words have meaning. They are how we order the world and understand the senseless chaos of this universe. Without words, without language and symbols and ideas, what is there? There's no meaning. There's nothing," The Punster said, and I entered a long hallway that was completely white from the floor to the ceiling to the blinding lights. There were several white doors lining both walls of the hallway that barely stood out from the rest of the whiteness. It was like I had walked onto the blank nothingness of a piece of white paper.

"Your father, he called himself 'Jack Titan.' He *chose* that. He called himself a Titan. And what is a Titan without monsters to fight? The media, they called him 'The Man of Myth.' And how can you have a hero of myth without a road of trials and temptations and dragons to slay? And a devil to face at the end of it all?" The Punster asked, and I didn't answer. I said nothing, and stood there in the nothingness, preparing for whatever fresh hell The Punster had ready for me.

"Words have meaning. Your father called himself a Titan, and I made monsters for him to battle. He wanted to be 'The Man of Myth,' and so I became the devil. And what do you call yourself?"

Countless videos and images of me washed over the walls and the floors and the ceiling and replaced the blank nothingness. This was yet another room in which every surface was covered by screens, and The Punster had used it to create an elaborate display of shifting images and video, all of me. I became a crimefighter right at the start of the Digital Age of Superheroes, and The Punster had hundreds, maybe thousands of pictures and videos of me to choose from online.

Both walls of the long hallway were plastered with a collage of my own drunken face. My wasted face grinned at me and looked down at me with dilated eyes and video played of me clumsily leaping across rooftops. There were dozens of camera phone videos and pictures, from all different angles and throughout my ten year career, of me pounding shots with The Millennials, of me dancing while high out of my mind on SUHP, of me throwing up in the middle of the street after drunkenly fighting Armadillotron. It was a mosaic of digital imagery and video, floating and rearranging across the walls and beneath my feet and above my head, and it was all dedicated to a decade of debauchery.

"You called yourself 'The Spectacle.' And what a spectacle you've made of yourself, son," The Punster said.

I walked through the hallway displaying the undeniable evidence of my abuse of drugs and alcohol, and I did my best to ignore it. My many injuries, the exhaustion, the blood loss, and the SUHP cocktail coursing through my veins, it all combined to create this experience that I wasn't walking in a hallway with screens on every surface anymore. I was walking through a tunnel of my own memories. I was struggling through a corridor in my consciousness that I really didn't want to see, and as soon as I got to the first door in the hallway, I opened it and tried not to make eye contact with the morphing montage of my inebriated eyes.

"Where are you going?" The Punster laughed. Behind the door was another much smaller and narrower hallway with a right turn only a few feet into it. It was also a white void of blank walls.

"You still don't get it, do you? I could end you right now. I could easily blow up this whole maze. I might not even be in this building anymore, did you even consider that?" The Punster asked, and I said nothing. More images and videos of me splashed across the walls of this cramped hallway.

This time, the mutating jumble of images and videos reminded me of every mistake I had ever made. There was a patchwork of photos of the time that I fought Dragon General and he threw a pickup truck at me. I was twenty at the time, just a kid, and I didn't think at all about where that truck would land after I got out of its way. Blog posts and internet articles and shuffling photographs flashed before my eyes as I turned the corner in the narrow hallway, and they all reminded me of the dozens of people that were severely injured when that pickup truck fell out of the sky.

Around the corner, the left wall was a cluster of photos of a fight I had with Captain Haiku. I was so distracted by the people filming me with their phones, so concentrated on showing off and looking cool on social media and firing off half witty one liners, I didn't even notice a van full of Syllabullies pull up and whisk their boss away. The photos of me smiling with fans and signing autographs afterward showed that I obviously didn't care that I lost him.

Every time I was just a fraction of a second too slow and an innocent person got hurt. Every time I was careless and accidentally let a supervillain get away. Every time I was a showboating asshole focused on getting as much attention as possible instead of doing my job. Every unprofessional and criminally irresponsible thing I had done that had been caught on camera, The Punster found them all and smeared them all over the walls.

"I could kill you any time I want to, but no. Not yet," The Punster muttered. The hallway ended in a dead end. I had to turn back and face my failures all over again.

"Because that's not the game, Spectacle," The Punster said. Still, I said nothing.

I returned to the larger hallway. As soon as I opened the door and reentered that shrine to my own public drunkenness, I realized that I couldn't remember which direction I had come from. I was lost.

"Uh oh…which way is the entrance? Or are you too *entranced* by yourself to remember?" The Punster taunted. I thought I heard his voice coming from one of the doors in the hallway. I opened it, and entered another smaller corridor of whiteness.

"You haven't got a clew, have you?" The Punster asked, and still, I said nothing.

More images and video appeared on all the surfaces of this new hallway, but they weren't pieced together in a rearranging collage anymore. Now, I was confronted by giant visions of myself that loomed seven feet tall on the walls, and they were depictions of me savagely beating supervillains.

There was a video playing on a loop of one of the many times I fought Master Boson. My fist struck Master Boson's face and knocked several teeth out of his radioactive mouth, and probably broke his jaw too. The video just kept repeating, my fist kept colliding with Master Boson's chin again and again, and it was hard to look at the agony in Master Boson's eyes and his utter helplessness and the viciousness of my own attack.

I walked past it, and on the opposite wall, there was a string of colossal photographs of an encounter I had with Professor Dinosaur. Each of the photographs focused on a super strength punch to Professor Dinosaur's midsection. I saw myself pelt his stomach and sides with punches that could have cracked concrete, and in the last photograph Professor Dinosaur fell to his knees and I kicked him right in his scaly snout.

The end of the hallway lead me left, and then right, and then left again, and throughout the snaking passageway, there were immense images and looping videos of a vigilante brutally thrashing supervillains and henchmen. I saw a superhuman man beating up costumed criminals that were much weaker than he was, that he deliberately chose to fight *because* they were much weaker than he was, and it filled me with nauseating shame. I came to the end of this corridor that was devoted to the cruelty of a superpowered bully in a mask, and I didn't want to believe that it was me.

"Your father was a violent man, too. I can't tell you how many times I woke up in prison hospitals with concussions and internal hemorrhaging because of the late, great Jack Titan," The Punster said, and the slightest twinge of resentment surfaced in his calming, grandfatherly voice. There was a door at the end of the hallway with a small camera above it. This door was also covered in screens, and it showed a digital reflection of myself, bloodied and burned and limping towards it with a trail of blood behind me.

"I guess the apple doesn't brawl far from the tree, does it, Spectacle?" The Punster asked, and any hint of sadness or humanity that had momentarily risen up in his voice submerged back into his detached, tranquilizing tone.

I opened the door, and still, I said nothing in response to another one of his absurd puns. The door opened onto the larger hallway that I had just come from. The Punster had just led me around a circle through that smaller hallway that forced me to look at the violence and brutality of being a superhero, and back to the larger hallway. He was toying with me.

My head was swimming. The long hallway that celebrated my intoxicated face in a shifting montage of hundreds of pictures was spinning around me. I braced myself against the screen covered wall. Its pixelated surface rippled underneath my fingers. I was bleeding profusely from glass cuts all over my body and the stab wound in my leg and gashes on my swollen face and Master Boson's glowing throwing star lodged in my shoulder. I had severe burns on one of my legs, and two broken ribs. And on top of all of that, I had just been dosed with a concoction of hallucinogenic drugs.

"Taking a little rest, Spectacle? The game's not over yet, son," The Punster encouraged. He was having so much fun.

I forced myself to walk. My drunken smile beamed down all around me, and I moved a little faster, breaking into a slow jog as I reached the end of the corridor. It bent left into a smaller passage, and now I was running, running towards the sound of The Punster's laughs. It wasn't coming from the speaker system anymore, it was somewhere up ahead, it was bubbling up from somewhere deep in the maze and resounding off the walls, and I pushed through the pain and now I was sprinting towards the laughter. I darted around tighter and tighter corners and forks and turns in the maze as the passageway became narrower and narrower, until the walls were almost squeezing my shoulders, and finally, when it seemed like I wasn't even going to be able to fit in the tiny tunnel anymore, I reached a door. I could hear The Punster's laughter behind it, his giggling which was somehow childlike and grandfatherly at the same time, and I opened it.

The Punster was standing in the center of a circular room next to a waist high Greek column. One of my father's golden wreaths sat on top of the marble column.

There was a ring of projectors hanging from the ceiling that flickered on as soon as I stepped foot into the round room. The white walls lit up with images. The curved walls of the room showed decades of conflicts between Jack Titan and The Punster.

There were newspaper clippings of Jack Titan fighting The Punster's gigantic Antdroid, blown up so huge on the walls that the Antdroid was almost life sized. There was grainy news footage of Jack Titan being crushed inside of The Punster's giant vise while the wordplay obsessed psychopath chanted "Jack Tighten! Jack Tighten!" in his face. There were photos cut out of an issue of Spandex that showed The Punster riding a tank-like sleigh across snowy city streets and towards Jack Titan with his Goons towing it like hazmat wearing reindeer. The caption read "The Man of Myth and The Punster's Slay Rides." There were forty years of murderous wordplay projected onto the round walls.

Jack Titan went from a young, vital man to an old, bitter man in a circle around me. He started as an inexperienced superhero in the 60's whose excitement and idealism was easy to read on his boyish face, even through his golden mask. He looked like he was thrilled to be alive, to be fighting back The Punster's Goons with their sedative goo harmlessly sticking to his breastplate and whipping around his Golden Sling. You could see it in his eyes. This is what he was born to do.

But as he aged in a ring around me, the fun drained out of his eyes. He dealt with endless pun-themed deathtraps, he fought The Punster again and again, and I don't know if it was the drugs, but I swear, I could see it in my father's eyes. He was trapped in a never ending cycle of fighting The Punster, and by the end of their forty year long rivalry, it had worn him down to a nub. And The Punster, his passion and frenzy and untempered madness was constant from the first photos to that very moment as he stood there in front of me. He hadn't changed at all, and there was no reason to think that he ever would.

"You know, I'm actually proud of you, Spectacle. I was so sure that you were going to die in that museum with all those ridiculous superhero souvenirs," The Punster said. He wistfully looked around at this circular shrine he had built to his lifelong obsession with Jack Titan.

"I almost had you a couple of times, too. If it wasn't for your metallic friend, you'd be dead right now and I'd never even get to use this maze that I've worked so hard on. I suppose we could call his death…a silver lining?" The Punster asked, and he winked at me. Still, I said nothing. I pulled my fist back and lunged at him. I aimed a punch at the old man's nose that was intended to knock him out and finally end this insanity.

The Punster caught my fist in his gnarled, arthritic hand.

"What? You were expecting a helpless, elderly gentleman?" The Punster asked. I tried to pull my fist out of his hand, but he gripped it far tighter than any ordinary man possibly could. His warm smile warped into a sneer.

"You're just like your father. Maybe even worse," The Punster said, and he jerked my whole body by my fist and flung me into the curved wall of the room. I slammed into the projected image of Jack Titan in his prime. The wall cracked with my impact, I slumped to the floor, and The Punster walked towards me through the soft light of the projectors. His shadow eclipsed the images of my father on the wall behind him.

"He would have done the same thing. Jump into a situation without thinking it through even a little. You followed me down here, Spectacle. You didn't have to," The Punster said while I tried to stand up.

"You didn't have to take that risk. You didn't have to blindly follow me down here, all by yourself. You're just like your father...arrogant. Immature. And stupid. Didn't you think that maybe, just maybe I would take precautions? That I would be prepared for you? For anything? Did you even consider the possibility that I would inject myself with a dose of liquid SUHP to even the playing field?" The Punster said as I barely managed to get up.

"...the temporary super strength won't last very long, but it'll be more than enough," The Punster said, and he hammered me in the face with an incredibly strong jab before I could even get my hands up. I fell back against the curved walls like a boxer on the ropes.

"I didn't want any of this. I tried to get you to work with me, Spectacle, to begin a new era of superheroics. I tried to bring order to the chaos of costumed crime, I tried to give it *meaning*. Your father died, and I realized that I wasted my whole life on this childish idea of the 'archenemy'. I wanted to move beyond that juvenile concept, and establish a legacy…but you're just like him," The Punster said, and he rained down super strength punches on my head. My back was up against the wall, the projectors were blinding me, and I did my best to block his punches, but with every blow to the head, I felt unconsciousness pulling me under like quicksand.

"You won't let it go," The Punster said and he stopped his barrage of punches. He was out of breath.

I pushed myself off of the curved wall and towards The Punster. He was bouncing on the balls of his feet with his weathered, bony fists up, and he had this look in his eyes, this look of hungry focus like a shark that smells blood in the water. Images of my father's life as a superhero orbited us. All of my injuries, the blood loss, the exhaustion, the hallucinogenic drugs…I could barely stand as I moved into the center of that room. It felt like a fever dream, like a slippery nightmare that you can only half remember when you wake up, but I remember one thing more clearly than anything I've ever experienced. I remember believing that one way or another, this was going to end right here, right now. One of us was going to die here.

The Punster fired a punch at me that could have dented solid steel, and I bobbed out of the way and fired back. My punch connected with his jaw and blood flew out of his mouth. The Punster was surprised only for a second, and then he was furious. He came at me with every last drop of drug induced superhuman power that he had. He threw super strength punches at me with such speed and ferocity that I could only avoid so many of them, and with every jab, with every uppercut and haymaker, I could feel the bones of his sixty five year old fists cracking. We circled around each other, both of us trying to beat the other to death with our bare hands, both of us ducking and leaning and bobbing out of the way, both of us taking shots to the head and the midsection, and this deadly rhythm set in, like we were dancing with each other.

I landed a punch right on The Punster's nose, right where I had aimed when I first entered that room, and I felt it break. The Punster was stunned, and blood streamed out of his nose. And suddenly…I was hit by this overwhelming clarity. I don't know if it was the sight of this old man in front of me bleeding all over his wrinkled face and his bright purple turtleneck. I don't know if it was the imagery of my father, of his decades of fights with The Punster and his pun motif weaponry, that circled us. I have no idea what it was…but I was struck by this realization.

I couldn't kill him. All around me, I saw my father trapped in a vicious circle. I saw him waste his life away with this rivalry, this obsession with beating The Punster at his own game. What did his attachment to this personal vendetta ever bring him? What did it ever bring him but the death of my mother by way of yet another childish pun deathtrap? What did it accomplish besides burdening him with crushing guilt and regret that all the SUHP in the world couldn't fix? If I killed The Punster, what then? *I am not a murderer.* Would the guilt kill me like it killed my dad? Would I end up an old man who never grew up, just like The Punster? Just like my own father? How long was this cycle going to go on? I just couldn't do it.

The Punster sensed my hesitation, and he punched me in the face so hard that his brittle, arthritic knuckles broke against my cheekbone. I stumbled, and collapsed to my knees. He kicked me in the jaw, and I heard his shin fracture with the force of the kick.

"Well…you know what they say…you can't make an omelette…without breaking…some legs," The Punster said as he tried to catch his breath. He just wasn't built to be using this much super strength. I almost blacked out from the kick…but now I knew what to do.

"You really are…the *spitting* image of your father," The Punster said, and he spit blood in my eye. He snatched Jack Titan's Golden Wreath off of the Greek column. He delicately placed it on top of my head, and he pulled me to my feet by my costume shirt. I said nothing.

"Say something you little shit!" The Punster screamed in my face. And still, I said nothing.

"This is it! This is the end of your life, and you don't have anything? You don't have any last words?" The Punster asked, and he laid into me with rapid fire punches to my rib cage. With every blow, I felt his frail knuckle bones crunching. The SUHP was wearing off. If I punched him once, it could kill him.

"This isn't fair. I created a pun masterpiece for you to die in, and you don't utter a single word? This whole goddamn thing was about words!" The Punster punctuated each sentence with punches to my face, and I drifted in and out of consciousness. All I had to do was let him burn himself out.

"This isn't how the game is played!" The Punster hit me again and again and again, and every punch was weaker than the one before it. All I had to do was stay alive long enough for the SUHP to run its course. All I had to do was keep my eyes open just a little longer.

"…just say something…" The Punster begged, and he raised a swollen fist that was cramping up into a knobby claw. He lobbed it at my face, and I swatted it aside.

The Punster had come down from his SUHP high. He flopped against my chest and clutched at me to stay upright. He was just a weak, crooked old man with frail, broken bones. It was over.

Finally, I said something.

"You're going to prison. There's nothing else to say, Punster."

I grabbed him by the collar of his purple turtleneck, and I dragged him out of the circular room.

"Prison? Please. No one will testify against me. No jury will convict a nice senior citizen like me," The Punster said as I pulled him through the narrow passageways that led to that circular shrine to my father. I felt extremely lightheaded. I couldn't stay conscious for much longer.

"I've got money, Spectacle, I've got millions. I'll get all the best super-criminal law attorneys. They'll get me out of any charges you throw at me. They'll say I'm a demented old man, they'll say I didn't know what I was doing..." The Punster said, and he kicked and struggled while I dragged him around the corners and turns and bends of the widening maze hallways. I had no idea where I was going.

"You walk out of here with me alive, and I'll never stop, Spectacle. I'll get out of prison eventually, and I'll come for you. I'll come for you and the people close to you, and I'll never stop," The Punster barked at me. Bloody spittle flew out of his mouth. I paused, and yanked him up towards my face.

"I'm not playing your game anymore, Punster. I'm done. You want to hound me for the rest of your miserable life? I don't care. That's on *you*," I said, and my pulse pounded in my head as I spoke to him. The Punster saw that I was blacking out, and he smiled, but I saw something too. I saw a trail of my own blood on the floor.

"A clew," I mumbled as the darkness slipped in at the edges of my vision.

The Punster kept ranting at me, he kept berating me and bargaining with me, but his voice faded to a dull hum. I followed my own bloody footsteps to the hallway of screens that glorified my own drunk face, I followed the red puddles across the artificial beach and past the birds sticking out of the painted wall by their beaks, I followed the trail through the SUHP fog filled corridor, I followed it up the stairs and out of The Punster's labyrinth, I followed my blood all the way to the exit of Amaze Toys with The Punster in tow, and then, on the super-battle devastated streets, I lost consciousness.

There's only so much a superhuman constitution can take.

Chapter 19: Renovation and Relaunch

The Kirby Museum of Superhero History was originally the Wertham Superhuman Correctional Facility. It was one of the first prisons designed during the superhero boom of the 60's, when SUHP was popularized and spread throughout the nation like a virus. Millions of people were taking this new drug, to expand their consciousness and transcend their physical limitations with temporary superpowers, and a tiny but significant percentage of these soupheads unlocked their dormant superhuman potential. Thousands of superhumans were being born every year. The Wertham Superhuman Correctional Facility was built to deal with these people. It was constructed to imprison some of the most physically powerful people who ever lived in a time when society was new to superheroes, when we didn't yet understand what it meant to be superhuman. The building stood for half a century, and we tore it down in half an hour.

It took over a year, a lot of bureaucratic red tape, and an extremely generous donation from the Superb 6 charity foundation, but they rebuilt the museum. This time, it wasn't constructed to incarcerate newborn superhumans whose only crime was not knowing how to control their abilities yet. It wasn't built to lock up soupheads whose powers were only temporary, who sobered up in prison cells and served out hard, long sentences because we still had more misconceptions about SUHP use than truth. This time, it wasn't built on a foundation of fear. This time, the Kirby Museum of Superhero History was built to remind us of our potential. It was built to show us the great and beautiful things we are capable of, to remember the terrible and horrific things we have done so that we might not repeat them, and to memorialize the fallen.

I was honored to be invited to the grand opening. When my father died, I probably wouldn't have been able to get into the event as a plus one. Now, almost two years later, I was attending with The Millennials as a "special guest." I was pretty surprised when I got the invitation in the mail, but I did make a modest donation of my own, so I guess I shouldn't have been so shocked.

"Do you think he would have liked it?" Insight asked me as we stood in front of one of the museum's new exhibits. It was called, "Jack Titan: A Life of Myth."

"I honestly don't know," I said.

It wasn't the largest exhibit. The exhibit dedicated to Beyond Man was at least ten times bigger. Queen Quantum had an entire floor for her royal gowns alone.

But it was good enough for me. It was more than I ever thought would come of my donation to the renovated Kirby Museum of Superhero History. I donated that cardboard box marked "Trophy Room." I kept the dozens of spiral notebooks that my dad wrote in, but I let the museum have everything else in that box. I expected them to use maybe one thing from it in a section of the museum devoted to obscure and forgotten superheroes. They used everything.

They had Jack Titan's silver breastplate enshrined in a glass case in the middle of the exhibit like a centerpiece. They had several versions of his Golden Sling that showed the evolution of its design, from early on in his career when it was just a couple of scraps of fabric, to the end when it was a monogrammed, gilded weapon tailor made for his hand alone. They had his Golden Wreath in a little glass cube next to a copy of the newspaper with the headline that named him "The Man of Myth." They even had all of his photographs arranged in a gallery along the walls.

There were dozens of the pictures that he collected in that cardboard box framed up on the walls with little metal plates giving you dates and information about them. It was a tour through costumed crimefighter history that showed a side of these people that we don't get to see much of anymore. It showed that these people, these iconic superheroes who have saved the world more times than we even know about, they were all young and irresponsible once. Even the founding members of the

Superb 6, they all liked to have fun, to be silly and reckless and party more than they should. They were just like the rest of us.

You could see Jack Titan posing with a souped out Sleight of Hand when he was still in his hippy, psychedelic wizard phase. There was a black and white photo of Doc Hyper and Jack Titan with their feet up on a coffee table at a Superb 6 after party, before the speedster had too many sneaker endorsement contracts to be caught drinking in public. There was even Jack Titan with his arm slung around Anhur, who hated to be photographed unless he was punching someone, both of them grinning and covered in ash after their first fight with Mistress Gorgon. You could see Jack Titan as a young man with the widest smile on his face. He was younger than me in a lot of these pictures. You could see him on the cover of Spandex Magazine, before he first fought The Punster, showcasing the rising stars of the superhero community. You could see my dad with so much promise and potential gleaming in his eyes behind his golden mask, before everything went bad for him.

"I didn't really know him," I said, and Insight leaned her head against my shoulder.

"I'm sorry, I couldn't help but overhear your conversation…wish I could turn down this Ultra-Hearing of mine, makes me feel like I'm constantly eavesdropping on everybody," Ultra Lady said as she walked up to us with a champagne glass in her white gloved hand. The reception for the opening of the museum was going on all around us with hundreds of people, most of them superheroes in full costume, mingling and conversing. The opening ceremony for the New Kirby Museum of Superhero History was a big publicity event for the Superb 6.

"He would have absolutely loved this, Spectacle. You have to know that," Ultra Lady said, and I believed her. Joe Metal looked at her with huge, starstruck eyes.

"Thanks," I said, and Ultra Lady smiled before gliding back into the throngs of people.

She was so at home schmoozing and networking with the superheroes and press packed into the museum. It was easy to see how Ultra Lady became the youngest member of the Superb 6 in the team's history. Not only was she incredibly powerful and talented, it seemed like she personally knew every single one of the costumed crimefighters and bloggers and journalists. She plucked the last shrimp wrapped in bacon off of a passing hor d'oeuvre tray at super speed, and then she hovered through the crowds back to us with a look on her face like she forgot something important.

"Hey, I just want to let you know, The Millennials have been getting the attention of the right people recently," Ultra Lady said to us in a hushed voice.

"Really? I mean, uh, *really.* We've been killing it recently. That makes sense," Joe Metal said, still starstruck out of his mind. He was so nervous that he was spilling champagne on his metal gauntlets.

"Yeah, really. Everyone in the Superb 6 has been really impressed. Insight, the way that you've gotten involved with the SUHP Addicts Anonymous program…all of the publicity you've done for the cause, the charity events for SUHP addiction treatment centers, the amount of awareness you've raised around SUHP abuse in interviews and podcasts with the way you're willing to talk about SUHP so openly, not to mention the crazy amount of money you've raised…it's really inspiring," Ultra Lady said to Insight, who glowed with purple telepathic embarrassment at the praise.

"It's not that big of a deal. I had a problem with SUHP. It was a real crutch for me. And helping people realize how serious an issue it is, it helps me stay clean, you know? It's really nothing," Insight said.

"Nothing? No, it's really not nothing, at all. Sleight of Hand, he had a serious SUHP problem in the 60's. He can't stop talking about how excited he is about the work you're doing, Insight," Ultra Lady insisted.

"…Seriously? Sleight of Hand said that?" Insight asked, and her eyes lit up with radiant, purple energy as she got excited.

"Yeah, he did," Ultra Lady said, and she waved to the retired Doc Hyper who she had just noticed across the room.

"And Joe, your social media experiment of streaming live video from the perspective of superheroes, almost all day, everyday…well, personally, I'm not a fan. But the Metal Network, your little website and app, you've got an absurd amount of people watching the superheroes you've convinced to strap cameras to themselves and stream video all day long. What is it now, a couple million subscribers?" Ultra Lady asked.

"4.78 million subscribers, but who's counting," Joe answered. He pretended to brush dirt off of his impeccably clean armor, and Ultra Lady laughed.

"Like I said, I'm not into it. I know the Metal Network's whole gimmick is in its slogan, 'Secret Identities Are Extinct', but I still prefer a little privacy. Wait…you're not filming this right now, are you?" Ultra Lady asked.

"Heh, no, we're not live right now, Ultra Lady. But we could be if you want—"

"No no, that's okay," Ultra Lady said, and she clinked her champagne glass against Joe Metal's armored shoulder.

"I'm personally not interested in putting my every waking moment on the internet, but the boys in the Superb 6 marketing department, they tell me that it might be the future of online superhero marketing," Ultra Lady said. She started to say something, but then she hesitated. She glanced around to make sure that no journalists or superheroes were listening, and then she continued.

"Listen, don't tell anyone about this, but the Superb 6 is expanding our membership. We haven't done any press or made an official statement yet, but pretty soon we're gonna be relaunching the Superb 6 under a new name and with a lot more teammates," Ultra Lady said, and now she was practically whispering to us.

“That’s…holy shit, that’s unprecedented,” Joe Metal said.

“Yeah, keep this to yourself though. That whole thing with The Punster, the way that the Superb 6 didn’t see that he was uniting all of the major supervillains in one organized group, the way that we couldn’t spare resources at the time to deal with him…it was a real failure on our part,” Ultra Lady said, and she looked at me with remorse.

“It’s alright. I mean, we understood that you guys had to prioritize. The safety of the entire world takes precedence over some old dude who likes wordplay way too much,” I said.

“The Punster still writes me from prison, by the way. He sends me a postcard every month, like clockwork, with a new stupid pun. You think he’s still mad that I testified against him?” I asked sarcastically.

“He might be, he just might be, Spectacle,” Ultra Lady said, and she looked at me with those x-ray eyes in the strangest way, like she was equally surprised and proud at how much I had changed since she first went to see why Jack Titan’s son didn’t show up to his funeral.

“But that’s the whole reason the Superb 6 exists, to solve large scale problems like The Punster coordinating with all the major league supervillains. And if we can’t do that, then…well, we’re fucked,” Ultra Lady said, still in a hushed voice. Joe Metal was paying extremely close attention. He was more focused in that moment than I’ve ever seen him.

"That's why we're rebooting the whole Superb 6 franchise. We're expanding the team to have way more than six members, so nothing like that can happen again. If The Punster can organize an army of supervillains, then we can organize an army of superheroes, right? We're calling it the Superb Society. And The Millennials is on the shortlist of superteams we're looking at for membership," Ultra Lady said quietly.

"So keep doing what you're doing. I'll be in touch soon," Ultra Lady said, she smiled, and then she floated back into the clusters of small talking superheroes.

"You should see your face right now, Joe," I said.

"This is...I can't even..." Joe stammered.

"I think she broke him, man," Insight said, and she laughed.

"This is so huge. I know we shouldn't get our hopes up or anything...I mean obviously it's not a done deal yet...but this is sort of what we were always working for, wasn't it? To be in the big leagues. To be serious, A-list superheroes," Joe Metal said, and for once, he didn't immediately return to scanning the social media feeds that his armor fed into his visual cortex. For once, Joe Metal was completely in the moment.

"Yeah. Mr. Mercurial would have said something funny or annoying right about now," Insight said, and her head glowed with purple energy. You could cut the telepathic sadness radiating off of her with a knife.

"You're right. He probably would have morphed his face into like, a cartoonish imitation of Beyond Man smoking a cigar or something, too. Wish he could be here for this," Joe Metal said, and we were quiet for a moment.

"He wouldn't want us to be sad though, that's for sure. That silly son of a bitch would want us to celebrate this news. Let's go to the Domino Mask. That's what he would have wanted," Joe Metal said.

"You're right, Joe. There's one more thing I want to see before we leave, though," I said.

"I think I know which exhibit you're talking about," Insight said, and the telepathic sadness flowing from her instantly changed into a sort of peace of mind, a sort of bittersweet sensation that might have been the kind of closure you'd feel at a particularly fitting funeral for a friend.

On the same floor as the Jack Titan exhibit, on the same floor that was dedicated to the many superheroes that fell in the line of duty, there was a metal statue of Mr. Mercurial. It was a little too tall. The color of the chrome they used was a bit off. And maybe his face was a little too angular...but they got his huge, silver smile right.

"I wouldn't be here if it wasn't for him," I said.

"You would have done the same thing for him," Insight said, and her eyes blossomed with telepathic energy as I felt her read my subconscious mind. I honestly never thought about it, but that purple, telepathic gleam in her eye as she sifted through my subconscious told me that it was true. I would have died to save Mr. Mercurial. I miss him every day.

"Let's get out of here, guys. Let's head to the Domino Mask and talk about old times, and tell bad jokes, and be ridiculous and silly as fuck, in honor of Mr. Mercurial. That's what that shiny clown would have wanted," Joe Metal said, and he'll never admit it, but I swear I saw a tear drop down onto that armor of his.

We had a lot of fun that night at the Domino Mask. We told a lot of stories about Mr. Mercurial, and the old days when we used to go to the Domino Mask almost every night. We didn't drink as much as we used to when we were stupid kids still playing superhero dress up, when we were still too young to understand that being a superhero wasn't all about partying as much as superhumanly possible, but we drank enough.

We drank enough to shake loose some stories about each other and Mr. Mercurial that kept us giggling until it hurt, like the time that Armadillotron tried to kill him with his armidillodrone swarm because he caught him sleeping with his girlfriend. Or the time that Mr. Mercurial was doing an impression of Supra that made everyone in the Domino Mask laugh their asses off, until Supra happened to walk up right behind him and tap him on his silver shoulder. We even listened to the rough cut of his comedy album, which he was working on before he died, and although some of his jokes were painfully bad, it was good to hear his voice again. That night at the Domino Mask, after hours of talking and laughing and remembering our best friend, I decided to write these memoirs.

Last call came around. We were all about to head home, and we walked out of the Domino Mask laughing about our friend and all the goofy shit he used to get up to. I was going to start writing as soon as I got back to my place, but right as we said goodnight outside of that old, dirty dive bar, several police cars raced by us with their sirens blaring. We just smiled at each other.

We knew that they were speeding towards another supervillain robbing another jewelry store or holding up another armored car or giving another grandiose speech about ruling the world. There's always another supervillain. Joe Metal's exoskeleton boots glowed and he shot into the air in the general direction of the police cars, Insight flew after him bursting with purple telekinetic power and she shouted that the last one there had to buy all the drinks the next time, and I leapt after them with only one thought rattling around in my head. You can go to Jupiter.

Made in the USA
Las Vegas, NV
03 July 2022